Until I Met You

S.L. SCOTT

ISBN 13: 978-1-940071-64-0

Interior design: Angela McLaurin, Fictional Formats
https://www.facebook.com/FictionalFormats

Cover design: Sarah Hansen of Okay Creations
http://www.okaycreations.com/

Cover photographer: Yuri Acrurs

Small Images: People Images, Dollarphoto.com, Stocksy

Editing:
Marion Archer of Making Manuscripts
Marla Esposito of Proofing Style

To my heart and soul—my husband and children.
I am, because of them.

Until I Met You

Prologue

THE BARS WERE rusted. The dingy paint was chipping on the inside of the windowsill, and her gown was fraying along the ties. She took in and then slowly released a long breath, even though the air she was breathing was stale. She wondered if the vent was blocked, but it was too high for her to reach. So she remained flat on her back on the bare mattress with the springs poking into her. Jude had a knack for lying very still for hours on end. This was how she stayed sane. This was how she survived.

Don't give them anything.

Don't give into them.

Fight.

Fight.

Fight.

Hold on.

One more day.

Hold on.

Love wasn't about reason.

Love wasn't rational.

The heart charged forth with love on its wings to spite the possibility of the bloodshed aftermath.

Chapter One

MAYBE IT WAS the music—an instrumental version of The Cure's "Just Like Heaven" played melodically through the Upper East Side apartment. Or maybe it was traces of the pink pills still in her system. Her mental freedom was slowly awakening her dormant mind.

Either way, Jude Boehler liked this party.

She liked the suits that surrounded her, the women who ignored her. She liked being invisible. *So wonderfully rare not to be under a microscope.*

Jude swayed to the music while nitpicking her way through the trays of food on display. She tried a few of the fancy appetizers but put back what she didn't like. Grabbing a celery stick, she dipped it in the creamy sauce next to it. *Nice.* She dipped again.

"You shouldn't double-dip," she heard a man say.

Continuing to swirl the celery through the dip in a figure eight, she looked up. While taking a large bite her gaze traveled over the charcoal-gray suit-clad banker type, and she swallowed. And smiled. Then laughed as she dunked her celery in the dip again as if she had never heard him. She took another bite, this time louder while looking into the eyes he hid behind black-framed glasses.

Lifting up on the balls of her feet, she tried to see them more clearly. Not appeased, she dropped back down and asked, "What color are your eyes?"

"Hazel," he replied flatly. A line between his brows, which had formed long before tonight, drew her attention.

Done with the celery, she stuck the remaining piece in the dip, leaving it sticking straight up, and took his hand, palm up, into hers. "You should buy me a drink." The tip of her finger traced a broken line that led from just above his wrist in a semi-circle around his thumb.

Pulling his hand back and shoving it into his pocket, he stated, "The drinks are free. The bar is over there."

His words screamed impatience and she wondered if he was always this uptight. She stood her ground with him and looked in the direction he was pointing. "You should offer to get me one. Isn't that the polite thing to do?"

His head jerked back. "You just put your germs in that dip and touched half the food on the table, thus contaminating it, and you're calling me out for not being polite?"

She nodded. "Yes. I'll take a Crown and Coke." Her back was turned to him as she picked up four different cookies to investigate the chip to dough ratio, and then settled on a brownie. She could feel Hazel's gaze and returned to face him. With an ironic smile, she curtsied. "Fine, I'll get my own drink. Since you're here, can I get *you* something while I'm over there?"

"No. Thank you."

"You're welcome." Before she left, she asked, "What do you do for money?"

"My profession?" He watched the peculiar girl twirl in front of him. Her skirt ballooned out and brushed against his gray wool-covered legs.

She stopped, smiled, and replied, "No, just in the general sense."

One of his eyes squinted, completely confused by the nonsensical question. "I'm an architect."

Jude's lips pursed, seeming to agree with him. "That makes sense." She left this time while he watched her go, but she didn't walk. She floated. She danced her way in red snow boots through the stiff crowd dressed in suits and evening attire. The girl wearing a chartreuse sundress with little pink flowers embroidered around the bottom in the middle of winter stood out at this party. *And* captivated him.

There were plenty of people he knew and some he should talk to, but he didn't move from where he stood. He waited for her. Shifting uncomfortably, he was confused as to why he was waiting, but he did.

Jude returned as if they were long lost friends, as if she had no doubt he would still be there, waiting.

Taylor stood next to the girl in the sundress in silence. Her brownie had been eaten, and a cocktail now replaced it in her hand, which she waved flagrantly to the music not noticing—or not caring—that liquid was spilling as she moved.

Finally speaking up, he asked, "How many drinks have you had tonight?" But he really wanted to ask if she was drunk. He had never seen someone so careless before, so *carefree* before. She twirled again, and he swiftly took the glass from her and set it down on the table. *For the safety of the drink, of course.*

"This is my first."

His expression may have questioned her answer, but he didn't say anything.

With a small smile, she asked, "What's your name?"

Her current smile was the most contained thing he had

witnessed about her tonight, and he found it endearing. "Taylor," he responded. "What's yours?"

"Judith. My family calls me Jude. You can call me Jude, too."

Watching the quirky girl in front of him, he examined everything about her, noting she hadn't even taken a sip of the drink yet. "But we're not family."

Nudging him with her elbow, she laughed. "We're not friends either, but we will be."

"We'll be friends or we'll be family?"

"I don't know," she said, her expression turning thoughtful. "Let's see where the night takes us."

Taylor almost argued that the night wasn't going to be *taking* them anywhere, but he couldn't. As he stood there, he started feeling a loss of his own senses. Somehow, pretty little Jude made him believe there was a possibility. Her free spirit was contagious, and in the middle of this repressed party, he started to relax. "What do you do, Jude?"

"Well, Hazel," she said with a smirk, "I'm glad you asked."

"Hazel?"

"Your eyes. They're hazel. Did you know that hazel is actually a very rare eye color? Most people think it's just an awkward brown that doesn't have any self-identity. But it does. *Your eyes do.*" She lifted up again to go in for a closer look. "Yep, Rayleigh scattering."

"Rayleigh scattering?" he asked, voluntarily widening his eyes for her to see them better. He finally just took off his glasses and tucked them into his jacket pocket. He liked to wear them for distance but didn't need them tonight.

She sighed, perplexed. "Hazel. It's just an impossible color."

Leaning in to see hers, he asked, "Green?"

"Blue, but mine too suffer from a variance that is often confused by what I'm wearing. I mean," she said, shrugging, "they really don't, but people like to say they change when I wear blue or green or whatever. But they don't change. My clothes do."

He nodded, almost lost, but managed to keep up. "Do you always talk like this?"

"Like what?"

"Like you're manic?"

"Manic or a maniac?"

"Manic. I don't think you're a maniac."

She seemed to ponder that and looked away. When she turned back, she asked, "So Hazel, what do you architect?"

"Homes. A few buildings around the city. Why are you calling me Hazel? Because of my eyes?" When a few seconds passed and she didn't reply, he realized she didn't tend to answer his questions, so he redirected the conversation. "And you?"

With surprise, her eyes went wide and her hand covered her chest. "Oh, I'm not an architect. Is that what this party is? A party for architects?"

Taylor was fully confused and shook his head. "No," he said, looking around. "It's a party for The Barretts."

Whispering, she asked, "What's a Barrett?"

Nothing about this woman made any sense, but he liked her chaos. He leaned over, pointed across the room at an older couple near a large fireplace, and whispered, "Those are Barretts."

"Ahh." Bringing the drink to her lips, she took a small sip as she watched them over the crystal glass, and then asked, "Never seen them before. Who are they?"

With his head almost touching hers, he leaned to her ear and whispered, "They're wealthy Upper East Siders who host parties for colleagues and charities *pretending* to be doing it for the cause, but really it's for the publicity."

Her eyes were fixated on the hosts, and it took great effort resisting the temptation to look at him. "And are you one of their 'causes?'"

"I am." Just as he answered, the Barretts, as if aware of their name being spoken moments earlier, came toward them. "Shit," Taylor muttered under his breath. He straightened back up and returned their smiles.

"*Taylor*, darling." The gray-haired woman with smooth skin and bright pink lipstick leaned in and kissed him on the cheek. "So glad you could make it." Her eyes focused on him, but sincerity seemed to be missing in her greeting.

"I wouldn't miss it."

Jude noticed how flat his tone was, and that the life in his eyes that had sparked when whispering with her had dulled in their presence. That was no good, and she hoped it returned once they left.

The older man shook Taylor's hand and patted his arm with the other. "How's the world of architecture?"

When they released, Taylor's right hand started to shake and he tucked it into his pocket. "I'm currently working on four projects."

"Good. Good. That's good to hear, son."

Mrs. Barrett asked, "Who's your friend, Taylor?"

Jude could tell the woman wasn't invested in the answer before he had a chance to give it. She was all too familiar with that judgmental, condescending tight-lipped grin. Taylor slid his hand down the underside of Jude's arm and weaved his fingers together with hers. "This is Judith."

The Barretts faced her and smiled. In unison, they said, "Hello, Judith."

"Hello," she replied meekly, feeling her body shrink away from their disingenuous gaze. As if Taylor understood discomfort, his hold on her tightened, causing her to look up. His smile was soft.

The architect made her feel safe, so she ignored the desire to flee, and stayed.

Their clasped hands were of deep concern to The Barretts judging from their critical gaze. "And how long have you known each other?" Mrs. Barrett asked.

Taylor was fast and confident. "Feels like our whole lives."

Mrs. Barrett continued to smile, but it stopped short of her eyes. "How charming. Hopefully we'll get to hear more about it over dinner soon. But for now, we must greet Mr. and Mrs. Stevens. They've been begging us to come to dinner. Speaking of, the food is being replenished. Please eat before you leave." Her hands held his shoulders and she kissed his cheek again before taking her husband's arm and making a quick getaway.

Taylor and Jude stood there silently recovering from the pretentious welcoming that just drove by and hit them. Peeking down at their still entwined hands, and then up, she asked, "Wanna get out of here?"

Chapter Two

IT WAS JANUARY second. The city was predictably cold and Taylor tightened his coat around him. Jude buttoned her purple coat and looked in both directions when they stepped outside. The awning protected them from the snow, but not the cold. Jude slipped on gloves, as did Taylor, and then she walked with the wind.

He was behind her, but double stepped until he caught up. Leaning his head down, he peeked at her. Her cheeks were rosy from the weather and snowflakes were clinging to her eyelashes, which she didn't bother sweeping away. He asked, "Are we going anywhere in particular?"

Her eyes teemed with happiness. "The world is our rainbow, Hazel."

He still had no idea how this girl's mind worked, but he was too intrigued to end the adventure. "What does that even mean?"

She laughed as if nothing bothered her in life. She was fascinating to Taylor and he stared. He had never met anyone like her before, nor understood how her blithe behavior carried her through life. She smiled so widely that two dimples appeared in her cheeks. "Let's find out together." Then like the snow, she flurried away.

When he caught up to her again, he asked, "What's your last name, Jude?"

She was an expert at avoiding what she didn't want to address. "When that man shook your hand, he called you son. Are you his son or was that him trying to relate to you?"

"I'm his son. You don't like to answer questions, do you?"

"I get bored with them. I'm asked questions all day long. How are you feeling? Will you venture outside today? Did you take your pills?" She turned to him. "See, boring. I get so sick of talking about myself all the time. Do you ever get bored of yourself?"

This was easy for him to answer. "All the time."

"Then you do understand."

He wanted to give her the smile he believed she wanted from him, but he was still stuck on the questions she's often asked. In particular, he was stuck on the pills question. "*Did* you take your pills today?"

Nodding, she patted him on the back. "Don't worry about me, Hazel. All is good. That's why I'm here."

Everything was a side effect of the previous topic with her. One thing led to another. "Why are you here exactly? I mean, why were you at the party if you didn't know my parents?"

She stopped in the middle of the sidewalk and put her hands on her hips. "Like I said, impossible."

Halting in front of her, he narrowed his eyes at the incredulousness of her comments. "Is this a reference to my eye color from earlier or to me now?"

"Aren't you one in the same?" Walking forward, she turned around to Taylor who was still standing where she left him. "You coming?"

He conceded and caught up to her once again. "Do you even know where you're going?" He walked steadily next to her. His long strides could easily out pace her shorter ones if he wanted. He just didn't want to. He couldn't fathom why, yet again.

"Do you want ice cream?"

She hit him with one surprise after another, and he replied, "It's freezing out here. How about a coffee?"

"I don't like coffee."

"Wow, a New Yorker who doesn't like coffee." Taking her by the arm, he stopped her. "Are you going to tell me anything about yourself?"

"I just told you I don't like coffee. That's something."

He sighed. "I'm serious, Jude."

His emotional sigh was wearing on her and she gave him the most honest answer she could. "Not if I can get away with it."

He looked into her blue eyes. Under a bright fluorescent light of a convenience store, he could see they were tinged in green with champagne centers. They were the most unique eyes he had ever seen. *She* was the most unique woman he had ever met. Now he felt bad for making her unhappy, so he broke his gaze away. "Fine. I'll limit my questions." And just to see her smile again, he said, "Ice cream it is."

She jumped for joy. "I know a great place a few blocks from here."

"Should we catch a cab?"

"No, I love the snow. It's magical."

Looking down the street and then back to her, he started wondering when he'd stopped seeing magic in the world. He could probably guess, but he didn't want to think about that time.

A half hour later, his hands were frozen but he still found himself eating pistachio ice cream with Jude for dinner. He bought the treats and joined her at a booth where she was contentedly licking her rocky road. As soon as he sat down, she asked, "I think you can tell everything you need to know about a person by their favorite ice cream flavor."

Taylor watched as her tongue came out and she licked the ice cream in absolute bliss. When their eyes connected, she grinned, catching him watching her. Having trouble hiding his own smile, he asked, "What does pistachio say about me?"

She paused in thought, then offered, "Maybe not in all cases."

Tilting his head, he said, "You have an opinion. You just don't want to share it with me. Go on. Don't hold back. I'm a big boy. I can take it."

Shaking her head, she grabbed a napkin and wiped her mouth. "No, it's okay."

He took one bite of his treat, and in all earnestness said, "I want to know what you think about me. I'm curious."

All the lightheartedness that existed between them disappeared and her voice turned somber. "I don't think you're pistachio at all. That's just what everyone else wants you to be."

"That bad, huh?"

Brightening, her expression showed her joy with a wide smile and that seemingly unattainable possibility was back in the depths of her pupils. "Have faith. It's not too late."

"Let's hope not." He looked down at his ice cream and completely lost his appetite for pistachio. Getting up, he threw it away and returned to the table.

Jude looked at her own ice cream. Rocky road. It had always been her favorite and still was until that moment. Suddenly she lost all favor for the flavor and threw hers away too. "What now?"

He laughed. "You're the one with all the crazy ideas."

"They're not crazy," she said defensively, and walked out into the dark of the winter's evening, the bell above the door chiming loudly behind her.

Taylor could tell he'd hit a nerve and wasn't sure if he should be relieved to find one thing that actually affected her or if he should feel bad. He went with the latter. "Hey, Jude. Wait up. I didn't mean that."

Shrugging, she looked up at him. He was handsome. Jude had noticed at the party. It would be hard not to, but now... with the faint light from the store surrounding him and snow falling over his head, he was stunning. Reaching up, she touched his cheeks with her fuzzy green-gloved hands. His breath appeared to stop like hers and she gravitated closer, the tips of her shoes on the tip of his. "Hazel?"

"Yes?" he replied as if that was his name now.

"Will you kiss me?"

Taylor had wanted to do that since he'd met her, but hadn't realized it until that moment. He took her cheeks between his leather-clad hands and leaned down without hesitation and kissed the girl in the chartreuse sundress. He kissed her until the snow flurried, their world revolving around them. He kissed her until her lips parted and a secret was shared. A secret that would always only be theirs to share. A kiss that said I like you... and maybe more. A kiss that spoke through emotions instead of words. A kiss that bonded them to this moment and to each other.

When Taylor pulled back, ever so slowly, he opened his eyes to find hers still closed, her red lips still parted, and her hands still on him. So he kissed her again.

And again.

Then he kissed her hands after taking them in his. "Jude?"

"Yes?" she asked in return, leaving her hands right where they were.

"Do you want to come back to my place?"

A playful smile crossed her lips. He had trouble looking away from them, wanting to kiss her again, longer this time. "Are you asking me because you want to sleep with me?"

"I'm asking you because I'm cold, but I wouldn't be opposed to sleeping with you."

Her smiled turned serene, warming him. "Okay."

Taylor didn't know what to expect from her, feeling very much like he was just along for the ride. Her answer was so easygoing and accepting that he found himself surprised by her again, but feeling lucky to have this quirky, pretty girl going home with him. Keeping hold of her hand, they caught a cab and headed across town.

Jude had been in plenty of nice buildings in Manhattan, but this one was nice, and still felt accessible, much like him. She liked that. The doorman was in a simple sweater and pants. No epaulettes on the shoulders of a brightly colored suit or check-in desk with a gatekeeper. This guy said hello to both of them and held the door. That was all and she was in.

Taylor lived on the fourteenth floor. As they walked down the hall, she said, "I like this building."

"Me too."

He held the door open and followed her inside. The apartment was modern, which didn't surprise her. He was an architect, after all. Clean lines. Simple color scheme of varying warm shades of brown. In contrast, paintings hung on the walls and offered large splashes of color, each room a different theme. Royal blue and turquoise in the living room. Yellow in the kitchen. She peeked back at him and caught his eyes on her. "I'm hoping red is in the bedroom."

"Then you won't be disappointed."

With a tilt of her head in approval, she walked to the large wall of windows and looked out. It was dark, but the city always remained lit up like false stars in the night. "Do you have blinds?"

"I do. Would you like me to lower them?"

"No."

Dragging her fingers across the glass, Taylor watched as Jude surveyed his apartment, secretly wanting her to like the place, *to like him.* Despite the fingerprint trail he would be cleaning in the morning, it didn't bother him. "Would you like something to drink?"

"Why are you acting so formally?"

"Am I?"

Her eyes locked on his. "You are. I liked you better when you spoke of The Barretts as things instead of people."

"I'm a Barrett."

"And yet, I still came here." Jude walked to an open door. "Is this the bedroom?"

"Yes."

"I'd like a Crown and Coke."

"Will Jack Daniels do?"

"I'll have wine. Red," she replied, then disappeared into his bedroom.

Taylor had stopped trying to figure her out back at the party, so her drink preference didn't surprise him. It took a few minutes to figure out which bottle he wanted to open. When he did, he poured them both a glass of Cabernet and joined her in the bedroom. He stopped in the doorway when he found her asleep on his bed. "Jude?" He waited a few seconds before trying again. "Jude, are you awake?"

Walking to the side of the bed closest to her, he set the glasses down on the night table and knelt in front of her. Her eyes were closed and her breathing was even and calm. Her coat was draped on a chair by the window and her boots were on the floor. The green gloves still covered her hands, so he carefully slipped them off, one by one, and set them by her coat before returning with a blanket to cover her.

Taking his glass of wine with him, he sat in the chair. Outside, the lights provided enough visibility to see her in the dark room. Her small form was curled on her side. Her lips were together. Her hair splayed over his pillow. He watched her, curious to know more about her.

He hadn't brought anyone to his apartment in a long time, and it had been even longer since anyone had been in his bed. But he found her discord refreshing compared to the monotonous tedium of his day-to-day.

This was the most alive he'd felt in forever. The high was addictive. The eccentric young woman more so. She had disrupted his peace and as he watched her sleep, he liked the way she made him feel.

He liked *her*.

Chapter Three

THE SMELL OF bacon and eggs woke Taylor. When he opened his eyes, it was still dark outside and his body was stiff. He sat forward in the chair and scrubbed his hands over his face. The bed had been abandoned and the blanket left balled up. *Jude.*

Getting up, he walked to the door and looked toward the kitchen. Her back was to him and she scrambled eggs in a skillet. "Good morning, sleepyhead."

She wasn't looking at him and he didn't know how she knew he was there, but he smiled lightly and joined her, sitting at the bar. "Is it?"

"Good or morning?"

"Either. Both."

"It's both," she replied, turning to greet him with a much more awake smile than his before returning to tend to the eggs.

Looking at his watch, he yawned. "It's two thirty in the morning."

"I like this time of day. I like being awake when the rest of the world sleeps. It's peaceful. There's no negotiating to be done."

As he stared at the back of her, her frame covered in wrinkled green cotton, he wanted to ask her about the negotiating, about the pills, about the turmoil she was hiding from. But he didn't because he liked this. Selfishly, he liked her secrets and her whims. He liked that she was cooking in his home.

Setting a plate of food and a fork in front of him, she asked, "Coffee?"

"No, thank you." He picked up his fork and looked up. "Thank you for the food."

She leaned forward, rested her chin on her hands, and stared at him. "You're welcome. Now stop being so formal, Hazel. You're making me uncomfortable."

He took a few bites, and then asked, "You're not eating?"

"I'm not hungry. I'm sleepy. I'm going back to bed." She whisked around the island bar, right past him.

"Why aren't you eating?"

She called from the bedroom, "I made it for you."

He took another bite and swallowed. Then asked, "So does that mean we're friends now?"

"Friends. Officially."

That made him smile. He finished eating and returned to the bedroom. When he walked in, he took off his pants and the button-up shirt he had fallen asleep in, leaving him in an undershirt and boxer shorts.

"Will you sleep next to me, Hazel?"

He almost argued that he didn't want to be called that, but everything with her seemed to fit, including suddenly having a name he didn't even like. So he decided to let it slide until morning and slipped under the covers. He felt her dress spread behind her, pushed it forward, and moved closer. He didn't wait to see if she wanted him touching her. He just did it. Selfishly, he put his arm over her, found her hand, and moved it so he was holding her around the chest, finding his own comfort.

Her warm breath hit his fingers lightly and he could feel the tenseness of her body. But he didn't move. He liked it too much to do something that selfless.

She whispered, "Who is the girl in the photo?"

Lifting his head up just enough to see the frame facing them, he inwardly sighed, not wanting to touch on that subject tonight. "Thank you for cooking. It was good."

"You're welcome," she replied, "to keep your secrets, too."

A small smile crossed his mouth knowing she understood him, and respected the need to keep secrets too.

They fell asleep in a comforting silence.

Hours had passed and Taylor was unaware of the hour. He removed the pillow from his head and looked up. Jude sat in the chair, her skirt billowing around her hips. The way her leg was bent exposed her body beneath the cotton. With a cigarette burning in one hand, her head rested on the other, she said, "What are we going to do about this, Hazel?"

"What's *this*, Jude?" He sat up, his back leaning against the headboard, and rubbed his eyes. With the morning sun shining into the room, he noticed her bright pink panties. "I don't allow smoking in my apartment."

She sighed and stubbed her cigarette into a coffee mug. "That's the 'do' I'm talking about. You're pistachio and I'm rocky road. They just don't mix."

"I could argue that, but I have a feeling anything I say wouldn't matter."

"That's where you'd be wrong." She took her boots in hand. Looking down as she slipped one on at a time, she said, "How long have we known each other?"

"We don't know each other at all."

"Ah," she replied, remembering. "Yes, that's right. You're a Barrett."

Bending his knees, he was getting irritated from this conversation. He wasn't awake enough for mind games. "And what are you again?"

"Hopeless. So very hopeless."

"And here I thought I was the impossible one."

That made her laugh. "Clever." Standing up, she took her gloves from the table, her coat from the chair, and put it on. As she buttoned, she said, "I called it the minute I saw it."

"Saw what exactly? My eye color?"

"No. Your soul."

He was starting to wonder if this conversation would have an ending or if she always talked in circles.

"I knew we'd be put in an impossible situation, a love affair that would mean more than it should, more than either of us could endure once it was over."

He got out of bed as she spoke and grabbed his suit pants. "Love affair? We've neither made love or had an affair tonight, so you are either overly confident or psychic."

"I'm neither. I just know what I feel and I could see what you needed." She walked past him as he buckled his belt.

Following her into the living room, he spoke to her back. "And what do I need that was so apparent to you?"

"Not just to me. To anyone who really looked."

"God, can you just answer one fucking question, Jude? You're leaving. Give me this."

While unlocking the door, she stopped and faced him. "For the record, everything you have said to me mattered. That's why I'm leaving." She walked out.

Jude was halfway down the hall, almost to the elevator when he said, "That seems like a reason to stay."

"Don't let them change you," she said as she pushed the elevator button. "They're trying to. They'll eventually win, but hold out as long as you can. Okay, Hazel? Hold out."

Watching her, he debated if he should follow. He debated if he should stay. He debated. He debated. He debated. He debated until she got into the elevator, then the debate was over.

He ran.

Hitting the button just before the door closed, he stood there, praying it would reopen. When it did, the cockiest grin he'd ever grown was solidly in place. She was standing at the opening and grinning herself. "Damn, Hazel, I actually thought you were going to let me go there for a minute."

He grabbed her around the waist and pulled her to him, laughing. "Nope, not letting you go." His lips crashed heavily into hers as he pressed her against the doorframe of the elevator. Until it started buzzing. Taking her hand assertively in his, he led her back to the apartment and then kissed her again and didn't stop kissing her until they were in his bedroom.

They parted long enough to catch their breath. Taylor looked at her red lips, then took her coat off. She kicked her boots off and stood in front of him, missing his lips, missing his breath, and liking his eyes on her, craving her. When her coat was dropped, he leaned in and kissed the side of her bare neck. His hands were holding her shoulders and covered most of her skin.

Sucking.

Kissing.

She closed her eyes, let her head fall back gently, and moaned. When his lips worked their way back up, his nose ran smoothly behind her ear, and the hand on her jaw held her to him. The other hand slipped her strap down over her shoulder. His lips replaced it as her opposite strap was lowered. He found the zipper with ease and slid it down her ribs. They let the dress fall, pooling at her feet.

He leaned back and looked at her bare breasts, at her body, drinking her in through his gaze. Taylor was so comfortable, she thought him an anomaly from the man he'd appeared to be at the party. At the party, he wasn't pistachio. Right now, he wasn't rocky road either. He was somewhere in the middle, maybe something smooth and definitely something delectable. Someone who got what he wanted, but who usually asked for it. She liked that he hadn't asked this time. She liked that he was taking...

His fingertip dipped into the front of her panties while he watched her eyes, watched for her reaction. The lips that were slightly swollen from kissing parted and her breath deepened. He kissed her until his lungs filled with the freedom she'd been inhaling.

Moving around her, he pressed his chest to her back and flattened his hand, sliding it down between her legs. Weakening under his touch, she reached up and from behind, she grabbed him around the neck, trying to keep her panting from breaking his lips apart from hers.

Taylor's mouth was at her ear, and he breathed, "You're so wet," emphasizing the T.

She shivered from his words. She shivered from the loss of control she had been searching for, and had finally found. Her mouth dropped open while her head fell farther back, giving him access to whatever he wanted access to. It didn't matter as long as his hands were on her body somewhere.

Gentle circular strokes coaxed each and every breath to leave harsher than it entered. She spun around in his arms and undid his belt. Watching him scrape his teeth over his bottom lips made her anxious and she hurried with the zipper. His pants fell to the floor and he stepped out of them. Cupping her face, he kissed her as he backed her to the bed until she sat and crawled onto it. Once she was settled, he took his boxers off and climbed to the middle where she lay, waiting for him. Centering his body over her, he kissed her.

Taylor squeezed her breasts, then bent down to kiss and suck each of them. He wanted to move lower. The light reflecting off the frame on the nightstand was in his eyes, so he lifted up, set it face down, and then returned to her body. She was soft under his touch. She was on the thinner side, but had fuller breasts, and wider hips. "Jude?"

"Yes?"

His face was between her breasts and he kissed her twice before asking, "What do you want?"

"I want you."

"How do you want me?"

She replied, "All over," while digging her fingers through his light brown hair.

"What do you like?"

"Architects. Ice cream in the middle of winter. Cooking for you. And your mouth on me. Anywhere. And everywhere."

A chuckle heated her chest, then he sucked good and hard. Maneuvering lower, he lowered her panties as he went down.

Reaching above her head to hold onto anything, she grappled to find something solid, but failed. His hands opened her wider and his mouth was on her. Jude's arms dropped to her sides and she fisted the blanket. "Taylor," she murmured, unable to keep his name inside her any longer. One of her hands took hold of his hair and she tightened her fingers in it. The straining pain on his scalp was harsh and encouraging, making him dip deeper, and press on her inner thighs harder. Each of her seductive whimpers was poetry to his groin and he bore down.

He loved to look at her. She was open and so completely tempting. As he tasted her, he found her pleasure. Reaching into his drawer next to the bed, he got a condom and put it on as she lay there, recovering from the riptide of tremors that coursed through her body.

Taylor settled between her legs, balanced above her on his forearms. As they looked into each other's eyes, she touched his cheek and lifted up to kiss his lids. Her lips were warm and plush, covering his eyes as he pushed inside her. He sighed. Relief and satisfaction became one as *they* became one.

When he dropped his forehead to the bed, he kissed her shoulder and pulled back out. Slowly. Slowly. Slowly he pushed back inside her welcoming warmth. Wrapping her arms around him, she rubbed the back of his neck, and down his spine. The muscles teetered between tense and relaxed as his arched back moved under her touch. Taylor's breathless voice called to her, "Juuuude." He repeated her name over and over until it got lost in the moans and motions of their bodies coming together and releasing.

Taylor fell to the side, a slight sheen of sweat covered his face, and when he kissed the rounded edge of her shoulder, he tasted her sweet and salty skin. "You're beautiful," he said in the light of day. January third.

Without opening her eyes, a satisfied smile covered her ruby, kissable lips. "You're sex drunk. Tell me when you're sober."

He could have told her she was beautiful again, right then. He wasn't sex drunk. He was more aware of who he was and what he felt, more life sober than he'd been in years. But he knew she wouldn't believe him, so he placed another kiss on her shoulder and rolled onto his back.

Jude scooted into his side and rested her head in the nook of his arm. She should leave, but *she* felt drunk on the sex they just shared, and didn't want what was pulsing deep inside her to end. The feeling was too powerful, entirely intoxicating, and utterly heartbreaking.

Even after squeezing her eyes shut, a flashback came anyway...

"No, Daddy. Please. I'll be good."

"We must abide by their wishes or risk breaking the law."

She closed her eyes before the tears could slip down and cleared her mind of the damaged parts of her brain. Instead, she went through the thirty-three flavors of ice cream at her favorite shop, until she figured it out. Hazel wasn't pistachio. No, that just didn't fit who she knew him to be at all. Smiling to herself when his arm wrapped around her, she knew exactly what flavor she would order the next time they happen to be out in the middle of winter wanting a sweet treat.

Chapter Four

"DON'T YOU HAVE to work?" Jude asked, her fingertips running freely over his chest.

"It's Sunday."

She sat straight up, her hands on the bed holding her upright and glanced at the time. Three fifty-three in the afternoon. Another second ticked by and she threw the covers from her body and raced around the bed. Grabbing her dress from the floor, she continued to the bathroom.

Taylor watched, rolling onto his side and propping himself up by the elbow. "You're leaving? Now?"

She came back out and turned her side to him. "Zip."

"Why are you leaving? Stay."

"I can't. I have dinner plans."

His fingers, holding the zipper, stopped halfway up her ribs and he tilted his head to the side. "Care to elaborate on that after having sex with me all night, morning, and day?"

Looking down at him, she giggled. "With my family. Don't worry. I'm not sleeping, eating ice cream, or having sex with anyone else tonight."

When she faced away again, he finished with the dress, and lay back. The edge of her dress was held firmly in his hand and he tugged twice. "Are you coming back?"

Exhaling loudly, she sat on the bed, her bottom pressed against his legs. Jude looked into his eyes, the hazel brighter, a tempting green. "Do you want me to?"

"I wouldn't ask if I didn't."

She leaned over him and kissed him. He grabbed her around the waist and flipped her onto the mattress next to him until he was on top. "Come back to me."

Her fingers weaved through his messy hair. "I like you like this."

"As opposed to what?"

"As opposed to being a Barrett."

"Oh, don't lie to yourself. I'm a Barrett through and through. All signs will lead me into temptation of societal acceptance and wealth at the expense of family, friends, and lov—"

Her finger covered his lips, stopping him from saying anything more. "Don't finish that thought. Don't give up before you've had a chance."

"A chance at what, Jude? Tell me."

"A chance at life. A chance at happiness." Her voice got so low he almost didn't hear her say, "A chance to love."

Dropping his head down on her shoulder, he took her hands in his and raised them above her head, and whispered, "Show me how to love. Until I met you, I think I've been doing it all wrong."

She kissed his temple and said, "When done right, love is felt, not shown." Sliding out from under him, she put her back to him as her feet touched the ground again.

He groaned from her absence. "Sounds complicated."

"It is. My family has shown me how much they love me to the point of smothering me."

"But you still leave me to have dinner with them."

She looked back, angling so she could really see him. "Maybe I've got love all wrong. Maybe it's supposed to be suffocating and hollow."

One of her delicate hands lay across her lap, the other on the bed behind her. He took the one that supported her, the one that would leave her relying on him, and held it. "What's your last name, Jude?"

Her head tilted down and she watched her feet, an overwhelming sense of self-preservation would slip away if she wasn't careful. "Let's not muddy the snow with such things that don't matter in the days to come, Hazel." Her fingers slipped from his as she took her coat and walked away. Standing at the crossroad of his bedroom and her goodbye, she said, "Sometimes you don't even have to find the end of a rainbow to find its treasure." Wiggling her fingers, she left him.

Taylor didn't debate whether he should go after her this time. This time he let her go because she was going whether he wanted her to or not. But before the front door could close, he said, "Come back when you can, Pretty Jude."

The door clicked closed and he was left with the scent of lingering cigarette smoke and the memories of surname-less Jude engulfing the rest of the space. For someone he'd known less than twenty-four hours, she sure knew how to occupy his mind. He'd never understood love at first sight, but it became conceivable in that moment. How she'd managed to disrupt his whole world, spinning it onto a new axis in such a short time was surprising. He smiled wanting to fully embrace this new trajectory.

In her absence, he watched the day deliver the night right to his window. Not even getting the courtesy of a golden winter evening, which was his favorite. No, darkness set in quickly tonight. And that was that.

Around nine, he stared at the turned-down frame on the nightstand. It reminded him of long-held anger from his past. An emotion he had forgotten while Jude filled the space, showing him there was a different way to live, a way to move forward.

Reaching across the bed, the mattress where Jude had slept, he opened the drawer and slid the frame inside, facedown, and slammed it shut.

There was no satisfaction in the action like he once suspected he would get if he had the strength to actually do that. No, none came. Just an emptiness he didn't know how to fill. So he ate. Frozen waffles that cooked in sixty seconds in the toaster. A can of soup he found in his small food cabinet for days when he was sick. Grapes he picked up on Wednesday. He was stuffed when he finished, but the emptiness still sat heavy in his belly, undigested.

Snow fell in rolling sheets, blowing across the wall of windows of his living room. Louis Armstrong and Billie Holiday wafted through the room as the hours ticked away.

By eleven, Taylor got up from the couch and stood with his toes touching the wall of glass. With a highball of Whiskey on the rocks in hand, he put his other on the window. It was cold, much like his insides. He finished the drink and sat at his drafting table in the corner. Sketching frantically before his hand would relent, he found himself drawing wide blue-green eyes and jagged brown hair. Taylor mixed two colors to create the shade of green he was missing the most about now. But before he had enough drawn to make sense of it, his phone rang.

He looked down at the phone as it rang until the number came into view. But it wasn't a number; it was a name. A name that he had thrown into the drawer earlier that night.

Katherine.

Katherine.

Katherine.

Turning the music off with the push of a button, he took a long breath. When he lifted the phone to his ear, he knew he shouldn't. He knew it was the same as opening the door to her, which he was doing to his own detriment, but couldn't stop. "Hello?"

"Taylor." Her tone was deeper, melancholy, trying her best to get to him. "How are you?"

He stayed quiet a minute, but gave in, into the weakness of giving her any of his time again, and snapped, "I'm still sick just in case you'd forgotten."

Her exasperated breath said more than her words. "I heard you were better."

"Depends who you're talking to."

"I'm sorry. I shouldn't have called. I just..." He remembered her using this ploy to draw him back to her when he was lost in his own thoughts. It didn't work anymore, so she said, "I miss you, Taylor. *I miss us.*"

He let silence reacquaint itself and took his time. Reaching for his glass, the ice had melted, but he hoped to find a few remaining drops of liquor mixed in. "Katherine, this isn't good." He swallowed the rest, and added, "We're not good."

"It's all my fault." He let her say what he thought she should have said a year earlier. "I was scared."

"You were scared? Katherine," he said, sighing. "I can't do this. Not right now."

"Maybe coffee on Friday then?"

"I'm tired. It's late." Dropping the colored pencils to the table, he let them roll down to the trench at the bottom.

"I'm sorry for calling so late. I've just been thinking about you. Please, Taylor. Coffee. Please."

Maybe it was that the hour was creeping toward midnight, or the Whiskey seeping into his system, but he finally relented. "Fine. Coffee on Friday. Meet you at Bean There at five."

"For old times' sake."

Old times' sake. He rolled his eyes. Taylor hung up, disappointed in his inability to say no to the woman who hurt him most when he'd needed her. He got up, set his glass next to the sink, and went to the door to lock up. There was no point in leaving it open any longer. Jude wasn't coming back.

As he brushed his teeth that night, he thought about the snowflakes on her lashes and how she'd made eggs for him. He wondered why she was at his parents' party, where she knew no one, and why she wore a sundress when it had been freezing outside. He rinsed his mouth and finished up. When he returned to bed, he left the blinds open and watched the snow fall until he fell asleep.

He awoke to knocking in the middle of the night. Jumping up, his heart racing from the disturbance, he rushed to the front door. Swinging it wide open, a drenched Jude stood there, looking a complete mess and dripping on the hallway carpet. "It's Boehler."

"What is?" he asked, restraining from grabbing her.

"My last name. It's Boehler."

A gentle smile appeared on her face when Taylor smiled. "Jude Boehler. Okay. Is that why you came back, Jude Boehler?" He hoped there was more, but had no idea how to read her.

"Yes. That, and because I wanted to kiss you again and I wanted you to kiss me like you did earlier."

Looking down and then back up into the eyes that seared his soul, he leaned his head against the open door. "I might not be able to replicate that kiss. What do we do if I can't?"

"We keep practicing—"

"Until we get it right." He took her hand and pulled her inside. She was soaked, but he didn't care. He hugged her tight, so glad she'd come back. The door was shut, the bolts locked, and her wet coat taken off and hung up. She left her boots at the door and her dress on the floor just outside the bedroom. His boxers were dropped by the bed, and their bodies connected, lips kissed— deeply—and moans were sighs of their coming together.

They were need and want.

Craving, and caring.

This was right.

They were right.

Chapter Five

"JUDE?"

"Yeah?" She yawned and looked at the time. Three seventeen. She yawned again.

"Are you on your cycle?"

"I don't even own a bike." She was taunting him. Three seventeen in the morning seemed like a good time to tease. *Not!*

"No." He sounded uncomfortable, but he finally worked it out. "Your menstrual cycle?"

"Medical speak is not my idea of foreplay. Try another angle."

"I want to know."

"Why?"

"Just tell me, Jude."

"No. I'm not."

He paused as it dawned on him. "Are you a virgin?"

"No, Hazel."

He was onto her tricks already. "Were you? When you came over after the party?"

"Maybe."

He pulled her even tighter against his chest and kissed her ear. "Thank you."

"Don't thank me for having sex with you. That's weird and feels like it's going to be followed up with a payment."

"I'm not paying you for sex, but I will kiss you again."

"Down there?" she asked, perking up.

"Of course."

Jude didn't leave Taylor's apartment that week, not even to get food or clothes. She wore his T-shirts. She ordered food. She smoked in the bedroom with a window cracked open since he didn't like the smell.

He went to work. He came home with groceries. He brought her flowers and air fresheners. He never complained about the smoke. He liked Jude too much to let her one vice bother him.

For that, he was welcomed home with pancakes and waffles, eggs benedict, and oatmeal for dinner. They ate in the nude. They ate on the couch and in bed. They made love while the snow fell outside and with the blinds wide open.

Friday came and he went to work. A black cloud had been blocking their sunshine and it was about to downpour. All week he hadn't really thought of Katherine or the coffee meeting. But here it was, and he didn't want to go. He sat at his desk, staring out the window of the high-rise office building where he worked. Ten blocks home. Three blocks to Bean There.

The ticking of his watch echoed in his ears and he looked down. Four fifty-seven. He set down his pencil and shutdown his laptop. Peering out the window while he put his coat on, he studied the weather and tried to think of any excuse he could to go home to Jude instead.

"It's gotten heavier," his co-worker Ben said. "I think I'll wait it out and get caught up on the Manger project."

"Good idea. Unfortunately, I've got to go. I'm meeting someone at five."

"You'll be late."

"Yeah, I'm okay being late to this meeting."

"Mysterious. You seeing someone new?"

Taylor smiled. He couldn't help it when he thought about Jude. Then he said, "Or did you get back together with Katherine?"

But *her* name wiped the happy gleam from his face. Pushing his glasses up his nose, he said, "I should go. Have a good night."

Ben got back to work, not bothering to get more from him. He knew he wouldn't talk about it if he didn't want to. And he had too much work to catch up on. "You too."

Taylor wrapped his scarf around his neck as he waited for the elevator. He thought about calling Jude, but he didn't have her number. It wouldn't matter. She'll be there when he got home. Content, she didn't ask him about his day or talk about hers. When they were together, they lived in the moment, and he loved every second.

As he rode the elevator, he wondered how practical that really was. Quite frankly, it wasn't practical at all. That was just it. They didn't make sense, but neither questioned what was going on. They just lived...

Taylor walked into the quaint coffee shop fifteen minutes late. He saw Katherine rise from a back table and wave him over. He started walking while taking his gloves off, but detoured to order a coffee before joining her. He needed to have something to hold, something to steady his hand. He hated faltering in front of her and she didn't deserve access to that side of his life anymore.

With his drink in hand, he sat down across from her, setting his gloves on the table. "Hello," he said, noticing her hair was shorter, not by much, but enough to see her differently.

"Hi," she said, keeping her voice intimate. She reached across the table and covered his hand that held the mug. "Thank you for coming. I wasn't sure if you were going to."

He pulled back, and eyed her. "I don't have long."

"Oh? I was hoping to catch up." When he didn't answer, she asked, "Are you seeing someone new?"

He looked away. He wanted to tell her that her photo had been discarded into the drawer. He really wanted to brag that he has someone waiting with bacon or some other breakfast food for him that she had cooked for dinner. And that the prettiest and messiest brunette he'd ever seen was there, waiting just for him, probably naked. This woman that made him laugh and think that a life, even one that could be cut short was still worth living, was at his place right now. But he didn't.

The very blonde Katherine stared at him, every strand of her hair perfectly in place. And he said, "No." He didn't feel right speaking of Jude to her. He didn't want to expose what they had to the outside world. He didn't know if it could survive beyond the walls of his place, past January, or beyond winter. So he held tight to what he cared about most and shook his head. "I just have a lot of work to do."

A wide smile showed, her white teeth brighter against the blood-red lipstick. "That's good to hear. I mean," she said, trying to sound casual, "about the work. You're keeping busy. That's good. Are you hungry? We can order something or go out to eat."

"No." He sipped his drink. "Why did you want to meet?"

"Like I said, to catch up. You're looking good. You look healthy."

"I'm healthier. Right now. But like you, it comes and goes."

Embarrassed, she looked down, her eyes on her coffee that was now cold. When she looked up, she steadied herself, and a small smile came along for the ride. "I'm sorry. I am. So much, Taylor. I miss you. I can't replace the past and the bad choices I made. I can only try to fix our future."

"We don't have a future to fix. You made sure of that when you fucked my friend while I was in the hospital." He sat back, feeling annoyed. "I'm surprised you didn't do it bedside while I slept."

"You weren't that close of friends from what I remember." He started to stand, but she said, "I'm sorry. Please. But you have to understand. You weren't the only one going through something, Taylor. I was going through it too—"

"Don't." He sat up, trying to keep his cool in a public place, but failing to keep his emotions in check. "Don't act like your life was on the line! You were put out. That's it. You were put out because your boyfriend was stuck in a hospital having every test out there performed on him and couldn't escort you to a fucking ball. A ball by the way that was hosted by my parents to support Parkinson's research."

A tremor ran through him and he released the mug abruptly, causing the hot liquid to slosh over the top. "I've got to go. It was great *catching up* with you," he said sarcastically as he stood up.

She stood and grabbed hold of his hand. Putting his between both of hers, she said, "I understand more now. I'm here." Her hands rubbed back and forth, his shaking subsiding. "I want to be here for you, Taylor."

Pulling his hand away, he tucked it quickly into his pocket, a habit he'd formed allowing him to hide tremors when necessary. "I need to go. I'm late." He walked away from her, weaving his way through the crowded coffee shop and out onto the street. He didn't bother tightening his scarf around his neck or even buttoning his coat. He just walked away from Katherine as fast as he could.

When he opened the door to his apartment, Jude stood up from his drafting table stool. Their eyes met, guilt tainting his heart. "Hi," he spoke first.

She fidgeted with the boxer shorts she was wearing, a royal blue pair he bought a month ago, and an old heather-gray college T-shirt of his with Brown across the front. "Hi." She hated feeling this way, feeling like when she was at home and was either in trouble or had caused trouble. "I made muffins. They're vanilla and jellybean."

"Jellybean muffins?" he asked hanging his coat on the hook behind the door.

"You didn't have any berries."

Walking slowly toward her, he said, "I didn't know I had jellybeans."

"You didn't." She shifted. "I did. In my pocket. I bought them last week."

"All right." When he reached her, he touched her waist gently. "I missed you today." Then he kissed her. Her soft lips opened for him and she pulled at his shirt until it was no longer tucked. Her warm hands slipped underneath and they got even closer. When they pulled back, he said, "I like you in my clothes. I like you here."

That eased her worries. "I like being here. Are you hungry?"

"Starved."

They kissed again, his hands sliding under her shirt and grabbing her breasts. A loud knock interrupted them, and he sighed into her mouth. She looked at him quizzically. "I can get it. You're hungry. Get something to eat."

"I'm hungry for you." He stopped her as she walked past, and went ahead of her. "No," he said, squeezing her perky breasts, her nipples hard under the soft cotton. "I'll get it. Have you eaten?"

"I was waiting for you."

Laughing, he reached for the door, and started opening it when he said, "We'll eat the muffins and then I'm going to eat yo—"

"Taylor." His head whipped around to the barely cracked-open door. Katherine stood before him. Guilt choked his words as he glanced behind him at Jude. When he turned back, Katherine said, "You left your gloves at the coffee shop." She held them out, but his hands seemed to be glued to the door. Her eyes searched past him before he stepped forward and started to pull the door closed behind him.

But it was too late. Katherine said, "Hello."

Taylor looked back into the apartment. It was as if Jude was shrinking into herself. She was fading like a Morning Glory in the hot sun.

Katherine added, "I recognize that shirt. It's the softest of all of his. It was always my favorite."

"That's enough," Taylor said, taking the gloves. "Thank you for returning these, but it wasn't necessary."

He started to close the door on her, but her hand landed on it with a thud as she took a step inside. "Oh, but it was. Very necessary I see. Who's your friend, Taylor?"

Wanting to protect Jude from Katherine's harsh glare, his tone turned adamant. "You're not welcome here, Katherine."

Katherine stood there, looking comfortable as she stared at Jude. "And you are?"

Jude gulped. The intensity of the beautiful woman in front of her wrecked her. She tugged at the shirt as if it could cover the lack of confidence under the cotton. Taylor. Gloves. Coffee shop. Katherine. It was too much. She excused herself, went into the bedroom, and closed the door.

Katherine turned, her hair flipping around and she smiled—big and broad. Tapping Taylor's chest, she said, "You can do better." She walked to the door and stopped just before exiting. "The place smells of smoke. I'm assuming with your health condition, you haven't started smoking. It was great seeing you today. Hopefully we can do dinner soon." She left and he closed the door, locking both bolts.

Dropping the gloves on the bar, he went to the bedroom and knocked lightly. "Jude? Can I come in?" He didn't wait for a response. He just opened the door and went in. She sat by the chair near the window and looked out. "I've overstayed my welcome." When she glanced back at him—a dark silhouette in the doorway—she said, "I tend to do that."

There was just enough light emanating from the kitchen that he could see her eyes were glassy as he approached and knelt before her. "You're welcome to stay here longer. We took things fast. That part has been hard to rationalize. But what others think of us doesn't matter to me. You do. You matter. I like you here. I like being here with you. I like being with you. Stay."

"It's not real. None of this is real." She closed her eyes and laid her head back. "It's a dream, all in my head."

"Then don't wake up." He rested his head on her lap. "Stay asleep with me forever."

His voice was full of passion and his words made her think that maybe they were possible, even if his eyes seemed stuck in the impossibility of it all.

She whispered, "I'll stay."

When he lifted his head back up, he grinned, amused, "So you snack on jellybeans?"

Her eyes shifted to his in surprise. "You don't?"

Chapter Six

THE WEEKEND. LIKE so many others, they felt the anxious anticipation of possibility as it hung in front of them teasing them into Saturday. While Taylor dressed, he said, "You need clothes. It's winter. I don't want you out in this weather only in a dress."

She zipped herself up. "I thought you liked this dress."

"I love it." He leaned against the door that led to the closet. "But I care about your health more."

Jude paused, her heart beating firmly in her chest. "You care about my health?"

He laughed, and then realized she wasn't joking. "Are you being serious right now?"

"Yes," she said in a tone that didn't feel much like herself when she was with him.

"Oh, Jude." He came to her and brushed her hair away from her face. "What do you think we're doing here?"

"What do you mean?"

"I mean, this week. It's been fun. It's been good." He looked at her wanting her to agree as she looked at him so innocently. "Has it been good for you?"

Happiness shimmered in her eyes. "Yes, it's been so good."

His arms wrapped around her waist. "So why wouldn't I care about you, care about your health?"

"I don't know." She glanced down, needing to get hold of herself before she spilled her real feelings for him and scared him away. "I smoke."

"And I hate it."

Confused, she asked, "Then why do you let me do it?"

"Because you like it so much. And sometimes, I think you need it." Swaying her hips back and forth, he explained, "We all have baggage, but your load seems to be heavier. So if a cigarette lifts that burden for a bit, I'm okay with that."

She gulped, not meaning to. It was loud and showed her discomfort. She hated talking about herself, her health, or her burdens. But when she looked into the depth of kindness in his eyes, she said, "Thank you."

A reward in the form of a gentle smile was given and he kissed her forehead. "Can I buy you some warm clothes today?"

Nodding, she said, "You know I have more clothes. Even some of the winter variety. I can go home and put them on."

Walking into the bathroom, he called, "Does this going home include me or is this something you would do on your own?"

"On my own." She didn't want to go into the many reasons she didn't want Hazel to come home with her. "I can meet you back here later tonight." She was sure she could. She just wasn't sure *how* yet.

"No, I don't want you to leave." *Me.* "We'll go shopping."

Underneath the sexy exterior of Hazel Barrett was a genuinely sweet man. And he made her wonder if he had a mean bone in his body. "You griped at me for double dipping."

"I didn't gripe. I simply pointed out the fact you were double dipping."

"Pointing out that I was double dipping makes it sound like I wasn't aware of the fact I had already dipped the celery into it once before."

"Were you? Were you aware, Jude?" he asked with a chuckle.

"Fully."

"I stand corrected then."

I stand corrected then. His words implied an open heart. *He didn't know the truth.* He stood in front of her, not knowing he could be hurt by a woman he barely knew, a woman whose family had determined she was responsible for hurting them all within her twenty-two years of life. Was this genuine sincerity a defect of his? Could he be that good? That good, to just accept her into his life so openly without questions or walls to protect himself?

She recognized parts of herself in him. He suffered from the aftermath of being hurt too. He was damaged just like she was. One day she would find out who did the damage and hoped she could protect him from it ever happening again. But for now, they would go shopping for winter clothes.

Taylor asked, "You ready?"

She nodded and walked to the front door. Before she put on her coat, she turned back to him and said, "What season would you be if you could be any season?"

Pondering the question, he smiled, and replied, "Baseball." He grabbed his coat and put it on. "I love everything about it from the hot dogs to the smell of peanuts to playing and watching it." He led her out the door enjoying the huge smile on her face.

His answer was so unexpected that she fell a little bit deeper in like with him. But was she possibly falling in love with him too?

Yes. *Hard.*

This new emotion momentarily paralyzed her more practical side, but they walked through the slush of snow as if it didn't affect them at all. Maybe it didn't. They were sunshine when together, both unaware of the gathering storm clouds ahead.

In a store off Fifth, Jude came out of the dressing room to a bored Hazel, who sat straight up when he saw her. She twirled in the lavender dress, the skirt ballooning out. With one raised eyebrow, he started to ask her about pants, sweaters, socks—*warm* clothes. But as he watched her, saw the smile on her face, he couldn't bring himself to do it. She didn't have any makeup on. Her hair had been brushed that morning, but was a mess from the windy day, and she was utterly breathtaking.

She searched his face for approval and then asked when he hadn't spoken, "Do you like it?"

"I love it."

She smiled even bigger and jumped. "Yay!"

After she disappeared into the dressing room again, his phone vibrated in his coat pocket. When he pulled it out, he saw a text from Katherine.

It was so good to see you. When can we meet up again?

He stared down at the words until another message came through.

It was better than old times. You look good, honey.

Cringing by the nickname she had for him, he sat there trying to figure out how to respond, failing to notice the brunette in front of him. She swallowed down the hurt, and barely above a whisper asked, "Do you like this one?"

Taylor had been caught. Somehow he had betrayed Jude even when he was the one receiving the messages. "It's not what you think."

The line of her mouth tightened. "What do I think?"

"You're thinking the worst." He held up his phone. "I didn't reply to her. I was reading them. That's all."

"But you were going to reply."

Feeling defensive, he raised his voice, "No, I wasn't."

The other patrons in the small store glanced their way before returning to their own lives.

Jude stood in front of him in an off white floral sundress that had lace straps and ended above her knees. She was sexy *and* demure. Her eyes though... her eyes said all she didn't, and guilt replaced his patience. He stood up, grabbed a brown sweater from a nearby table and threw it at her. Her hair blew from her face as the sweater hit her in the chest. "Damn it, Jude! What do you not understand about winter?"

The millisecond he released that sweater he felt like shit. The second it traveled across time and space, regret filled him. He reached out to stop the damage he was about to do, but it was too late. The sweater hit her. The shock on her face that morphed into pain would haunt him.

Jude held the sweater where it had landed, staring at Hazel. Her eyes did not leave his. "Winter. Got it."

"Jude? Wait." He reached for her, but she hurried back into the dressing rooms.

That didn't stop him. He went after her until a petite older woman sidestepped into his path. With her arms out, she said, "Stop. There are other women changing in here."

"I don't want her to change." *Not referring to the clothes at all. I like her just the way she is—inside and out.*

"Sir, please. Step outside before I call security."

He stood his ground for seconds before reason returned. "My apologies." He walked out, distressed, and ran his hands through his hair, impatiently waiting for Jude.

When she did, she was dressed in the clothes she'd come in, her coat buttoned to the top, and her boots laced properly. Taylor had only known her a week but already knew this wasn't good. She saw him and signaled to the store's entrance. When she pushed it open, he said, "What about the dresses?"

The door closed behind them and he stood in front of her. She wasn't looking at him. She was looking at everything and anything other than him and he hated it. "I'm sorry. I didn't mean it. You looked beautiful in the dresses. You should get them."

Her arm went up and a cab was there in an instant. "I'm going home."

"No, don't." He grabbed her hand and held it tight. "I'm sorry. I'm sorry. Don't go."

She had tried to hide her inexperience from him when it came to matters of the heart, but she didn't know what to do. Feeling vulnerable, she fell back on what she did know and hid her hurt feelings in the form of a smile. But Jude couldn't hide the truth when she looked at him. She liked him a lot and her eyes warmed to his. "I'll be back."

Taylor didn't believe her. Her soul was lying to his. He could feel it in his gut. "Don't go, Jude. I want you to stay with me." It was a whispered confession that conveyed every honest moment of his life.

She was pulling away from him, her body already free from his desperate touch. She got into the car and shut the door. The window was cracked open and she said, "I'll see you soon, Taylor."

The taxi drove off and as the impact of his real name hit him, he knew she was lying. "No!" he shouted not knowing what else to say to stop her from leaving. He yelled again and then saw the cab stop ahead at a red light. This was it. This was his chance. He ran. He ran over the slosh and skidded along the icy patches. He took his chances and ran into the street where the heat of the cars had melted the snow and ice.

He could see her big eyes, staring back at him. Then she closed them and turned around and the cab drove through a green light leaving him in the wet and messy remains of what was bliss just an hour before.

Punching the sky, he yelled, "Fuck!" and kicked the freezing air.

A cabbie yelled at him as he drove by, "Get out of the street, you crazy bastard!"

Taylor flipped him off and moved back to the sidewalk.

His phone vibrated again and he pulled it from his coat pocket. When he looked down, there were another two messages from Katherine.

The Castors are hosting a benefit on the 16th. Maybe we can go together?

I bought a new dress you'll love. It's your favorite color. This will be fun. Call me back.

Katherine's manipulation didn't work on him anymore. He saw her for what she was and he wasn't interested. Her lack of acknowledgment of his illness still bothered him. She seemed to live in a world where he would recover and they could go on their merry way. Her ignorance astounded him, but pissed him off more.

Besides that, Taylor had no idea what color she thought his favorite to be, but he knew her dress wouldn't be chartreuse. *Dresses.* He marched straight into the shop and bought the two dresses Jude had loved and left the brown sweater behind. He walked home leaving the texts unanswered. There was no point. They weren't from the one person he wanted to hear from.

It was past lunchtime and he was hungry but didn't have the energy to eat alone in a restaurant. Holding out one last hope, he didn't have any motivation other than to get home to see if Jude was waiting for him.

When he walked in, the stale air hit him. That's when he knew she hadn't returned. She made air come alive just by breathing it. She made *him* come alive just by existing. Aimlessly, he shut the door and walked inside. He left his coat draped over a barstool as he walked to the couch and sat down. After setting his phone down on the coffee table in front of him, he stared at it, willing it to ring.

It didn't.

He had never given her his number. She had never given him hers. He had never seen her with a phone, and didn't think to ask about it.

Evening came and he lay down sideways, watching his phone, feeling she could overcome any obstacle; obstacles like not knowing his number, and still be able to call him.

The day passed and darkness shrouded his apartment as it infiltrated his heart. The light had left and gone home with her.

Chapter Seven

JUDE RANG THE bell outside the large black doors of the historic Lenox Hill brownstone. She stepped back and held on to the large concrete railing and shifted nervously. She hated this part. *Hated it.* She prayed Roman would answer and not Nadia.

Her breath stopped short when the door opened. When Roman looked out, she started breathing again. "Well, c'mon in, Hummingbird. Get upstairs and get cleaned up. Your parents have been in a foul mood all week and are due for tea soon."

She walked in through the open door and looked around. The coast was clear, the black and white marble tiles sparkling, and Roman, her personal gladiator, a welcoming comfort. He'd always been there to help her fight her way back. "Thank you." As she started up the main staircase, she said, "How bad will it be?"

He shook his head and looked away. That told her all she needed to know. But as she went up the stairs, he asked, "You've been taking your medicine?"

Nodding, she lied, "I have."

He smiled. "Good. And, Hummingbird?" She rounded the case and stopped to look down at him before continuing. "It's good to see you."

"It's good to see you, too." She then dashed up the rest of the stairs and ran down the hall to her room. She shut the door and leaned against it, resting. She wished she could lock it but that privilege had been taken away from her years ago.

She went into her bathroom and started the shower. Standing in front of the mirror, she unzipped her dress. It would forever remind her of a certain hazel-eyed guy. Something about seeing it come off now made her sad, made her feel the loss of him in her bones. Trying not to think about it, she hopped in the shower and scrubbed her body clean and quickly washed her unruly hair.

After she was squeaky clean, she dried off and blew her hair dry. She liked her hair down and natural, but she suppressed that small joy and her movements became automated. Rote. She pinned it back into a French twist and straightened her bangs, then neatly sprayed it so no hair was loose. Jude put on a pastel yellow shift dress and a matching cardigan, her pearl necklace and earrings. Horribly uncomfortable kitten heels were slipped on right after she applied her makeup meticulously until her skin was flawless to everyone. Everyone but her. Her dream life with Hazel switched off as she switched off the lights and went downstairs, descending into the darkness of her life.

Outside the formal living room, she took a deep breath, then rounded the corner with her hands clasped together in front. Classical music played in the background as her stepfather, mother, cousin Isla, and Aunt Leslie talked in a mannerly fashion to each other. Their teatime was like a modern day scene ripped from an Austen novel. They were so pretentious. Nobody worked harder than her family to appear like they were part of blue blood high society. Seeing them made Jude roll her eyes. If her father were still alive he would have laughed at this sight. It had been too many years since she had heard such a genuine and loving laugh that she feared she had forgotten what one sounds like. Her brother Ryan got his laugh. As Jude stood there, she realized all she had gotten was this charade of happiness.

All four looked up at the same time, her cousin's mouth dropping open. Isla stood up. "Judith."

Judith pushed down her fear and joined them, choosing to sit next to her aunt and across from her stepfather. Isla and her aunt moved in two years ago after Jude's uncle died. They were lonely upstate, took up two guest bedrooms in the house, and never left. Isla and her mother were sandwiched between them on the antique couch. The chair she chose always overwhelmed Jude's petite body and she felt like a child. But it beat being at the other end of that sofa. She reached for a cucumber sandwich and said, "Hello."

Her mother, Renee, looked down at the napkin on her lap, clearly at a loss for words for her only daughter. Her stepfather wasn't though. "Judith, where have you been? We've been worried."

She finished the sandwich she had shoved into her mouth and wiped her fingers on the tea towel. "I was at a friend's apartment." *The dreamiest of friends with the most captivating hazel eyes.*

Nadia entered the room and set a teacup down for Jude, gave her an incriminating glare, turned on her heel, and then left them to finish the conversation. When Jude reached for the cup, her mother found her voice. "Do we know this friend?"

"I'm not sure you've met." *And you never will if I have my way.* She filled her teacup, and as if the whole room wasn't waiting for answers, she dropped two sugar cubes into the hot liquid.

"How long have you known this friend?" her aunt asked.

But her stepfather added to the questions before Jude could respond. "Did you meet this friend at the hospital?"

The creamer clouded the tea and Jude smiled, loving the art of watching the white blossom in the light gold liquid. She laughed. It was loud and unexpected, a burst of amusement. "No, Brewster," she said, still giggling. "They aren't crazy like me, so no need to worry yourself over that."

"What do you mean, Judith? Of course we worry." Her stepfather spoke deliberately, his tone trying to control the anger that edged it. "You are our responsib—"

"I'm your responsibility." She raised her tone, not meaning to. "I got it. I know. I don't have to be constantly reminded. I have no free will. I understand completely."

Her stepfather stood up. "Apparently you don't or you wouldn't have gone missing all week."

Jude set her teacup down, and then flattened her napkin on her lap by brushing her hands over it several times. "You allow me no freedoms. If I don't disappear I won't ever live again. Is that what you want?" Her voice shook. She hated fighting. She hated confrontation. She hated having to defend herself and her actions. But she did it because she had to. "I'm home. As you can see, I'm fine."

Her mother slapped her hand flat down on the cherry wood table. "Stop this! Stop fighting." When her clear blue eyes met Jude's startled ones, she said, "All we want is for you to live. That's why things are the way they are. You know this, Judith. You know we love you. We can't risk..." she lowered her voice. "We can't risk losing you again. I won't survive it."

"That's ironic since I would be the one technically not surviving, Mother."

That earned Jude a harsh glare from everyone except Isla, who favored sympathetic today. Isla spoke in her softest, calmest tone. It was natural for her. Out of her family, she was the most compassionate to Jude's plight, if not ignorant to it. "We love you,

Judith. Please. Please stop the fighting."

Her stepfather had finally sat back down and Jude stood up. Looking down at the untouched tea, she felt a pang of disappointment that she wouldn't get to drink it. "I'll be in my room."

Her stepfather asked to her back, "For the night?"

And with her back still to them, she replied, "For the night."

"I hope you're not lying. I don't want to have to call the hospital again." It wasn't a threat when he said this. It was a fact. Brewster Boehler had to hold up his end of the court order. She tried not to resent him for this, but she did. She'd never understood why her mother married him so quickly after her father's death, much less gave him a say in Jude's life. Jude continued back to the room where she was allowed no locks on the inside.

It was evening, two hours since she'd left Hazel, and every minute that had passed weighted her to a hopelessness she hadn't experienced in more than a year. Lying spread-eagled on the pink bed under the pink canopy, she stared at the small white posies adorning the matching fabric and matching wallpaper. She once counted them, counted every last posy in her room. Twelve thousand, three hundred, eighty-six. It was a number she struggled to forget. It was a time in her life she wished she could wipe from her memories, but being in this room did nothing but remind her of those days.

Nadia entered the room without knocking, like she always did. She waltzed in with the silver tray in her hands and spoke in her thick Russian accent. "You should respect your parents, Judith. They care for you. One should be so lucky to have such love." She set the tray down on her vanity, then put her hands on her hips and tsked. "Look at you. A mess." She came over to Jude and pulled her up by the arm. Fixing her hair, she said, "Your father will be in shortly."

"My stepfather," Jude amended.

Nadia twisted her lips, but ignored the correction. "Eat. Get your strength and your answers straight. No more of this foolishness. Do you hear me?"

"I do," Jude responded, staring past Nadia as she scraped her scalp with a bobby pin.

Stepping back, Nadia approved of her work and smiled, but it was stilted, like her personality. "There. Don't lie down. Go eat and wait for your stepfather."

Jude didn't say anything else, but she did roll her eyes, wondering if Nadia was born this cold or if the cold world had made her so.

The door shut and Jude was alone again. She got up and walked to the vanity, eyeing the food options. Nothing appealed to her, so she sat at the pretty table and touched up her lipstick before her stepfather arrived to have another talk.

She wasn't kept in suspense for long. Her stepfather knocked and politely waited outside her door until she told him to come in. He cleared his throat while he entered. It was a tick she knew only led to bad things. Standing up, she said, "I'm sorry. I should have called."

"You should have come home. What are we to do with you, Judith? We tell you to stay, you leave. We let you have a choice of the hospital or here and you always say here, but you continue to sneak out. The hospital seems to be the logical place for you—"

"No. No. Please. I'll stay put."

"You've promised this before."

She would try anything, so she defeated her pride and said, "I will, Daddy. I'll stay. I promise. I'll only go out when you say I can. I'll be here when you say I have to be."

He remained near the door though it was closed, shaking his head. "This is not a punishment, Judith. This is your mental health. Do you understand how much pain and worry you have put this family through?"

His tone... she knew it well. Too well. Her stomach twisted into knots. "I do. I'm sorry. I'll be better. I won't worry you anymore." She thought of Hazel and the blissful bubble she'd lived in this week, realizing how it was all so fleeting. "Please, Daddy."

"I'm sorry."

She froze and stared at him. "Why are you sorry?"

"They think you should be evaluated."

Tears pricked her eyes instantly. "No. Please," she said, rushing him. "Please. I'll be better. Please. Please. No. I'll be good. I'll be the best. You'll see."

He turned his head away from her. "I'm sorry. We have no options here. The hospital can demand an evaluation at any time under the court order. We must abide by their wishes or risk breaking the law."

"Daddy," she said as tears ran down her cheeks. Her mascara blurred her vision. "Please. Help me."

His hand was on the doorknob. He opened the door and said, "I'm sorry, but we'll see you off in the morning." He left her standing there.

Begging didn't matter. The subject was closed before he even came in. She dropped to her knees and fell forward on her hands. Trying to stop the sad sobbing that wracked her body, she closed her eyes. *Warm hands caressed her, pulling her body to him. She sat up, keeping her eyes closed to keep the memory alive. Reaching up, she touched his cheek. His breathtaking hazel eyes halted her tears and she lifted up to kiss his lips.*

Hazel evaporated and she opened her eyes to her miserable

reality. Out of breath, she panted from panic, but knew what she had to do. She had to see him again. She had to escape. She jumped up and ran to her closet. She pulled off the cardigan and dress and pulled on jeans and a sweater. He would like her in a sweater. *He will take me back if I wear a sweater.* She pulled on warm socks and her coat, grabbed a fuzzy hat, and her gloves. Hazel would approve. He'll be happy she finally listened to him. She did what he wanted. She'll be warm and stay healthy. Yes, he'll like her again. *Want me again.*

She grabbed her wallet and her lip balm, tucking them into the large pockets at her sides. She couldn't wait here any longer. She had to get out of here before they came in the morning. "I can't go back," she murmured over and over.

He was her only answer. She would go to him and kiss him until he took her back. She would have to be sneaky, her sneakiest of all time. She opened her bedroom door and stopped, her body unable to move. Jude tried to shut the door, but the men put their hands out and prevented her from closing it. "Ms. Boehler, you need to come with us."

From their white clothes to their overly composed voices, she knew she was in trouble. Her eyes flicked to her stepfather, who looked away, and then left. "There's been a mistake," she cried. "I've been doing everything I was asked."

"Ms. Boehler, there's no mistake. We only want to help. Your parents only want to help you get better."

"I'm fine!" she shouted. "Please. I'm fine." Something flashed, the light reflecting and that's when she saw it—the needle. "No, please," she pleaded. "I'll go willingly. Just please. Please don't give me a shot."

"It's procedure. We're sorry, Ms. Boehler."

She ran for her bathroom but was caught before she could

enter. Pinned to the ground, she felt the sharp needle enter her body, and screamed. But that was all she remembered...

Chapter Eight

THE SADDEST MUSIC Taylor had ever heard crooned through the speakers of his apartment. He pressed stop. Jude had an affinity for the blues and she had reprogrammed his stations when she had been there.

He took a sip of his coffee that had gone cold. Setting the mug down on the bookcase next to his drafting table, he spun around and pressed play again, willing to take the hit to his heart.

It was snowing outside again. January sixteenth. Would it ever stop or was this winter going to be as harsh as his life had become?

One project wrapped earlier in the week, but he still had three that needed updates. Every day he had meetings. It was seriously cutting into the time he wanted to be thinking about Jude, wondering if she would return to him or not. He tapped on his phone until a bazillion Boehlers popped up. While scrolling down the list for Jude or Judith for the fiftieth time, a text came through.

Katherine: *The Castor's party is tonight. Hope you haven't forgotten. I'm all dressed and will meet you there since I'm on the other side of the park already.*

Staring down at the text, he shook his head. He never agreed to go with her. As a matter of fact, he had forgotten all about her and the Castors altogether. He quickly typed out his excuse.

I won't be able to make it. Not feeling well. Send my regards.

It wasn't a total lie. He moved his phone off to the side and looked at the house he was designing. Right when the tip of the lead pencil touched the paper, his phone vibrated again.

I can come over and bring you something to eat. Maybe you're hungry. I remember you always getting caught up in work and forgetting to eat.

Annoyed, he typed, **No. It's okay. I'm okay. I'm going to bed early. I've had a long week.**

Taylor hoped that was the end of it. But he knew Katherine too well. There would be at least one more message to deal with. He waited for it. And waited. Then it came: **I can join you...**

He left that text unanswered. There were only so many ways he could say no. His music shuffled and Alessia Cara's "Here" came on, changing the air in the apartment. The playlist of songs were heavy, emotional songs and he loved them because she did. These songs had played on repeat when he'd touched, tasted, and made love to Jude's body.

His eyes closed and he could see her, almost touch her. He lay down on the leather couch, closing his eyes again and turned the music up loud enough to drown out his sadness. Above him, beneath him, behind him, in front of him—Jude surrounded him. Her scent penetrated his deepest desires. The girl he barely knew was the same woman he knew wholly—inside and out. When he reached out for her, she disappeared and his hands came down on his chest, empty.

His eyes opened and he stared at the ceiling. The music played loudly while shadows crawled across the walls as the gray of the day changed to night. Eventually it was dark inside and out. No lights were on, but enough shone through the relentless snow just beyond the glass.

He wasn't aware of the hour. He wasn't aware of hunger or thirst. Taylor lay there, lost in the lyrics, in the pain, in the loss of the little brunette who had stolen his daylight.

Convinced he was asleep despite his eyes being wide open, he remained laying there, empty. He remained until the phone vibrated, crashing to the floor. He remained long past the knocking became pounding. He remained until the door was opened and his building supervisor and Katherine stood over him. She was talking, but he heard nothing. He heard nothing... until the music was abruptly cut off. "Mr. Barrett, are you okay?"

Taylor blinked. Twice. And their faces came into focus. "No. I'm not."

"Would you like me to call an ambulance, Sir?"

"Will that bring her back?"

Katherine snapped. "He's fine, Chuck. I'll take it from here."

Taylor slowly sat up, placed his feet on the ground. His back was sore from being in the same position for so long. He scrubbed his face and watched Katherine shut the door after escorting Chuck out. "Leave, Katherine."

"I'm not leaving. What's wrong?" She scanned the place, looking for the same person he was looking for. "Is it that girl?"

"Yes." He stood up, annoyed. "Get out."

"Stop being rude to me. I was worried. You weren't answering your phone or your door," she said.

"Next time, take the hint."

She gasped, offended. "What has gotten into you, Taylor?"

"Jellybean muffins, blues, greens, purple, red boots, and lips that can make me forget myself, forget my disease, and forget you."

"Okay, fine. You're in a bad mood, but you don't have to be an asshole."

He stood in front of the large windows, his arms crossed over his chest, his feet apart, and his eyes focused on anything but here. Not sure how long he stood there, he rolled his neck and found he was stiff.

When he finally turned around, the apartment was empty. No one was here but him and he wondered if he had been arguing with ghosts. Walking into his bedroom, he stripped, and crawled under the covers. Tonight he closed the blinds before going to sleep.

JUDITH BOEHLER WAS always surrounded by the finest money could buy—houses, vacations, clothes, schooling… always the finest, only the best would do where her family was concerned. So as she stared at the bars traveling vertically up her window, she smiled.

The bars were rusted steel. The cream paint was chipping on the inside of the windowsill, and her gown was fraying along the ties. She released a long breath, relieved. The air she was breathing was stale and she wondered if the vent was blocked. It was too high for her to reach, so she remained flat on her back on the bare mattress with the springs poking into her. Jude had a knack for lying very still for hours on end. This was how she stayed sane. This was how she survived.

Don't give them anything.

Don't give into them.

Fight.

Fight.

Fight.

She rolled over and looked down the space between the metal

bed anchored to the floor and the dirty wall. Chewed up, dried pills were piling up. She took what she needed. She took the white one. The pink ones—she didn't like. The recovery after the pink pills was tougher. They made the details harder to decipher. They were only about the big picture, the moments lost under the influence.

One more day. Hold on. One more day.

Friday finally arrived. January seventeenth.

Jude entered the foyer and waited, too weak to conquer the journey upstairs alone. Like every other time, she was returned worse for wear. Roman took her arm and helped her up the large staircase. She could have taken the elevator, but he knew she liked to walk, to regain her strength, to regain herself as soon as possible.

The door to her bedroom was open, the bed perfectly made. The damn posies mocked her return, taunting her. Roman released her and set her bag on the dresser. It contained her meds and a toothbrush. She wasn't allowed anything else.

She stood there.

They had found her pile of pills in her room the night before and had watched her, forced her to take the pink one that morning. She struggled inside her own body, scratching at the shell that restrained her sanity. She screamed as loud as she could, but her mouth refused to open.

Feeling came back slowly, entering her pinky first and she wiggled it. Her feet were shoed in lead, but she pushed against the tidal wave of stagnant air of superiority that engulfed her. On her bed, she rolled to the side, every limb thick with her transgressions. Her thoughts were heavy with hazel eyes and kisses down her neck and lower, lower, and lower until she was sweating and breathless.

He had thanked her for giving herself to him—the first person she had given herself to willingly—and she missed him. Jude knew she had been reckless with his emotions. She knew it would end in tragedy. He was her very own Romeo, a tragedy to match his impossible eyes.

She closed hers to the daylight that shone through the open, sheer pink curtains. She closed her mind to the crazy thoughts. She closed her heart to the dangerous emotions Hazel had made her feel. She tried to block out the twelve thousand, three hundred, eighty-six pink posies. Smothering herself with her pillow, she was finally able to scream, her voice loud despite the down feathers.

Tears pricked while she went hoarse. She threw the pillow, her capacities working again. The frame on her vanity went crashing to the ground and she stilled until she realized what made that sound. Scrambling to her feet, she ran, dropping down into the broken glass, blood from her knees spotting the carpet.

The paper was scratched, the photo ripped at the corner. Holding it to her chest, she rocked, apologizing. Her brother deserved better than this, better than to be a ripped picture in his lost cause of a sister's room. If Ryan were still here, they wouldn't be here any longer. They'd be long gone. He'd promised. He'd promised her California and sunshine. He'd promised her so much... and broken all of them.

Standing up, she took the photo and the frame to the vanity and sat. Carefully she placed the photo back into the frame, knocking out any remaining glass before she closed the back and set it down. Seeing his smiling face, she felt conned and almost knocked it over again.

Catching her reflection, she stared into the large mirror. Standard issue results from her "stay" at Bleekman's Recovery Center: Dark circles with a side of heavy bags, dirty hair, and cream-colored paint under her nails.

She simply stared, her mind flitting between the things she loved. Her stepfather came. He went. Her mother visited, sitting on the end of her bed, talking to her. Jude heard nothing. Ghosts that came in and out, mere reflections in the mirror. When it was dark, Nadia came in, stood behind her, resting her hands on her shoulders.

Jude was put in the shower, stripped of her clothes. Her dignity had been stripped away long ago, stolen during her first "stay" at Bleekman's. Nadia scrubbed her clean of the recovery center, but failed to scrub deep enough to take away the scars beneath the pretty façade. Those were permanent. She would live with those as instructed through hushed tones as she floated away to happier times.

She emerged at dinner, sat politely, dressed up, her hair styled by Nadia, her nails with a clear coat of polish, her lips a pale pink. No dark circles. No bags. All as they liked her, loved her, in fact, reminding them of happier times. *Their* happier times.

Her appetite had been suppressed by the drugs running through her system. For her parents' peace of mind, for show, she ate her soup and tried her best to stomach the roasted chicken. She was stuffed before finishing half. They didn't complain. They knew the routine by now.

When she was excused from the table, she retreated back to her room. The shattered glass swept away before anyone would notice, much like her broken insides.

She took her pearl earrings off and set them on the jewelry tray. Sitting down at the vanity again, she took the makeup removal wipes, took two out, and dragged them slowly over her face, pulling her skin until she started to recognize more of herself, the distorted happy person she once was. Two days. She would feel better in two days. The countdown began...

Chapter Nine

JANUARY EIGHTEENTH.

The snow had turned to rain, ruining the carefully orchestrated arrangements Mrs. Stevens had planned. Dinner was moved from the conservatory to the formal dining room. The acoustics would suit polite dinner conversation better in the wood-paneled room.

The Barretts were the first to arrive. Betsy Barrett's timeliness was better than Big Ben. Harold Barrett had just hung up the phone after telling his only son to hurry. Taylor Barrett reached the landing and shook Mr. Stevens's hand and kissed Mrs. Stevens's cheek, then her daughter, Clara, on the cheek, but Clara angled her head and his lips nearly landed on her mouth. They had known each other since they were four. They slept together at seventeen, on a drunken night in The Hamptons. And Clara had never forgotten the handsome Barrett boy.

The Barretts were ushered into the library and had drinks in their hands before their coats were taken away.

At twenty-five, Taylor didn't feel like he fit in with the "adults" at the party. He smiled when he was supposed to, nodded whether he agreed or not. Except when his illness came up. He hated being discussed, dissected. He hated being their poster boy for charity, their platform for social climbing, the subject of idle chatter. Tonight he didn't argue. He didn't have the strength. The last week had worn him down. There were no Jude Boehlers in New York. He was angry: at himself, at her, at their perfect week. He hated the memories of her in his T-shirt. He hated the smell of smoke that lingered everywhere. He hated his kitchen where she cooked in the nude. He hated his bed where they fucked and made love, slept, and where he'd held her. He hated *her*. He wanted that week washed away so he never had to think of the frivolous girl again.

To Mr. Stevens and his father, Taylor nodded, trying his best to act the opposite of how he felt. He even managed to not let Clara's sexual innuendoes bother him. He was a wall, unbreakable by anyone anymore. He would stand tall, stand firm behind his own emotional fortress. Jude had gotten to him and now the anger inside him raged for being duped. He wouldn't fall for such novelties again.

No, he had been fooled into thinking life didn't have to be this affected. For a short week in time, he believed in something other than a life built on a superficial foundation. But tonight he was back, serving the term he had been sentenced to. So when Clara's hand wandered over his backside, he didn't move away. He didn't yelp when Mrs. Stevens grabbed his ass. He smiled and had another drink. He was finished with two by the time The Moeklers arrived. Three by the time the last guests showed up thirty fashionable minutes late.

But he and Clara were upstairs by then. Taylor fell back, his drink upright, and spilling onto the comforter, when she pushed him onto her bed. Crawling over him, she kissed him. She touched him through his pants. She whispered how much she had missed him and didn't know where the years had gone.

He lay there—*letting her*.

He lay there until he sat up just enough to take another drink from the glass in his hand. She went down like the amber liquid, and said, "I'll make you feel so good." The sound of his zipper was the only noise he heard after that as he felt a loss in the pit of his stomach he knew Clara Stevens couldn't fill. Closing his eyes, he could imagine another, so easily.

A loud knock interrupted them. "Clara, dinner is being served. Your mother has requested Mr. Barrett's and your company."

Clara huffed, but then smiled. "Don't worry. We can pick up where we left off after dinner. Maybe you can spend the night."

Taylor sat up. "Maybe," he lied. When he stood, he adjusted his cock and pulled the zipper up. He set the empty glass on her dresser as they left the room. That would be all he would drink tonight. He was losing his senses, his better judgment. Almost drunk was not a feeling he liked.

They entered the dining room and greeted everyone already seated. Fourteen guests and two empty seats near the far corner, the kids' end of the table. Taylor held Clara's chair out for her and then took the empty seat next to her. He took his napkin from the table and spread it across his lap right as Clara's hand joined it.

Conversation at the other end of the table picked back up and he finally looked up at the company that sat across from him. His breath collapsed in his chest as he looked into the blue-green eyes that had demolished him. Her ruby lips were parted just enough for him to hear a harsh breath escape. He leaned in and inhaled. When her eyes left his and looked at Clara, he felt sick.

Her gaze drifted back to him and Jude ran her finger subtly over her mouth, and he knew. Knocking Clara's hand away, he grabbed his napkin and scrubbed at his mouth until fuchsia lipstick was smeared across the white cloth. The blonde to his right had marred him so deceitfully. She knew what she had done. She had staked claims where she had no right. And now he sat in front of the only person he would never want to hurt, hurting her.

Clara, bubbly, completely unaware, introduced them, "Taylor Barrett, this is Judith Boehler and her cousin Isla Boehler. Judith and Isla, this is Taylor."

Isla spoke first. "It's very nice to meet you, Taylor."

He stood, reached across the table, and shook her hand. "It's nice to meet you." He remained standing, turned his full attention on Jude and reached his hand out for her, palm up. It was the only offering he could give, and he hoped she accepted. "It's very nice to meet you, Ms. Boehler." His voice might have cracked, his nerves sneaking out, but he wasn't sure.

She placed her hand in his and when their hands embraced, her lids dropped closed, the heat, the memories, the attraction almost too much. The long greeting was not awkward for them. It was needed. It was wanted. But Clara did not appreciate the extra attention shown to Jude.

Clara asked, "Have you met before?"

Taylor waited for Jude to answer, not sure why they were pretending.

"No," she said, releasing him and leaning back in her chair. She raised her glass of water to her lips to hide the quiver of her bottom one.

A distraction was needed and one was provided in the nick of time for Jude. Bigger than life Rufus Stevens walked in, apologizing for his lateness. He'd been working. His grandiose entrance garnered smiles and happy chatter as a chair was added to the head of the table along with a place setting.

There was a time when Taylor liked Rufus, but many years had passed and dirty deeds had tainted the relationship. Rufus was a womanizer of the worst kind—he paid for sex with jewelry and expensive dinners and treated all women as if they were subservient. His expectations never exceeded a good blowjob and fuck. Taylor had spent more than a few nights comforting the women he'd abandoned at parties where they had been picked up, used, and dumped for the next conquest. There was something about a woman in tears that Taylor had trouble ignoring, even if she did know what she was getting into.

But more than any other woman, Rufus was the same "friend" that had slept with Katherine when Taylor was in the hospital. An engagement had been looming, the pressure from both families firmly planted on Taylor's shoulders. When he told his friend, his "friend" did what any enemy would do: pursued Katherine, and when he got her, when he broke the happy couple up, he dumped her.

Her tears were the only ones Taylor never consoled. *Would never console.*

His mind was occupied on other things. He had his illness to deal with. A broken heart was just another part of him that he hoped to find a cure for one day.

Rufus and Taylor greeted each other with faux-civility. The former friends had not been in contact since Taylor's disease had been diagnosed, and since the betrayal had made the rounds of social gossip circles.

Their salads were promptly served and their glasses topped off. Taylor ordered a Whiskey on the rocks, knowing there was no way he could make it through this dinner without something to slow the bombarding thoughts bouncing around his head.

Not wanting to focus on his foe, he turned back to the brunette who sat directly across from him, suddenly his heart feeling exposed. When she dared to look up, she was met with a fury of emotions, all seen so clearly in his eyes, and she looked away.

He didn't.

Her hair was pulled tight, up in the back. Her bangs hung down to her eyebrows then fell softly across. Her lashes were darker, her lids lined with a thin black line. Pink graced her cheeks, but this pink was unnatural to the blush she had given him. This pink was the opposite of when she was tired, worn out from making love, and sated with their love.

Her pearl necklace covered the divot in her neck that he loved to lick, to suck, to caress. Small, delicate pearls adorned her ears and matched her pale silk dress.

Taylor stared at the brunette across from him, not recognizing her at all. He watched her over the soup course, over the salad course, over the main course. Over dessert. He watched her all night hoping to catch a glimpse of the girl who had ransacked his world.

She ignored his eyes. She ignored the animated conversation going on around her. She ignored the nudges from her cousin. She ignored most of the food in front of her. But she couldn't ignore *him*. He'd given her seven days of happiness. He'd given her seven days of acceptance, of love, of trust. She could avoid his eyes, but no, she couldn't ignore the man that had consumed her days and nights. That consumed her memories.

And she looked up, straight into his hazel eyes and smiled just for him, for her, for them, and the memories they had made.

In the eye of the hurricane, only the two of them existed, the others lost in the deadly winds that swirled around them. It became hard to breathe as she stared into the eyes of the one person she couldn't have. She couldn't destroy him. *She wouldn't.* She had to let him go, for good.

His hand slowly reached for her and her fork fell, clanging against the plate. The hurricane was gone, everyone sitting in silence and staring at her. Everyone but Taylor, who stood. "You've gotten something on your dress. Here," he offered, along with his hand, "I can help you."

She took his hand and lightning struck twice, her heart failing to fend off the currents. "Okay," she replied, barely audible.

Clara laughed at the ridiculous notion. "Sit down, Taylor. The help will get that out. Just go into the kitchen, Judith."

Taylor ignored the snob seated to his left and held tight to the only woman that mattered to him. Their arms were raised above heads as they walked out of the room refusing to let go of the other. Through the swinging wood door, they entered the kitchen, and kept walking until they exited the other side and walked down the hall into the conservatory. They stood in the dark room, the rain beating down loudly on the glass that surrounded them. The harsh weather drowned away the world outside their bubble. And for a few seconds in time, he saw his Jude again.

Not wasting time, he said, "You didn't come back. You said you would."

Then she disappeared again...

"I'm sorry," she apologized, adding him to the long list of people she felt she had disappointed. "I would've if I could."

"Why couldn't you?"

Her hand slipped from his and she walked to the window, the other side covered in battering drops of rain. "Does it matter?" She pressed her hand to the glass, feeling the cold, feeling the pressure of heavy droplets hitting it. "You and Clara seem close."

"Looks are deceiving."

"I guess," she replied, her expression lackluster. She shrugged ever so slightly.

"Don't do that! Don't act like that week didn't matter, like *I* didn't matter." Anger was taking over despite his best efforts to remain calm around her. His hurt had morphed and this was what he was left with. "Everything about you makes sense now. That's not you at all. My parents don't *even* recognize you from that night. You look different and you're acting differently. Where's your beautiful chaos? Where's the wrinkled sundress and the snow boots? You're not the girl who unapologetically crashed both a party and right into my world." He looked at her and said, "Tonight, you're stunning, but I don't recognize the woman standing before me at all."

Desperately wanting to find that girl as much as he did, she whirled around to face him. Her smile was gone when she realized her skirt was fitted and wouldn't twirl. "This is how everyone wants me to be. Am I not perfect? Am I not prim? Or proper? Presentable?"

"You're all those things, but you don't get it. Where is the girl *I* met?" He went to her, got as close as he could while holding back so he wouldn't touch her. He was weak for her and he needed to be strong. "Where's the girl who double dips and cooks in the middle of the night? I want her back."

Becoming frustrated, he had finally set her off. "So do I, but that's just too bad, Taylor!"

"Don't call me that, Judith!" He raised his voice right back at her. "Speaking of, I thought you said your family called you Jude. Everyone in there calls you Judith."

She was insistent. "My real family does."

"You make no sense. You're fucking crazy. I should have gotten the hint at the last party."

She grit her teeth as she stared at him. She became a woman possessed. Maybe obsessed was at the root of her affections, her anger toward and for him. "Don't call me crazy."

Her reaction took him aback. The colloquial phrase had slipped from his tongue with no thought behind it and he looked at her, really looked at her. Then he said with his hands up, "Calm down. We need to return in a minute and I don't want to explain how *well* we know each other. Not to any of them."

Offended, Jude turned on her heel and walked to the door. "No explanation necessary. To your parents, we've known each other forever. Wasn't that what you said? 'Feels like our whole lives'? For everyone else, we met tonight for the first time." Her voice was cold, matter-of-fact.

Nope, not the Jude he recognized at all.

Walking out, she went into the bathroom across the hall and locked the door. A light knock on the other side caused her to take a step back from the door. His voice permeated the enclosed room, like it permeated her chest. "Jude?" he said so softly she barely heard. "I didn't mean what you think. I just meant I don't want to share what we had... what we *are* with them."

"What are we?"

"Lost."

"It's best to cut ties now then. Save ourselves the trouble." *Save our hearts any more pain.* Taking a deep breath, she steeled herself, refusing to cry over him. She leaned her head against the inside of the door, closed her eyes, and said, "Don't worry, Taylor. Our secret is safe." *But my heart never stood a chance.*

Chapter Ten

TAYLOR SAT AT the table, mindful of the worthless conversation that surrounded him, included him, and angered him. His foot was tapping uncontrollably as he waited and waited for Jude to return. Clara reached over, put her hand on his knee, and whispered, "Stop. We can hear you."

He pushed back from the table, and away from her. He couldn't sit there any longer, across from the empty chair. He didn't care what people thought. He needed to find Jude. He was about to stand up when she entered from the main hall. A smile was placed on her face, her eyes blank as she made her apologies. A small, wet circle on her ribs drew everyone's attention to her dress. No food. No stain. An acceptable cover.

Mrs. Stevens said, "I've got a great dry cleaner if you need a reference. They will make your dress look new again."

Jude quietly replied, "Thank you," and went to her chair.

Taylor stood. His fingers pressing so hard against the wood the tips whitened.

Rufus eyed Taylor and stood up as well, buttoning his jacket as he did. The dinner guests watched the two men. Their competitive stance was obvious to everyone except the girl they were competing for.

Jude kept her eyes on the full wine glass at her place, but before she had a chance to sit, Rufus walked around and said, "We're done in here. Would you like to join me in the conservatory, Judith?" His proffered arm hung in the air between them. Seconds ticked by as her gaze drifted over the antique lace covered banquet table and up the navy blue pinstriped suit to eyes on fire, eyes that burned for her, eyes that scorched her from the inside out.

She knew it was pointless, but she tried to steal her heart back and slipped her arm around Rufus's. She was escorted from the dining room and down the hall with the *adults* continuing to the library and the *kids* following their lead into the glass room where she'd just been.

With an unflinching glare, Taylor bore holes into the back of Rufus's head. Then turned his attention to the woman who walked in front of him. His gaze flowed down the curve of her neck and over her back. He wanted to caress her bottom while bending her over and fucking her until she called out "Hazel" at the top of her lungs. He wanted to melt into her heat, into her mouth, into her world again.

His arm was pulled and he looked at Clara who signaled toward the stairs. "I want to cash in that rain check."

"It's still raining." He pulled his arm away and followed Jude into the conservatory.

"Taylor!" she screeched.

He ignored her.

The lights were turned on. Music filled the large room and Taylor walked to the bar and made himself another drink. He'll feel like shit in the morning, but he didn't care anymore. Morning had no significance when tonight was saddled with this much turmoil. Clara slithered up to him. "What is going on with you tonight?

You're not acting like yourself."

"That's good, right?"

From across the room, Isla's laughter broke the tension and Taylor looked over at Jude, who was watching him. Taylor's gaze skimmed down her arm to where Rufus was touching the inner part of her forearm, the same place where Taylor had touched her that first night, had tasted her at his place, had licked her sweet sweat.

Clara draped herself on his shoulder and poked him, the wine going to her head. "This is so boring. Let's get out of here, Tay."

His eyes never deviated from Jude who he watched leave Rufus and Isla to stand at the window. She stared out into the garden that was now lit up, and wordlessly he joined her, standing so close his chest pressed against her back. Her eyes met his in the reflection. She wanted to say so much, to tell him everything that had happened. But as the pink pill wore off, she started seeing the pain in his eyes, and the damage she had done.

Barely moving his lips, he whispered, "I need to see you."

Turning around, her chest to his, she looked up. "You're seeing me now." She stepped around him and left the room, left him standing where he was, staring out at the rain-soaked gardens alone.

Rufus called to her but didn't bother leaving the company of Isla, who had been chatting nonstop since walking into the room. Clara bumped into Taylor and remarked, "For such a pretty girl, she's moody. Let me know when you're ready to go upstairs." She stumbled away and fell into a chair next to Rufus. Taylor could hear her tinkling laugh behind him, and the sound grated on his nerves.

Outside, the rain had stopped and a small familiar figure stepped into the moonlight, her hand running along the hedges as she walked. Taylor hurried from the conservatory.

The house was a maze and he ran checking doors until he found a maid who directed him through the sunroom on the lower floor. He swung the door wide open and ran into the night until he reached Jude. Grabbing her, he pulled her into the shadows near the trimmed rose bushes and kissed her.

He kissed her despite her hands against his chest.

He kissed her holding her to him.

He kissed her until she stopped pushing him away.

He kissed her until she kissed him back.

In the dead cold of winter, their bodies heated as they reconnected. Jude felt alive. She felt stronger than the drugs. She felt wanted. She felt loved and lusted after. Holding him to her, she kissed him until her thoughts fogged and he was the only thing that remained clear.

They shifted and the chilly air came between them. "Why did you leave me?" Taylor asked, feeling the curse of time beating down on them.

"I had no choice. I wouldn't choose to." She stepped closer, preferring his heat to the cold.

"Nothing makes sense."

"Including us."

Staggering back from her, he needed space, needed clarity, needed to feel less insane. "Who are you?"

"You know me, Hazel."

"I don't. I only know what I've seen tonight and Judith is not the girl I spent the best week of my life with. I don't know you right now."

The best week of mine, too. Tears welled in her eyes. "You know me. You just have to look closer, deeper, underneath..." She started choking on her words and looked down. "Underneath what you see before you."

He was losing his mind like he'd lost his heart. He ran his fingers through his hair and pulled at the crown. "What is going on, Jude? Please tell me." He stumbled into the light and his face looked fragmented, shifting between torture and concern.

"You've drunk too much tonight."

Arrogance slipped out, and he snapped, "I haven't even gotten started."

Images of him staggering into the dining room with Clara Stevens produced a new emotion, one she had never felt before—jealousy. "You started before I even showed up. That shade of lipstick did nothing for you," she mentioned offhandedly.

"Fuck! Why won't you talk to me? You came into my life, disrupting my peace—the peace that took me years to find—and destroyed it."

"You were living in the past. A disruption is what you needed to finally put that picture of your ex-girlfriend away. I think I'm owed a thank you." Her insides untied and she calmed, hating that these would be her memories of them, replacing the magical ones they had once made. "Why are we fighting? You can kiss who you want. You can fuck who you want. You owe me nothing, Taylor."

He swayed, unable to stop the storms that raged inside. "Stop calling me that!"

"This is why we're no good. This is why I couldn't come back. We know nothing about each other and we're fighting like we have that right, like we have a future."

"We know each other." Rushing forward he took her by the arms and bent his legs until he was eye level with her. "Look at me, Jude. You know me. I know you. I know the *real* you. I know everything that's important about you."

"You don't know the dark that follows me like my own shadow. It's a part of me that can't be fixed."

"Then show me your shadow, show me the dark. When I told my parents that it felt like we'd known each other our whole lives, I meant it. You gave me that and now you're taking it away. It doesn't work like that though. What we had you can't just erase. That week meant something to me, even if you act like it meant nothing to you."

She shook her head. "You only know a medicated girl you met at a party that made you feel alive for a short time. I can't be that girl." *I can't go back to the center. I can't drag you down with me.* "I can't be her anymore. Not even for you. This is me. This is the only me that is left."

"You keep saying that, but I don't believe you. I don't know who this Judith is tonight, but that's not who you are. Medicated or not. You showed me the real girl that week, so I'm not going to believe your lies now."

Her glassy eyes stared into his impossibly gorgeous eyes, and she weakened and said, "Jude is gone. Judith is all that remains. Don't you see? You met me under a drug-induced haze of pink pills. Save yourself the trouble and let that girl go." Just as a tear slipped down, she glanced up and over his shoulder.

He followed her gaze and saw Clara and Rufus watching them from the conservatory, their bodies silhouetted by the light that shined behind them. Rufus drank from a glass that sparkled and Clara walked out of the room. Rufus gave a lazy salute, then left as well. He wanted to ask her about the pink pills, but something more pressing was threatening. Taylor turned to her and swallowed hard. "He'll destroy you, Jude."

"No more than I already am."

Walking side by side, he stopped with his shoulder against hers, not able to look at her. "I cared about you."

"I know. That's why it's called a tragedy."

The reference to the devastation to his heart did nothing for his mood or the pain he felt. He didn't want to live a real-life tragedy. He'd been living that long before her. Taylor walked back to the house, leaving her standing there.

Minutes later when Jude entered the house, her parents clapped their hands in delight at the other end of the hall. "Oh good, you're still here," proclaimed her mother.

"Of course." She walked to the front door. Voices carried from the library drawing her attention to the left as she passed the dark wood-paneled room. Taylor stood leaning against the mantle, a fire roaring in the fireplace, his back to her. Clara was talking vividly to a man she was too clueless to notice wasn't listening. Rufus sat on a chair opposite Isla, facing the hall. He grinned and raised his glass to Jude, who kept walking.

Her stepfather smiled, and asked, "Are you ready to go, honey?"

"I am. Thank you so much for having us. Dinner was lovely," she said, the robotic response programmed when she was young.

Her parents got into the car and then she got in. When the door shut, she glanced up and saw Taylor, her Hazel, watching her through the tall window. She couldn't see his eyes, but she could feel the heat of his gaze on her. A fire started in her heart, an attraction that would burn them both. The car drove away and she started breathing again.

Her mother patted her hand. "You did good, honey. You did good."

As the buildings rolled by outside, one after the other, she replied, "Thank you."

Back in the library, Clara ran her hand up Taylor's back, and over his shoulders, squeezing his muscles. "Come with me."

"Have you no dignity?" he asked and jerked out of her hold. Walking to the door, he took his coat from the rack and opened the door. Letting the cold air hit him, he walked down the steps to the sidewalk, leaving the front door wide open. He put his coat on and headed for the corner where he hailed a cab.

Shortly after, Taylor entered his apartment and poured himself another drink before removing his coat. He didn't even bother with ice this time. The warm liquid coated his insides, fanning the flame that burned inside his chest. Boehler. Brewster. Renee. Judith. Boehler. He set the empty glass down on the bar and took his coat and suit jacket off.

He fell onto the bed and kicked off his shoes. His pants followed and he lay on his back in his shirt still buttoned and his tie still in its Windsor knot. He lay there alone, fucking alone again. He missed the unpredictable girl he met weeks earlier.

Boehler. Boehler. Boehler.

Judith. Judith. *Jude.*

He missed her.

And he wanted her back.

Reaching down into his pants pocket, he pulled his phone out, and flipped to his photos. He regarded the photo he took of her when she hadn't been looking. It was the saddest picture he had ever seen. Jude was listening, looking at Clara at dinner. But her eyes held no life, no energy, not the girl he'd met at his parents' party. She looked like no one at all. Not even Judith. She was empty.

All night he fought against exposing them to the others, revealing that not only did he know her, but that he might have real feelings for her. But when they were apart, something happened to her, something distressing, something destructive.

But what?

Chapter Eleven

PRIVILEGES WERE EARNED.

Like a child, Jude earned back her freedom half hour by half hour. After an acceptable day, she was rewarded thirty minutes to leave on her own. Two days after that, an hour. She waited, counting the days, until she had earned two full hours. It took seven days, but that's what it would take to get there and back in time.

The second Monday after she had last seen Hazel, she sat at a deli across from his apartment building. She only had fifty minutes left to risk. Traffic was too unpredictable and she didn't dare be late.

The first day she had spied on him, she made it back home with ten minutes to spare. She only wished her heart had been spared in the process. She didn't know why she chose to sit and wait opposed to knocking on his door. Maybe she only needed to see him happy—happy without her—so she could walk away once and for all. She could take their week together and pocket it like she pocketed all the things that mattered most to her. Like her brother. She had thought the hole her brother had left in her heart was healing, but it throbbed without Hazel, a constant reminder of the gaping wound.

On the third day, she figured out why she hadn't been able to go to his apartment. She knew she had to stay as far from his apartment as she could. Her favorite memories resided there. And if she were brave enough to talk to him again, it would have to be in neutral territory. By the following Sunday she was in full stalking mode, determined. But it was Sunday and by the time she arrived, she didn't know if he had already left his apartment or if he would leave.

Another hot chocolate was ordered and she sat on a barstool facing the street. When he appeared, coming out of his apartment building, she spilled her drink just as she took a sip. Just seeing him again sent a thrill through her body. The last time she'd been dealing with the effects of mind-numbing drugs. In hindsight, she wished they would've worked on her heart instead.

Jumping up, she threw the cup away and ran outside. She only had five minutes. Five minutes left before she had to leave for home, so she ran across the street, jaywalking, and almost getting hit by a cab.

The honking of the car didn't faze Taylor. It was Manhattan and honking horns were a part of the melody here. He shoved his hands into his pockets and kept walking. Until...

"Hazel! Wait!"

He'd been hurt. There was no sense in hiding it anymore. He never believed his own lie anyway. But hearing that name stung, deep. He didn't want to assume, but when he heard it again, and again, he couldn't stop himself from turning around. His mouth opened in surprise as he saw Jude running toward him, arms flailing, causing a complete scene.

And he smiled.

She stopped just short of him, out of breath, and bending over at the waist to recover.

He said, "You're here."

Looking up at him, she looked relieved. "I am. For you."

"Why?"

"Because I owe you an apology. I'm sorry. You deserved better than I gave you."

Seeing her now, he struggled to be mad, and considered the good times they'd shared. "You gave me everything I needed."

She shook her head. "I mean at that dinner." Finally in control of her breathing again, she stood up straight. "I hated that you saw me that way, but it happened. I just need a few minutes to explain." She checked the time on her watch. One minute left. "But I can't today. Maybe another time?"

"Why? Why not now?"

"I have to go."

"No!"

His anger and pain vibrated though her, her heart still tethered to the man before her. "This is not what I wante—"

Stepping closer, he almost touched her to see if she was real. "What *do* you want, Jude?"

"I want you to live a gloriously happy life. And that can't be with me."

Only the tips of his fingers touched her coat, but the sensation spread throughout her whole body. He whispered, "One week wasn't enough."

"One week is all we have." She backed away, needing to leave, but not wanting to leave him again. She has to fight her instincts, to protect herself from what will happen if she doesn't. "Maybe we shouldn't meet again. I don't want to hurt you any more than I have."

"I'll meet you. Just say when, Jude. I'll do it. I'll take what I can."

She understood his desperation. She felt that for him, but she had no idea until just then how much he felt for her. She couldn't refuse him, just like she couldn't refuse herself this one last taste, this one last time with him. He'll hate her soon enough. She would savor any time she could get. "Tomorrow? I can meet you between eleven and two."

"I have two meetings tomorrow. Can you come over tomorrow night? We can make dinner and talk."

"No," she said, "I can't." Flustered, she started walking backward. "I have to go, but soon."

He stepped forward. "Don't leave. We can talk now."

Holding up her arm and touching her watch, she tried to explain, "I can't right now. I'm sorry. Soon."

"I'm going to hold you to that, Jude Boehler. I've got your name and number now." He smiled so innocently, but Jude's blood iced in her veins.

"No!" She stopped suddenly, in the middle of the sidewalk and went back to him. "You can't come for me. Promise me you won't come over."

Her rapid transformation sent up a million red flags of concern. He'd have more to address than her constant disappearances the next time he saw her.

"Okay." He told her what she wanted to hear, but it pained him to agree. He wanted to see her. This was his Jude—all over the place, a crazy hat on, wrinkled skirt, and red snow boots—and he was holding himself in place so he didn't grab her and take her inside to talk now. Instead, he watched her nod as she backed away again.

In return, she gave him a small, familiar smile, then blew him a kiss. "Soon," she said. "I promise."

While she walked away from him, he realized how much he had missed her, missed Jude. "Tuesday," he yelled down the street. "Meet me here on Tuesday at noon."

She waved, and even with the distance between them, he could see that life had returned to her eyes. She was vibrant. Kodachrome. She was that rainbow she'd spoken of the first time he'd met her, come to life. "I'll be here," she called back to him before rounding the corner.

He couldn't stop his smile in return.

On Tuesday, Taylor left work early to get back to his apartment by noon. He didn't want to be late. He didn't want to keep her waiting, so he took a taxi. The cab pulled up out front and he saw Jude leaning against the wall looking from left to right for him. She didn't notice him right in front of her until it was too late. He cupped her face and kissed her. When he leaned back to look her in the eyes, he said, "You use impossible a lot. Well, I find it impossible to resist your lips." He kissed her again. "Let's go upstairs."

He grabbed her hand and started leading her against the breeze to the door, but her feet were planted and she didn't budge. "No, Hazel."

Turning back to her, he questioned, confused why they had stopped. "What? Why not? I thought we were going to talk?"

"We are, but somewhere else."

"Why not my place?"

"If I step foot in that apartment, I don't know if I'll be able to leave."

With a playful grin, he pulled her hat farther down her forehead, and said, "I don't see the problem."

Jude blushed, which was part of the problem. He did things to her... he made her want to do things she couldn't want to do anymore. *Mustn't want anymore.*

That was the natural pink he'd missed. Bending down, he kissed her on the cheek. "I'll go wherever you want to go, Jude."

She looked around and suggested, "What about the new gallery two blocks up?"

"Okay."

They held hands as they walked, neither protesting. They had minutes left together and they didn't want to waste one of them.

Taylor felt happy, happier than he had in weeks. Jude appeared happy to him as well. She was trying hard not to look at him, but he would catch her eyes on him every now and then, and he liked it. He didn't know how today was going to go, but he was ready with an arsenal of reasons of why they were worth a real try.

When they entered the gallery, she took a pamphlet, folded it, and tucked it into her pocket. He followed her in and while she stood in front of the first installation, tilting her head all the way left, he watched her. Her long neck was beautifully curved, her hair falling unevenly to the side, her feet together, and hands behind her back. Standing upright, she turned over her shoulder, and asked, "What do you think?"

"Beautiful."

She scrunched her nose and looked back at it. "Really? I think it's gross." When she stepped to the side, he could see the mass of green mold covering the compost contained in the acrylic box. "But you know the old saying, 'Art is in the eye of the beholder.'"

He started laughing, sort of embarrassed she thought he'd said rotting food was beautiful, but he didn't correct her. "I thought it was beauty? Beauty is in the eye of the beholder?"

Pondering that, she shrugged and smiled. "Well I have no idea then. But I still think it's gross."

He got up and they walked side by side to the next installation—a series of very tiny paintings, landscapes. They stood very close to the wall and took in each one, moving around each other to see the intricate detailing. She bumped him and he staggered a step over. Laughing, he returned and bumped her. Harder than he meant to. She ran right into a very serious-looking man who didn't appreciate the distraction from the art. Jude brushed her hand down his arm, and said so sweetly, "I'm so sorry. I lost my footing."

He snapped at her, "You should have that checked out."

So Taylor stepped in, brought her into his side, and said, sternly, "She apologized. You should be grateful she bothered."

He eyed Taylor and walked away.

New Yorkers. So jaded, Taylor thought. He kept his arm in place and said, "I don't have much time. We should talk."

Jude nodded, dreading the conversation she never wanted to have. As they walked silently through the gallery, holding hands, they looked everywhere but at each other. Finally they reached a terrace on the second floor, and even though it was cold outside, they chose to talk out there.

She spun around once with her arms in the air before leaning against the railing and pulling him to her by his coat. His expression was soft while his body was pressed hard against her. "Kiss me," she said.

To Taylor, Jude was irresistible. So he kissed her. But *the talk* hung over their heads, casting shadows on them. When their lips parted, she kept her eyes closed and her lips ready, waiting for more from his.

"Where did you go?" he asked, wanting to kiss her more than he needed answers. But the questions still plagued him. "Why did you not return?"

"I did return. I'm here."

"*Now*. You're here, now."

Leaning her cheek against his chest, she replied, "Yes, Hazel. I'm here now. Hold me."

His arms wrapped around her and they swayed together, the sonata of the street below played their song. Minutes passed before he finally spoke. "Are you going to leave me again?"

"Not if I have a say," she whispered, her arms tucked between them.

"Can I see you tonight?"

The heavy burden of her life weighed her down twenty-two hours a day. She didn't want it to be a part of the two hours she lived for, the two hours she survived for, the two hours that kept her breathing. But he deserved more, even if it was more than she could give. "No."

His arms tightened around her and he kissed her forehead. She had become a puzzle that refused to be solved, but remained the answer to the most important questions in life.

In his arms, she could hear him gulp, gulping down the protests that she herself felt confined by. There was no good answer she could give to ease him, so she closed her eyes and listened to his heartbeat instead.

Quietly, he asked, "You're not going to give me anything, are you?"

She placed a kiss on his chest though he couldn't feel it through the layers of fabric. "I'm giving you all I can. The rest, we'll have to trust to the future."

Taylor understood blind faith. He lived with it every day, just like he lived with Parkinson's. When he felt the tendons begin to shake, he held her tighter to stop the onslaught. "Trust is like the wind, my sweet Jude. It slips away before you have a chance to catch it."

She sighed. "I wish we had met in another time and another place. Life would be so much easier if I wasn't broken."

"Life is tragic," he said, knowing this too well.

"Love is tragic," she whispered, feeling lost to the life she lived.

"Love is devastating to one's heart."

She looked up at him, resting her chin on his chest. "You say that as if you've loved before."

"I say it from feeling it." *With you.* He backed away from her and took hold of the door. "My lunch is over."

Chapter Twelve

TOGETHER, JUDE AND Hazel's time became an interlude to their lives. Each day, they sneaked away to spend a precious few minutes, if lucky, a few hours with each other. But they never went to his apartment and he never came to her home. They went to all the galleries in the area, and visited coffee shops, saw a movie that made Jude cry on Taylor's shoulder, and they walked through the park.

The park was her favorite. It was wide-open space. When they were there she felt free. She felt like she could breathe.

They sat on a bench together and he read a book while she rested her head on his lap and stared up at the sky. "Do clouds have souls, Hazel?"

"Yes. How else would they hold their sadness in until the next time it rained, Jude?" She loved that he never hesitated to answer her questions. She also loved who he was with her. His calm and fury; his passion and love. He made her laugh and made her feel something other than pain and betrayal for the first time since her brother's death.

Taylor closed his book and looked up at the sky. Clouds floated by and he realized that these times together, just the two of them, two against the world, the quiet times and the times they talked for hours, was what he had been missing his whole life.

It was then he understood that it wasn't her chaos that had drawn him to her. It was her soul.

The depth of her heart.

The width of her imagination.

The breadth of her knowledge.

The gravity of her pain.

They all made up this beautiful woman whose head was in his lap. He reached down and touched her cheek, choosing the peace of the park to any chaos she conjured. Yes, he preferred this Jude to medicated Jude any day.

January melted into February and on a random Thursday, Jude looked at the tall man to her left, who was reading over her shoulder. She loved how handsome he was. She knew she shouldn't care about things that were so shallow, but he was very pleasing to the eyes. She especially liked that line between his eyebrows, the one he got when deep in thought. Wanting to see it, she said, "Did you know there's a phone app that distorts your face so much that you're almost unrecognizable?" Jude scrunched her nose. "Isla has it. It makes her skin so smooth and removes every mark that makes a person who they are."

Taylor chuckled. "Everyone wants to look perfect."

"Perfection is an ugly beast. It's our blemishes that make us pretty. Never be perfect. Okay, Hazel? I like you just the way you are." She lifted his glasses and kissed the light line between his eyebrows.

He laughed again. "I'll try not to be, but some days it's a real struggle."

That made her laugh and she wandered to the next aisle of books at the store. Military. He followed behind, following the girl he'd follow anywhere. "Why don't you have a phone?"

"I do. I just didn't have anyone to call."

"You've had me for over a month."

"I *have* you?"

"You do. Completely," he said, grabbing her and giving her a kiss that would lead to more right here in the middle of a bookstore if they weren't careful.

She pushed him gently and flitted away, saying, "Well, maybe I'll give you my number then."

He caught her in the Family Psychology section with her nose pointed down at a book. "Whatcha reading?"

Quite quickly, exhaustion seemed to creep over her beautiful face, "I tried to kill myself." Desperately needing to get it out there. Desperately wanting him to know her deepest secrets, tired of hiding it from the one person she wanted to be completely honest with.

Taylor was shocked. His mouth dropped open, and he leaned his hands against the shelf, needing some sort of support. His eyes knit together and he looked down. His voice was low and calculated, too controlled when he asked, "When?"

"Two years ago."

He could tell he was going to have to pull every detail out of her. She had turned away from him to put the book back on the shelf. "Why?" he asked, his voice sounding croaky. He hated his easily exposed emotions.

Jude leaned her back against the books and looked at him, then turned so she was leaning against him instead. The fabric of his pants was smooth as she ran her hand over them. She loved him in suits and this gray one was especially sexy on him. Her only mistake was opening a can of worms that would take the rest of his lunch hour. He'll either stay or leave, but she needed to give him that choice. Taking his hand, she led him to the fiction section, feeling more comfortable in the land of fantasy. "My family blames me for my uncle's death."

"Why would they do that?"

"Because they didn't want to know the truth. The truth is damaging and drives people away. It's better to live in the lies."

"That's not true." He got frustrated, yanking her to a standstill. "Is that why you haven't told me before? You thought you'd drive me away?"

"We have... oh, I don't know anymore, Hazel. Things feel too easy for us."

"Nothing is easy for us. We meet for an hour each day and then a few on the weekends. We're pretending this is normal. It's not. What happened to the week we had? What happened to spending time together in private?" Taylor surprised himself. Pent-up feelings were unstoppable now. "Why can't I come to your house? Why can't I pick you up for a date? Why can't we have sex again? When you say it feels too easy, there is nothing that feels easy to me when it comes to you. But I'm here. I'm willing to do this how you want because when I meet you, it's the best hour of my day."

Jude hadn't realized how affected he was by the change in their relationship. She should have, but she knew so much more than him and never wanted that to taint their time. "I'm selfish, but your mere presence is comforting to me."

"Because you don't have to live in the lies with me."

Smiling, trying to distract him, she said, "So that's why this feels so good."

He didn't return the smile, still caught up in the details. "Why did you try to kill yourself?"

Anxious, Jude looked around to make sure no one was listening to their conversation. "We don't even have to talk. You just let me be and you give me security," she confessed.

Rubbing the bridge of his nose, he said, "Don't shut this down." Taking her hand, he took her outside to the busy street where no one cared about them. "I need more. Please."

Offhandedly, she said, "My uncle, the one who died, Isla's father, he... he did things to me. He touched me in ways that no one should touch you without your permission. There it is, Hazel."

Jude heard the harsh breath he sucked in when he backed them to the nearest wall. He felt like shit for being so hard on her. "I'm sorry, Jude."

"So am I."

"What do you mean your family doesn't believe you?"

She angled away and hugged her body, closing herself off. "I didn't encourage him. I swear I didn't."

"Oh God, Jude." Standing behind her, he rubbed her shoulders. "Of course you didn't. I believe you. I'm sorry if you thought I meant—"

Looking over her shoulder at him, she asked, "You do?"

"Do what?"

"Believe me? You believe me?"

"What? Of course I believe you."

"Why?"

The relief she was seeking came quickly. "Who would ask for that to happen?"

Shaking her head, she lowered it. "I asked him to stop, but he said he would tell my parents that I had instigated it. I should have let him tell. Maybe things would be different now."

Strong arms embraced her and she slid into his warmth, into his love. With her head against him, she listened to his steady heartbeat. He kissed the top of her head, and asked, "You thought killing yourself was the only way out?"

"I was dirty. I couldn't get clean enough. *He* made me feel dirty. I was sixteen and excited about finally being able to date, to hang out with my friends, to get my independence, and he stole all of those dreams, those rights from me. He stole my innocence before I had a chance to give it away."

He rubbed her back, but didn't say anything.

She said, "We had a family celebration that night on my birthday. He came into my bedroom later when I was changing into my pajamas. He told me not to say anything. When I tried to leave, he slapped me, and filled my head with threats of how he would hurt me, hurt my brother, and destroy my family. And I believed him." With tears in her eyes, she looked up at Hazel. "I believed him."

"You're not at fault. Do you hear me?" Taylor was mad, infuriated. "I don't know what they've done to you since, but they've fucked with your head. You're not to blame, Jude. He was a psycho pedophile."

Her throat staggered over a deep breath, and she said, "Every time they would visit, he would get more aggressive. I knew what was coming next. I knew he would rape me. I watched him over dinner. I saw how much he was drinking. I saw him watching me, how he looked at me. I knew."

Taylor looked around, not wanting this to play out on a dirty city street. "Let's go around the corner." She walked, her head against his bicep with his arm around her. They rounded the corner to a tree-lined street and went to a stoop and sat. He sat one step down and looked up at her. "What happened?"

She spoke as if she couldn't wait to get it off her chest and out of her heart. "I stopped talking to my brother. I ignored the friends I had. I had nightmares of him sneaking in and... I felt ashamed of what I looked like. My breasts had to be to blame. They were tempting him. I was responsible for him doing that. If only I didn't look like *this* things would have been different."

His heart hurt so badly that he didn't want to speak. He couldn't say anything that would help her, or heal her. Instead of words, he held her, hoping that would suffice.

"I went to my parents' medicine cabinet and took twenty-eight pills from two different prescriptions. I didn't even know what they were. I just knew I didn't want to exist anymore." Her shoulders hunched down, her body closed in on itself. "When I woke up at the hospital a day later they were so happy to see me." She laughed humorlessly. "And then my parents told me I owed my life to my uncle since he was the one who found me." She let that hang in the air between them.

It was clear what happened, but Taylor still voiced it. "That bastard found you because he had come into your room to violate you."

With a grin, she said sarcastically, "But I now owed my life to him. Oh the irony."

"If he wasn't dead, I'd kill him."

Jude had never heard that tone from her Hazel. He had always been kind even when he'd been angry with her that night at the Stevens's. So when he said that, she believed him. "My brother walked into my bedroom one night to show me his acceptance letter to NYU. It was his dream school. He wanted to be a movie director. He was always filming us when we were younger. He made some amazing short films in high school and even won an award for one."

"Jude?"

She had disappeared into memories for a minute, but was back, and exhaled. "He saw me pinned. My uncle had his hand over my mouth..."

"You don't have to say anything else if you don't want to."

"My brother walked in and saw my uncle touching himself over my body while I cried."

Taylor stood up, not able to sit still. She watched him, as if the fury couldn't be contained. He kept his back to her as he paced. Then, he turned around and squatted down with his head bent forward. She expected to see sympathy.

She expected that.

But she got anger, eyes that blazed in a way that almost scared her—*almost*. Looking at her watch, she wanted to calm him, to comfort him. "Time's up for today, Dr. Barrett."

"Don't make jokes." He was serious.

She smiled, attempting to laugh, but unable to. "Jokes are exactly what we need. Know any?"

Rolling his head to the side, he shook it. "I'm fresh out."

Trying to downplay the whole thing, she said, "That's okay. I'll see you tomorrow. You can make me laugh then."

"I'm not leaving you. I can't, knowing this."

They both stood up. She then went to him and wrapped her arms around his middle to give him the comfort he always gave her so effortlessly. "But I can't stay." She looked up, and gave what she thought was a reassuring smile. "I'll be okay. I just need to go. Like you do before you're even later."

"What can I do for you, Jude? Tell me and I'll do it."

"You're doing it already."

Chapter Thirteen

VALENTINE'S DAY FELL on a regular Thursday. Hazel showed up to the park a few minutes late. Jude wasn't worried, but she hated they didn't have more time. When she looked up from her book, he stood there with a pink rose in his hand, and she said, "I didn't think we would do gifts."

He waggled his eyebrows. "It reminded me of you. Anyway, it didn't cost much so don't worry about it."

As she took it from him, he sat down. With the flower to her nose, she closed her eyes and smelled. "Thank you."

"This reminded me of you, too." He held out a small box.

She knew it was jewelry just from the square shape of it. "No, I can't take that." She bit her lip and glanced between the box and him.

"Yes, you can, Jude. I bought it. You take. You open it. You say how much you love it and then you wear it. See? It's that easy."

A smile finally surfaced. "I used to love surprises."

"Maybe you'll like this one then."

Bumping him with her elbow, she laughed. "Maybe. Guess we'll see," she teased. She had no doubt she would love it. It was from him, so that was already guaranteed, but she also had no idea what it would be.

Taking the small box in hand, she lifted the top and pulled out the little velvet box. Her breath stopped when she lifted the hinged lid and saw a ring.

"I know it's presumptuous to give you a ring, or maybe a terrible idea that I had one late night when I was lying in bed alone when all I wanted was to be lying there with you. But I liked it and..." His eyes met hers. "I hope you'll keep it, even if you don't wear it."

She took the delicate band of diamonds from the case and held it between her fingers. "Hazel, I can't keep this."

"There's a necklace. One you can wear it on so no one knows, if that's what you're worried about."

A million thoughts ran through her head, pros and cons of a gift of this magnitude, of this sentiment. But looking at him and then at the ring, the answer was obvious. Her heart spoke through racing heartbeats straight to his, and she slipped it on her finger.

He admired it on her. "A perfect fit."

Yes, you are, my love, she wanted to say, but didn't. *For now.*

Turning to him, she placed her hands on his face and kissed him. As their lips came together, winter took its last walk around the park and spring had announced its arrival through a warm breeze. When she looked at him, the cold had returned, but her body stayed warm cloaked in his love.

Jude leaned her head on his shoulder, and stared out. "Thank you."

He nodded. "You're welcome."

When she sat up again, she said, "Hazel?"

"Yes?"

"My family can't know about us. They'd never let us be."

"You're twenty-two, Jude, not twelve. They can't stop me from seeing you."

"They can." She stared down at the sparkling ring wrapped around her finger, much like he had her wrapped around his. He just didn't know it yet. "They think I'm crazy."

"What do you mean?"

"I've been in and out of an asylum they call a recovery center at least fourteen times over the last two years."

He sat up, concerned. "Why?"

"Because they hold a court order that says the hospital can evaluate me at any time. My stepfather tells them when I do anything wrong and then they decide if they come take me away."

"What are you talking about, Jude?" He sat up, needing the full story, trying to understand. "You're not crazy."

"I'm not. I swear to you. I'm not, but they treat me like I am."

That line she always noticed when he asked questions appeared, deeper than usual this time. "Where do they send you?"

"Bleekman's. It's a terrible place. They try to turn people crazy so they can collect the money from wealthy families. I see it. I know what they're up to. It's a private facility. The drugs, the... doctors."

He noticed her hands shaking as much as her voice. Unable to face his fears, he looked away when he asked, "What do they do to you? Tell me."

"Not today. It's been such a beautiful day." She held her ring out again and smiled. "If I don't wear it on my finger, I'll wear it close to my heart. Always."

Clasping her ringed hand between both of his, he looked her in the eyes. "Jude, I need you to tell me what they do to you."

The spark left her eyes and a haze replaced it. She struggled to keep eye contact and tried to pull her hand away, but he wouldn't let go. He leveled his eyes on hers and though she knew she could trust him, she could see his anger building before she even spoke.

Taking her free hand, she touched his wrist and stole an ounce of his strength before saying, "They force me to take drugs that numb me, numb my mind and body. Then I get locked in a room with a window that has bars and peeling paint. I actually feel safe in there, in the isolation. Until the door is opened in the middle of the day, after lunch at twelve fifteen like clockwork, and the doctor does a *check-up*."

He swallowed down the will to suppress this conversation and asked what he wasn't sure he was prepared to have answered. "What's involved in the check-up?"

"Let's just say the abuse didn't end with my uncle's death." She got up, book and box in hand, and took the path toward the street.

"Be honest with me. Is that the reason you don't want to go to my apartment? You don't want to be intimate with me?"

"I don't go to your apartment because if I don't return home, I go to Bleekman's."

He sat there, feeling like he'd been punched in the gut. Today's information hit him hard. This girl he was falling in love with was wearing a ring he'd just given her and yet, he wasn't protecting her like he should. How did he not know any of this before now? He tried to control his anger, but that wasn't going to happen. "You're not going back to Bleekman's," he shouted.

He followed her. She turned around when he got close, and said, "Don't you see how much I love you, Hazel?"

Love was in the air, in her heart, and filled his, but her forthright declaration surprised him.

Through the cleansing of the darkness, she was looking at him bathed in light. The spark returned to her eyes when he neared and his hands went around her waist. He lifted her up, eye level with him, and kissed her. When he set her down, he said, "I love you more."

With a teasing smile, she said, "You said your gifts didn't cost much."

"It's only money, Jude. Money doesn't matter. Love does."

Jude started opening up after that. The stories were hard to hear, but he would listen, would ask questions, and would comfort her the best he could. He just wished he could open up as easily. Telling her about his illness seemed like a daunting burden he didn't want to place on her. She had enough to deal with.

In late February, they were waiting in line, a coffee for him and hot chocolate for her, outside his work on his lunch hour, when she said, "You would have liked my brother Ryan."

He tried not to make a big deal when she offered these insights into her life up, but it was hard to just wait to see what she would say. "Was he like you?"

"No. He was strong."

"I think you're strong."

"You say that because you don't see me but for a few hours each day."

"I say that because you've survived and still have the ability to make others smile." He smiles and points at it.

That made her laugh. He loved hearing her laugh. She laughed quite often with him and it made him wonder if she laughed when they were apart. "Tell me more about Ryan."

"Ryan was a lot like you—handsome and smart." She rolled her eyes. "Girls were all over him all the time. It was quite annoying actually. He was two years older than me and would have done great things in life, if given the chance."

Sensitive to the subject, he whispered, "How did he die?"

"He didn't have a fitting death for the life he led." They moved up in line. "He was hit crossing the street here in the city. Two cars racing. In Manhattan. It would have never ended well. Someone was destined to die. I just wish it wouldn't have been my brother."

"Me too." Taylor put his arm around her shoulders and they ordered their drinks. When they walked away, the moment had passed, and Jude was onto another topic. Each time she shared a little more of herself, of the life she hid from him, he started to feel he understood why she kept them hidden.

Mid-March. On a Saturday that couldn't decide if it was winter or spring, Jude felt very much that she and Hazel were star-crossed lovers. One day felt like perfection, the next complications from their secret affair overshadowed their day. Despite the mixture of emotions, she stopped when she found they were walking by The Plaza Hotel. People were coming and going, rushing past them as she stood there, looking up into hazel eyes that adored her. "We should go in."

It wasn't a suggestion and he took full advantage of the offer. "How much longer do we have?"

"Two hours left."

He didn't run, but he might have rushed the doors and up to the registration desk. "One room please."

The woman behind the counter glanced to Jude and then to Taylor, for whom she smiled. "Certainly. One room for the night. Check-out is eleven in the morning."

The plastic of his credit card slapped against the counter, and he replied, "That will work."

Taking the card in hand, she looked at the name and up to him. "Very well, Mr. Barrett. No luggage?"

"Nope. Spur-of-the-moment trip," he said, smiling.

Jude lifted up on her toes and whispered, "Are you sure?"

"Never more so."

Looking around the lobby, she knew it was time, so with her

back to the desk, she said, "I want to have you over for dinner with my family."

"Really?" he asked, shocked.

"I'll tell my parents about us tonight."

"Do you want me there?"

"No," she replied, coyly. "I should break it to them first. I'll have to explain when I've been seeing you. I haven't been telling them the full truth. I tell them where I go, but I don't tell them who I'm with, so I don't know how they'll react."

He took her hand and kissed it. "That's why you take the brochures?"

"That's why."

Jude spoke to the front desk attendant, "Can we have champagne sent up to the room. We're celebrating."

Peeking up at Taylor, he had one eyebrow raised, then said to Jude, "Yes, we are. Several times over if we have it my way."

"Have I ever told you how much I like your way? Especially when you have your way and move your tongu—"

"Sir!" the woman said, interrupting. "Your card. Please sign here and here is your room key."

Taylor signed for the room and took the key. After listening to brief directions, the two walked together toward the elevators, a shared secret on their lips.

Chapter Fourteen

THE FUNNY THING about fate is one can't outrun it. No matter how much they try, setting their sights on a different outcome, they will always end up exactly where they were meant to be.

Rufus Stevens had just left a hotel room at The Plaza after giving his regular Saturday rendezvous a diamond bracelet to keep her coming back, and more importantly, to keep her mouth shut. For, Mr. Rufus Stevens had a sexually experimental side that wouldn't go over well with the blue-blooded debutantes he preferred to *date*, or rather, to be seen with in public. So he took his sexual transgressions out on highly paid call girls instead.

More recently, the Stevens family, namely his parents, had started to put pressure on him to settle down. They'd even offered a high-paying position at the family-run business and free access to the estate in the Hamptons as a wedding gift. Even after getting off, he felt like a dead man walking just from the thought.

That was until he saw a certain old chum of his across the lobby heading to the elevators with one sexy piece of ass under his arm. Taylor Barrett had been a thorn in his side since Rufus faced a rape accusation back in high school. Taylor Barrett had backed the girl instead of his friend. Daddy Stevens paid the family to shut it down, but it took nine years to get the satisfaction Rufus wanted. When Rufus nailed Taylor's soon-to-be fiancée in a supply closet of the hospital where Taylor was recovering, he had finally gotten his sweet revenge.

"Taylor Barrett?" he called, stopping and making a scene. "Hey, is that you?"

Jude and Taylor took a step away from each other on instinct, their bodies disengaging. Taylor looked back, but he knew the voice before seeing the face attached. As they turned around, they both held their breath unintentionally. Taylor put on a smile and waved. "Hey, what a coincidence running into you here." *Not at all.*

Under his breath, he whispered to Jude, "I'll handle this."

She felt a tightening in her chest. She knew. She knew before he even opened his mouth that there was nothing he would be able to say that would explain what they were doing there... together.

When Rufus reached them, the two men shook hands and acted as if this was a happy coincidence, though neither felt it. Rufus eyed Jude. "Judith Boehler, right? Wow. Look at you." He checked her out from head to toe. "You look... different. Why didn't we keep in touch after that dinner?" Taking her hand, he pulled her forward and kissed her on the cheek.

"I've been crazy busy," she said, stepping back, wishing Taylor could wrap his arm around her again and make her feel safe.

Rufus turned to Taylor. "So what are you guys doing here?"

"We were grabbing lunch." Taylor didn't offer more than requested. Liars got caught by offering too much. But more importantly, he didn't trust Rufus. Ever.

Rufus's eyebrows knitted together. "Really? The restaurant is that way and you looked like you were heading for the elevators. This isn't a date, is it? Oh man, I'm sorry." He raised his hands in a cautious way. "Seems I've interrupted a little afternoon delight."

Rufus winked at Jude, making her stomach churn.

Taylor bit back, "You've misunderstood. We were going to the restaurant. As a matter of fact, we're going to be late. It was good to see—"

"Oh good. Then you don't mind me joining you? I'm starved."

Jude swallowed hard. "Taylor was helping me with a problem. A friend of mine's problem. I wanted to offer her advice, but don't know how to go about it. So if you don't mind, I'd like to talk to him privately over lun—"

"Taylor is great with the advice as long as it benefits him. Maybe you want an unbiased opinion." Rufus swayed his hand toward the restaurant while putting the other on Taylor's shoulder and redirecting them. "Let's eat and I'll be happy to help."

The three of them started walking across the lobby, Jude and Taylor much less eager than Rufus. She tried to catch Taylor's eye, but she caught Rufus's instead and he grinned at her. "Sure is good to see you again, Judith."

She didn't reply, but she felt it in her gut: nothing good could come from this. Debating on bowing out, she walked toward the sunny windows ahead, drawn to the outside. Unfamiliar fingers took her elbow, her skin crawling under his touch, and guided her back on track to the restaurant.

They were seated at a table in the middle of the restaurant. Very public. The couple thought it was perfect. There was no way to get too personal when there were so many ears that could hear. Rufus would have to stay checked with his insinuations.

Taylor and Jude sat next to each other at the table for four. Rufus took the seat on the other side of her, cozying up closer to her corner. Jude hated this. She couldn't see Hazel's eyes without being obvious. His eyes gave her security, made her feel safe and beautiful. In his eyes, she saw a future that she couldn't see with her own.

Bending her head down, she read the menu, taking her time to help distract her nerves.

Once they placed their order, Rufus clapped his hands together and said, "So what's the big problem your *friend* has?"

Jude, startled from the loud clap, and stuttered, "Um, well..." She closed her eyes hoping to see the lie that needed to be told, but her mind was blank.

Taylor saved her. "It's a remodel issue with her friend's boyfriend. If they can't blend their two styles, is their future doomed?"

Rufus stared at him like he was looking at a three-headed alien until his beer was served and he took a long pull.

Jude took the split-second reprieve to steal a glance at Hazel. She was fidgeting and her nervous energy was spreading. Taylor reached under the table and squeezed her hand gently before placing his napkin in his lap and pressing his knee against hers. Unfortunately it was the only gesture of reassurance he could give without Rufus noticing.

Jude sipped her wine. She shouldn't be drinking in the middle of the day, but she needed something to calm her nerves.

Rufus finally said, "Are you for real? People fight over this stuff?" He sat back and scanned the restaurant. "As long as the place doesn't have florally shit everywhere, I don't give a shit how my wife wants to decorate. It's her place. A woman's domain, and all that. Let her have at it. Women love that crap. Right, Taylor?"

Jude looked at Hazel just as interested in his answer as Rufus. Taylor's tone was reflective of his feelings toward Rufus. "I think it's important for couples to find balance so they both feel at home. I've found many solutions for couples that couldn't decide on styles. The last thing a couple wants starting a marriage is strife."

"Are you saying that because Jude's here? 'Cuz that was a real pussy answer."

Taking a deep breath, he released it and said, "I'm saying it because I believe my wife's opinion matters and I know mine will matter to her."

"Speaking of wives, I saw Katherine last week." *Bam!* There it was served so blatantly, so purposefully to hit Taylor where he thought he could hurt him most. "She said you guys have gotten together a few times."

"One time," Taylor corrected, glancing at Jude.

"I say smeegal. You say smigel. Semantics." He leaned forward, directing his hand in a very purposeful manner. "My point is—"

"I don't give a fuck what point you're trying to make. That topic is off the table."

Jude's knee started bouncing again and Hazel pushed forward with his until hers stopped. She drank her wine and didn't join in the conversation that had made all three of them tense.

Rufus pushed on. "I was just going to say it's good to see you're working it out. I think she'll appreciate you more this time."

Taylor couldn't stop from watching Jude as she finished her wine in silence. He wanted to explain everything. He wanted to tell her he wasn't seeing anyone but Jude, but he couldn't, and Rufus knew that. Rufus knew what he was doing, leaving them two choices—come clean, or continue the lies.

They ordered another round of drinks when their lunch was delivered. Taylor glared at Rufus. Rufus grinned at him, and then crossed a line. "Judith?"

She looked up, surprised he was addressing her directly.

He asked, "We should go out sometime. Got any plans tonight?"

Taylor's hold on his knife tightened. He turned his wrist so the utensil was turned upside and he stabbed downward. His vision briefly blurred and he almost lunged across the table, wanting to take him down, but this time Jude's hand landed on his thigh, her soft touch strong enough to hold him in place. "Actually," she replied, looking directly at Rufus. "I already have plans."

"With Taylor?"

"No. With my family. We spend a lot of time together."

"Oh. That's... quaint."

The fork made another pass over the salad she ordered, but Jude could barely eat. She checked her watch and saw their opportunity passing too quickly. She thought of the room upstairs and how she could possibly get Rufus to leave so she and Hazel could enjoy it. But like a leech, he stayed to suck every second out of their time together until Jude finished her wine again. "I'm sorry, but I need to go. I promised my family I'd be back by four." She rubbed her forehead. "And I'm not feeling that well."

"That's an hour from now. You have plenty of time," Rufus said, touching her hand. "Stay a while longer."

Her skin burned in an entirely different way than when Hazel touched her. "I'm catching the subway and I need to find a station."

This was news to Taylor. He was just about to suggest a cab, but Rufus spoke first, "Stay a bit longer and I can have my driver take you home. Let's just finish lunch first."

He wasn't asking. He was telling her, and Jude had no excuses come to mind. She didn't dare look at Hazel. She knew he was boiling inside. He had a jealous streak, a possessive side that she was first introduced to the night of the dinner. It was a side she saw in spades that night, but hadn't seen since. Until today. His knee knocked into hers, hard.

A sure-fire way to shake Rufus was with the obvious. She coughed, and then said, "I have to make a stop for girl stuff on the way home. So thanks, but I'll be fine." She stood up abruptly and dropped her napkin on her plate. "Thank you for your help with my friend's problem." She looked at Hazel, only Hazel, and said, "I'm sure they'll find a way to work it out."

"I'm here, if she needs help. Please let her know. She can tell me anything. Anything at all and I'll work with her to come to a resolution to keep them together."

"What the fuck are you guys talking about?" Rufus asked, finishing off his third beer.

Her gaze lowered as disappointment set in, their afternoon a lost cause. She glared at Rufus. She hated him. Everything about him reminded her of the other men who took liberties at her expense—her uncle, the doctor, her stepfather.

When she turned back to Hazel, she replied, "Thank you for everything."

She started digging into her pockets for money, but Hazel said, "I'll take care of your lunch."

"Thank you again."

Hazel stood, being polite. Rufus remained seated. "See you soon, Judith." The way he said her name made the hairs on her arms stand on end. She nodded and left, hurrying as fast as she could.

Her head was beginning to spin and she was starting to feel confused. In the lobby, she stopped and touched her temples. She hadn't taken her meds that day. She didn't need them. She never really had, but she felt woozy like the last time she tried to commit her life to the ever after.

She ran outside and had them hail a cab. Hopping in, she gave her address and leaned against the window, trying to catch her breath. Each breath was weighted in her chest. This wasn't right. She hadn't mixed. She knew better. These days she had too much to live for. But when she was dropped off in front of her home, the driver went and knocked on the door, as she stood there motionless at the bottom of the stoop. Roman took one look at her and his lips wavered down. He paid the cabbie and took Jude by the arm, helping her inside.

"Why are they doing this to me?" she asked, staring blankly ahead as she walked up the stairs, counting each step to the pink bedroom. She started to cry as the wave of her reality, of her life, came crashing down inside her head. Roman shook his head and in his quiet sympathy, she got her answer. "They've been drugging me all along."

Chapter Fifteen

JUDE MADE HERSELF throw up. She wanted to sleep it off, but she wanted this feeling to go away more. But no amount of sickness would expunge the betrayal. She tried to lean against the wall next to the toilet to rest, but the knife in her back hurt too much. So she remained leaning on her arm across the seat and rested her cheek on her wrist.

Nadia came in a short time after, or maybe it had been hours. She wasn't sure of the time. Nadia helped her up and wiped Jude's face with a cool cloth. Jude's voice was soft, so soft when she made the accusation, "You knew, didn't you?"

"I did know." Her reply was curt. She was always direct and to the point. Jude never much cared for her because of it. Nadia added, "You don't need the medicine, do you?"

Jude shook her head. "They're making me take drugs for problems I don't have."

"I'm sorry, Judith."

And for a moment when their eyes connected, she saw behind the stiffly starched uniform and hard lines on her face. Through her jaded vision of her, she finally saw empathy for the first time. That made Jude want to cry, but she held it in, for both Nadia's and her sake. "You don't have to do it, not anymore. Not for them."

"I do as I'm told. This is a good job."

And like that, the gentler side she had shown was gone again.

Forty-five minutes later, Jude sat on the other side of a formal tea, across from her stepfather and cousin. Her mother and aunt were out shopping. Her stepfather chewed methodically—sixteen times each bite. Her cousin refused to meet her eyes because she knew all too well what was going to happen and she was never one to stop it.

"Wine," her stepfather started, "is a violation of the order for good reason. You could die. You could overdose. Mixing alcohol and these medications could kill you, Judith. We can't let you die."

You're killing me every day. The thought came to her, but she didn't voice it.

"The hospital recommends an evaluation."

Jude closed her eyes as her fingers dug into the velvet chair. "Please. No."

"It's a violation."

Her eyes flashed with anger as they locked on his. "I didn't know I had the drugs in my system, did I?"

"We've told you not to drink. You were doing so well, even passing it up at the last dinner party. What made you drink today?"

A knock on the front door interrupted them and her stepfather got mad. "Do they not know it's tea time?"

Isla jumped up and peeked out the window. A broad smile appeared. "We have a visitor."

Roman, not thirty seconds later, announced, "Mr. Rufus Stevens."

Isla rushed around the crudités and greeted him with both hands and a kiss to the cheek. "What a pleasant surprise."

Rufus and Jude set their eyes on each other, but Jude

immediately looked down. He sounded happy when he said, "I came by to check on Judith. She wasn't feeling well at lunch."

Her stepfather looked between the two of them. "I didn't know she had lunch with anyone."

"Yes, Sir. Taylor Barrett and I were honored with her company today."

"You and Barrett, huh. Interesting." He smiled at her, and said, "Why didn't you say so, Judith? I'm glad to see you're making proper friends."

Jude's gaze glided from her stepfather to Rufus, who stood grinning at her. "Yes, Judith. You should tell your family how we spend time together." Full of arrogance, he added, "I actually wanted to take Judith out tonight, but she said she had made plans with her family. I love my family immensely so I understand the devotion."

"We have no plans tonight."

Jude stared at her stepfather as a sinking, sickening sensation dropped to the base of her stomach. She could see it playing out before she could stop it.

Her stepfather continued, "You should go, Judith. It will be good for you to get some fresh air. We can finish our discussion tomorrow."

Isla was eager. "We should all go. Won't that be fun? We can invite Taylor. Maybe Clara."

"Clara's in Boston. The four of us can go," Rufus said. "How about I pick you up at eight?"

"Perfect," Isla chimed. Turning to look at Jude, she said, "Isn't that perfect?"

"Perfect," she replied, not willing to give a smile. Rufus Stevens was considered a *proper* friend? Rufus Stevens, the snake, was what got her a get-out-of-jail-free card for the night? She wished she had a chance to speak to him about Hazel first.

When Rufus left, Isla ran upstairs to get ready.

Jude stood up to go to her room, but her stepfather said, "This is a good opportunity to solidify these new connections, Judith. I'm willing to overlook today's incident this one time." She turned back to him, shocked. "Barrett and Stevens are well-respected names in New York. This could be good for all of us. Your thoughts are clear?"

"Yes. Never more."

He smiled. "That's my girl." As if this wasn't about him and his social-climbing goals, as if he was doing her a favor, he added, "I think some fun will do you some good. Go be young tonight. Youth doesn't last forever."

She gulped down the relief that filled her and fed his ego. "Thank you, Daddy."

"You're welcome. Stay with your cousin. Don't stray, okay? I'll handle the hospital."

"Okay." She left the room not sure if she should be happy or sad. Rufus seemed intent on her, but Isla seemed intent on him. And how did Hazel fit into this mess? She was scared to find out, but excited to see him again.

Isla made sure Jude was on time and Rufus and Taylor arrived promptly at eight. Isla swung the door open, cutting Nadia off before she had a chance. Jude stayed back a few feet, but when she saw Hazel, she smiled. Rufus cleared his throat and greeted Jude and then Isla with kisses on the cheek, then said goodnight to Nadia right after. The four of them got into a limo. The guys sat at the back and the girls on the sides.

Taylor asked Jude, "Are you feeling better?"

She blushed. She couldn't help it around him. "Yes. Much better. Thank you for asking."

"You're welcome."

Rufus poured drinks, whiskey all around, then asked, "You girls ready to party?"

Isla responded, "Can't wait. Right, Judith?"

"Yes, Isla." Jude was starting to hate her cousin. She was too chipper for Jude's good, too oblivious to what was happening right in front of her. *Or was she?* Jude looked at Isla, sitting blissfully unaware of the demons that haunted her every move and wondered what it must be like to live so frivolously. They had tolerated each other since her uncle died, but now she felt a stronger emotion.

Taylor watched Jude sitting in the seat ahead of him, her legs exposed to the thigh. Dirty thoughts were taking over as he looked at her skin and the shape of her legs. It had been months since they'd been together and he'd missed being between them, having her open for him. He'd missed her so much, but he ended that train of thought since it would only make him embarrassingly hard.

Eyeing her, he noticed she was wearing makeup and looked seductive. Her hair was styled but down, the way he liked it. Her red full lips were licked innocently, then her eyes met his and she quickly looked away again. He liked that she couldn't stare back. Every other girl could. Their experience taught them that trick. Not Jude. Jude's innocence pervaded her to the bone.

Taylor forced himself to look away, to look at anything but the woman in front of him. He was never good at charades and now he was forced to play some never-ending game of it. "Where are we going?"

Rufus laughed and hit Taylor's leg. "Relax, man. We got all night. Boehler even said so." Taylor didn't like the way he said that. Rufus's eyes locked on Jude like she was prey. Rufus glanced out the window. "Anyway, we're here. Let's go."

Jude followed Isla and Taylor followed behind her. He wanted to touch her so badly that just the thought was making him harden. It had been too long since the last time they had been together at his place and after earlier in the day, when they were so close to that hotel room, he didn't know how long he could take this torture. Tonight would be a true test of his willpower, indeed. He eyed her again, brazenly as they walked, while he could get away with it.

Rufus paraded them in front of a long line on the street and past the bouncer. They entered the club and were led by a hostess to a rounded booth that sat one level up from the dance floor. Rufus tipped her and allowed the girls to slide in first, then sat next to Jude, leaving Taylor standing at the end.

"Sit, my friend. We're in for a long night."

Taylor glared at him and then slid into the booth next to Isla. Bottles were brought to the table, mixers, and snacks. As they made cocktails, Isla leaned in front of Jude and said, "I want to dance. Let's dance, Rufus."

Jude turned to her left, leaned back and her eyes landed on the most handsome man she had ever seen. When Hazel smiled at her, her heart quickened, and she felt love embrace her.

"I don't dance," Rufus stated loudly. "Take Taylor."

"No," Taylor stated firmly. "But you should dance. Maybe Jude... *ith* wants to go."

His slip caught her attention and she looked at him momentarily again before glancing Isla's way. "I'll dance with you." *It would beat sitting next to Rufus all night.*

The girls slipped out and Isla led Jude by the hand to the packed dance floor.

As the men watched them, Rufus, as if he was truly interested, asked, "What's going on, Barrett?"

"What do you mean?" He took a drink, not wanting to talk to him at all.

"You know what I mean." His snake like eyes narrowed on Taylor. "Fucking in The Plaza in the middle of the day, all the bullshit over lunch, the casual, unaffected attitude that shows how affected you really are." He finished half his drink before he finished speaking. "You're banging the Boehler girl and for some reason you don't want me to know about it. For some reason, you don't want *anyone* to know. Why is that?"

"First of all, I'm not banging her. Secondly, you're losing your edge. There's nothing going on. You've misread everything you think you've seen."

Evil flashed in his delirious eyes. "So you're okay if I bang Boehler and you get the cousin?"

"Stop calling her Boehler."

Rufus smirked. "What should I call someone I fuck and throw away? Judith?"

"A hooker. Judith isn't a plaything to entertain you until you get bored. She's a good girl."

"I know. That's why I have this insane desire to turn her into a bad girl."

Shaking his head in disgust, he said, "You're fucked in the head. Have you ever cared about anyone other than yourself?"

"No. You shouldn't either. You're a man, not a girl."

"Fuck you." Anger rose in Taylor's chest, making him feel hot in the club. He wiped the sweat away from his forehead and angled away from him.

The two men watched the women dance, arms up, arms down, swaying, turning, laughing. Rufus refilled his glass and said, "I'm going to fuck her, Barrett, unless you can give me a reason not to."

"You fucked my girlfriend. There's nothing I can say that would stop you from trying to fuck Judith. You have no boundaries. You never did, which is why we're no longer friends."

Rufus laughed loudly. Pointing his finger at Taylor, he said, "See? I knew there was a reason you came tonight. And considering you just said we're not friends, that means you're here for one of them. And my gut tells me it's not the cousin."

Taylor rubbed one of his temples. He sucked at lying, but would do anything to protect Jude. "Take her. You can have Judith." The one thing he knew about Rufus for certain was that he didn't want to be *given* anything. He'd happily pay for sex, but when it came to dating, it was all about the chase, the unattainable. Taylor just hoped he fell for his play and rejected his offer.

Eyeing his enemy, Rufus chuckled. "Since when do you *give* me anything?"

"That's right. You prefer to take."

"You're damn right. Just like I fucking took Katherine. Had her begging for my cock. Had her begging to marry me."

"You're an asshole, Stevens." Taylor stood up and started to leave.

"This asshole is gonna fuck your life over and over."

Taylor stopped and turned around. "Why? Why are you after me? This can't be about a girl when we were seventeen. That was a long fucking time ago."

"I'm sick of your fucking face. I'm sick of the golden boy getting all the attention. I'm sick—"

"You're sick?" Taylor slammed his palm down on the table. "You're fucking sick? *I'm* sick. You win, Rufus. Don't you see? I die in ten years and you get to live. You win, so this path of revenge you're set on will end at my funeral."

Rufus drank his drink, watching the girls dance. Taylor might be right, but he wouldn't rub it in. He couldn't. He had to protect what he and Jude had, but his insides twisted. Watching Jude out there with a smile on her face, life not burdening her, he wanted that for her always. But selfishly, he also wanted her. When he didn't respond, Taylor walked away. He went down the steps in a hurry and crossed Jude's path, making sure he caught her eye. When he disappeared down the hall, she told Isla, "I'll be back. I'm gonna use the restroom."

"Want me to come?"

"No. Keep dancing. I'll be right back."

Jude hurried to the hall, then slowed down, her heart beating out of her chest. Suddenly, she was grabbed and dragged into a bathroom. The door was locked and she was pressed against the cheap wood. Taylor's lips were on hers, his hands roaming her body. Her heart was racing and her body was frenzied. She'd missed him so much. She'd missed *this* so much.

She came up for air while he went down on her chest, kissing the chain that held his ring over her heart. His hands went under her skirt. Panting, he warned, "Don't wear this skirt again. Do you understand me, Jude?"

"I do," she exhaled. "I do. I do." Then it occurred to her and she lifted her head to look at him. "No, I don't understand. Don't you like it?"

Just as his hands covered her thighs, he stopped and burst out laughing, leaving her against the door and out of breath. The faucet was turned on and he splashed his face twice with cold water. While he patted dry with a paper towel, he watched her lick her lips. "And that. Don't do that anymore either."

"What?"

"Lick your lips."

It was becoming clear. His comments were becoming clear to her. She cocked an eyebrow and said, "So, no wearing of aforementioned skirt." She dragged the edge of it up her thigh slowly, oh so slowly. He was following the deliberate rise with his eyes. "And no licking of the lips." She licked her lips, dragging her tongue over them.

Turning abruptly he slammed the bottom of his fists against the painted cinder block wall, then tossed the towel. "You're driving me fucking crazy, Jude, but I'm not gonna fuck you in a filthy bathroom."

"Where are you going to fuck me then?"

Taylor paced back and forth twice before he said, "I want you to come home with me. I know you'll say you can't, but please don't."

"Is it that you miss me or you miss having sex?"

He laughed, but it was tinged with desperation. "I'm not going to lie to you. Both. But I want you in my bed again any way I can get you. I want to make love to you and I want to wake up to you." He caressed her face, his body against hers. "Come home with me."

His breath was inebriating. His heat awakened her body. Her body became alight with desire for this man. Everything that she had tried so hard to protect him from, everything she'd kept hidden, was for him. And here he stood pressed to her, weakening her defenses. He was worth the wrath she would face because she never stood a chance. She kissed his temple, his forehead, the side of his mouth. "Okay," she whispered against the edge of his lips. "Okay, Hazel. For you. All for you, I'll come home with you."

He kissed her again, a smile showing as their lips parted. "Let's go." Taking a tight hold of her hand, they left the bathroom much to the relief of everyone in line, waiting for it. He pulled her through the dancing crowd. The music thumped louder, or it was his heart in his ears. He wasn't sure anymore. The flashing lights kept him from thinking rationally. The only thing he knew to do was to get Jude out of here, to get her to his place, to make love to her. *To love her*. Again and again.

Taking one last look back at Rufus, the enemy's eyes fastened on Taylor. Rufus held his glass in the air as a toast, or touché. Taylor knew Rufus had gotten the better of him, but there was no going back now. They would face whatever battle they had to together, repercussions be damned. Glancing down at Jude, he knew he loved her too much to go back anyway.

Chapter Sixteen

EVERYTHING ABOUT JUDE—the mystery, the secrets in her eyes, her body, her lips—all of her attracted Taylor like no other. She was different from the girls he had grown up with, dated, was expected to marry. She was uniquely her. She was Jude. And she was his.

"How did we not know each other growing up?" he asked in the car ride to his house, meaning to ask her this long before now.

"We lived upstate until I was fifteen. My stepdad got a promotion and we moved to the city." She didn't look at him when she replied.

He didn't like that. He could see how anxious she was getting and it made him feel bad, like he was taking advantage of her. That was the last thing he wanted to do. "I can take you home."

She turned to him. "I want to be with you."

"I don't want to cause you any more problems."

Her hand slid across the seat until she found his. She was quiet for a few blocks and then said, "We can go to mine. If you don't mind sneaking out before morning."

"I'll take my chances if it will help you."

"It will make tomorrow easier."

"Are you sure you want to do this?"

"I'm sure."

Thank fuck, thought Taylor.

She unlocked the front door and snuck Hazel upstairs. It was late and no one was awake. Apparently staying out late was perfectly acceptable if she was with Isla. She rolled her eyes at the ridiculousness. When they entered her bedroom, she left him standing by the closed door in the dark until she reached the lamp on her bedside table. When it flicked on, she said, "Ignore the pink explosion. It was here, furniture and all, when we moved in. Ryan got the green room. I got stuck in here."

Taylor stood there in astonishment, not only by the large size of the room, but by the décor. This was not his Jude. This room belonged to a ten-year-old. He was horrified. "Good God, Jude. They're keeping you young forever."

She got embarrassed. "It's just a room. It means nothing." She didn't know why he was angry, but she felt it rolling off him in waves. Her teeth scraped over her lip, tugging it in and she stood there awkwardly.

He wasn't sure what to think about this, but he could see her discomfort so he tried to push the other feelings down and went to her. "I'm sorry. Just from what you've told me... and now seeing this. It's a lot to take in."

"I loved being at your place. It felt more like home than this room ever has."

His heart lurched and all he wanted to do was love this woman the way she deserved to be loved, for as long as he was able to love her. His few years would be better than having her stay here. He wanted to save her, to protect her, and to love her. "Jude?"

"Yeah?" she whispered.

"Marry me." He didn't whisper.

"What?"

"I want you to marry me." He pulled her toward the bed and sat, holding her hands as she stood in front of him. "I'm not sex drunk. I'm not drunk at all. I love you. I want you with me."

She smiled. He always had a way of making her smile from the inside. "Is this because you want me out of this room?"

Not just the room. He wanted her out of the house that had stolen the life from her eyes. He could see it. "I do want you out of this room, but I wouldn't marry you for that reason."

She sat on his lap, and ran the tips of her fingers over his mouth. "Have I ever told you how wonderful these lips are?"

He was used to how her mind worked and let her go down this path. "No, tell me." He reached around her and undid the clasp of the necklace. Sliding the ring he'd given her off the chain, then listened to her while placing the ring on her finger.

"They're full and kissable, so very kissable." She kissed him. "And they say the sweetest things to me and they ask me to marry them. When I look at them, I have no restraint whatsoever. So if they really want me to marry them, I will."

He got up, so she stood. Dropping to one knee in front of her, he said, "Jude, I love you more than anything or anyone." Bringing her hand to his mouth, he kissed her palm, the ring she was wearing on her finger, and placed her hand on his heart. "I feel you here. I feel you in my soul. I feel your absence when you're away. I don't want to be away from you anymore. I promise to love you always. I promise to protect you all of my days, my entire life. Please say yes. Will you marry me?"

She moved her hand to his cheek and kneeled down in front of him. "I'd be honored to marry you, Hazel Barrett."

He kissed her long and hard until they parted, breathless and restless for more. Her top was the first thing to go, his next. Shoes. His—hers. Her skirt. His pants. Her bra. Things slowed and he undressed completely standing in front of her. She undressed the rest of the way standing in front of him. Her fingers danced across his hard abs that twitched under her touch. It had been so long, too long for both. Her hands slipped around his neck and she pulled him closer until their bodies were together. She whispered, "I missed you. I missed thi—"

He kissed the rest of her words away, leaving her relying on him for air. Large warm hands covered her sides, up and down. He felt his way, reacquainting himself with every inch of her torso.

Pulling him toward the bed, he stopped her just before they reached it. "No, not in that bed. I can't. I won't."

The tears that pooled in her eyes reflected each beat of her heart that cried from his kindness. Loved. Protected. She felt both under his gaze. She went to her closet and pulled down a blanket and two pillows. They each took a corner and spread it out on the floor. Hazel lay down first and beckoned her. She kneeled down and then bent forward to kiss his chest.

Loving seeing her hair down, his fingers wove into it. He loved when the ends touched him when her mouth was on his body. She went lower until her mouth was around him. Closing his eyes, his mouth opened and his breath hit harder.

Opening his eyes, he watched her. When her eyes met his, he pulled her up. "I want to come inside you." He sat up and they traded places. He also wanted to take it slow with her. For her and him.

He was between her legs, looking down over her body—so open, so willing for him. Only him. Forever. He started on her hipbone. He kissed, and then sucked the tender skin of her belly until a red mark appeared. His tongue tickled her belly button and he moved up to her breasts, covering each one with his mouth. Kissing the outside of her breast, he sucked until the blood rushed just under the surface. He kissed her lips twice and had to stop himself from marking her neck.

With his head between her legs, he sucked so hard that she grabbed his hair and moaned his name when she came. Turning to the side he sucked the inside of her thigh until her body gave in and a deep red mark appeared. His tongue ran over it several times until he kissed her sweetness and the pulsing gave way. He should care about safety... about protection. But with her, she made him lose himself before reason could catch up. Upon her, he nipped at her neck and pushed inside her warmth. His breath was jagged, the feeling almost overwhelming. When he looked at Jude, her lips were parted, her head tilted to the side, her eyes closed.

Her name escaped his lips as a moan and she opened her eyes to him. "I love you."

In the middle of the ecstasy of it all, she smiled, her hand pulling him by the neck down to her. When their lips kissed, she said, "I will love you 'til my dying day." *Kisses.* "I want to be on top."

Their bodies were adjoined and they rolled over. She sat atop him with her hands on his chest controlling every roll of her hips, every lift, and fall. Her eyes stayed fixed on him while his hands traveled over her skin as he rediscovered the landscape of her body. Each dip and curve led him somewhere even more provocative until he was losing his senses, the storm clouds gathering. He grabbed her by the hips and thrust hard twice before he crashed, his soul shattering inside her.

When he lay there with her head on top of his thudding heart, he realized Jude was right. Taylor was drunk—sex, life, and otherwise. He was completely intoxicated by this woman. He couldn't get enough. She had become another drug his body needed to survive despite the warning signs to be careful, to slow down.

Could they sustain this high? It was all too good. He felt too alive. Life tasted too sweet. They were moving so fast. An endless merry-go-round that neither wanted to jump off. He held her tighter, and closed his eyes.

An hour later after they had rested, she held his hand above her. "Your lifeline is too short," Jude noted as she traced the different sections of the broken line on his palm several times. He closed his hand tightly, wanting to hide his Achilles heel. He should tell her, but he couldn't bring himself to add to her misery. He held her hand above his head, looking at hers. She didn't squirm or move away. With her head against his shoulder, she stared at her open palm like he did. "And mine's too long."

Frustrated, he put her hand down and sat up. "Why do you say stuff like that?"

Her eyes flashed to his, but she stayed with her head on the pillow they had been sharing. She was tired and didn't want to argue with him. "Nobody really believes that stuff anyway."

Leaning forward against his bent knees, he stared at the pink wallpaper with the little white flowers. He finally closed his eyes and shook his head at himself. Lying back down next to her, he said, "I'm sorry."

"I'm not upset, Hazel. You don't have to apologize to me." She turned on her side, facing him, and closed her eyes. "Let's get some sleep. You'll need to leave in two hours."

Turning toward her, he slid down until they were eye level. He kissed the tip of her nose, and closed his eyes. "Goodnight, Jude."

"Sweet dreams, Hazel."

Two hours felt like seconds. Taylor rolled over and groaned. "No. I need sleep."

Jude shook him again. "Wake up. You need to go." She kissed his bicep, then squeezed it. "I like your arms," she whispered near his ears. Her hand roamed over his chest and stomach. "And your body." Lower. Lower. "And this part of you especially."

A sleepy smirk crossed his lips. Rolling onto his back, Taylor said, "And here I thought you loved me for my heart."

"I do. I love you for your heart. I like you for your body."

He sat up and she sat up with him. Kissing her, he said, "You're gonna be my wife."

"I am, but not if you don't get out of here now."

He rubbed his erection against her leg and glanced at the clock by her bed. "It's four thirty-seven. We have time. I'll be quick."

"I don't want you to ever be quick. I want it long and slow, hard and passionate."

"It will be all those things, except slow. C'mon, I'll make you feel so good, baby."

The sound of *baby* rolling off his tongue so easily when referring to her made her heart cartwheel in happiness, but he needed to go or happy would be the opposite of what she would feel. She pushed him gently, and said, "You need to go. We've got plans to make and I need you alive to make them."

With a heavy sigh, he got up. "I'll go, but I'm coming for you, Jude Boehler, and I'm never letting you go again."

"Swear?"

"I swear to you. Never letting you go again."

When he was fully dressed, he kissed her goodbye at her bedroom door and then she led him to the foyer downstairs. But she couldn't let him go without another so she took him by the shirt and pulled him to her again. Planting her lips on his, his hand went into her hair at the back of her head. They leaned their foreheads together before he kissed her there.

A light was flicked on overhead, and a woman's accented voice said, "Good morning, Judith."

Jude's heart stopped at a standstill in her chest. Taylor looked at the woman in her robe staring at them as Jude's hand fell away from him. Nadia added, "Mr. Barrett."

"Good Morning," he replied, not sure if he should say anything at all.

Nadia eyed Jude before turning her full attention on Taylor. "I suggest you go before the house wakes." She walked past him and started opening the door.

Jude stood, terrified. Taylor brushed his hand against hers, and whispered, "I'll see you soon." When she finally looked him in the eyes, he smiled at her. "I promise."

She nodded and watched him go.

Nadia added, "Good day, Mr. Barrett."

He glanced back once, then headed outside. The door shut and Nadia tightened the belt of her robe before turning back. Her hair hung down and her face was clean of makeup. Jude had never noticed how pretty Nadia was before. She assumed because she didn't tend to notice such niceties about her enemies. "You should go upstairs, Judith, and don't come down until you're dressed and ready for the day. I suspect today will be a long one." She passed her and went back down the hall from where she came.

Jude remained, her heart now beating wildly in her chest. Then she ran as fast as she could up the stairs and into her room. She shut the door quietly behind her and leaned against it until she caught her breath. Seeing the pallet they had made, the place where they made love, and commitments of forever, made her smile so big that she flopped down on it and hugged the pillow to her chest. When she took a deep breath she caught the scent of her forever still lingering. She curled around the pillow and closed her eyes, wanting to live in this bliss until she could be with her Hazel again.

Chapter Seventeen

JUDE SAT AT the other end of the table from her stepfather. Her mother flanked his side, but her place had been sequestered four seats down. This had been where she and her brother had always been relegated, but since he died, she sat down there alone. Some mornings Isla sat by her. This morning Isla wasn't here. She hadn't returned from her night out.

After her glass was filled with orange juice, she picked it up and moved her entire place setting down the table until she was across from her mother and next to her stepfather who sat at the head of the table. "What are you doing?" he asked before eating his toast.

"I don't want to sit alone." She eyed the juice wondering if that's how they were drugging her.

Her mother put her coffee cup down and smiled at her daughter. "How was your night, Judith? I heard the Stevens and Barrett boys took you and Isla out. That must have been a nice change."

"It was. About Taylor," Jude started.

Her stepfather put his tablet down, and said, "Who's Taylor?"

Jude tried to hide her nerves by eating and reached for her fork. "Taylor Barrett."

"Oh," he replied.

Her mother said, "He seemed nice at the Stevens's dinner." She lowered her voice as if Taylor would hear her. "So sad about his illness."

The forked strawberry touching Jude's lips was lowered as she raised her eyes to her mother. "What do you mean?"

Her stepfather was agitated. "Can you save the gossip for when I'm gone?" He set his fork down and finished his coffee as her mother watched him and Jude stared at her mother. He stood and walked away from the table. As soon as he was gone from the dining room, Jude, feeling sick to her stomach, asked, "What do you mean sad about his illness? What illness?"

Her mother picked up her coffee cup again and signaled for Nadia, who came and refilled it. Nadia's eyes were on Jude, the exchange between them one of caution. Surely Jude was misreading her, but she didn't care about that right then. "Mother?"

"Yes, Judith. Let me get my coffee. The Barrett boy—"

"Stop calling him that. His name is Taylor."

"What has gotten into you today? She set her cup down and looked exasperated. He has Parkinson's."

"What? Parkinson's? No." She shook her head. "I thought you had to be older…" She knew nothing of Parkinson's disease other than the obvious—tremors. She had never seen him tremor.

"Yes. I'm pretty sure that's what his parents told us at dinner. He was in and out of hospitals for a few months until they gained an accurate diagnosis." She lowered her voice again as if they were conspiratorial sisters. "That's when his fiancée cheated on him with his friend." She made a face of distaste. "Such a scandal. I almost wish we would have known them then. It would have made tea time much more interesting."

Jude sat there, staring at her, staring through her.

"Are you not feeling well, darling?"

Jude snapped her gaze down. Though she was hesitant to drink anything she had not served herself, she drank her juice to coat her drying throat, Hazel's words echoing in her head. *"I promise to love you always. I promise to protect you all of my days, my entire life."* Then her words. *"Your lifeline is too short."*

"I had no idea. How is he? What did his parents say?"

"You tell me. How was he last night?"

Blissful. Romantic. Handsome. Sexual. *Marry me?* She pushed her plate away. "He was happy."

Her mother smiled. "Well, that's nice. Maybe it doesn't bother him anymore."

Jude became impatient and stood up. "I don't think Parkinson's works like that, Mother."

"His mother, Betsy, asked me to co-chair a fundraiser for research in June. I think I'll accept. I've been bored with the usual charities."

Holding back what she really wanted to say, Jude said, "Charities aren't for entertainment. They're important in raising awareness and funds. But since you're bored and all..."

"Jude?" her mother called after her.

Jude stopped under the arched doorway, her hands on the molding. She turned around and asked, "What?"

With her back to Jude, she asked, "What is that ring you're wearing?"

There was nothing believable Jude could say, so she didn't say anything at all. Just as she turned to leave, her mother added, "I married your father for love."

Turning back around, Jude asked the question she had always wondered, "Why did you marry Brewster?"

"For security." Her mother turned to meet her only daughter's eyes and asked, "What will you marry for?"

Jude paused to think, but decided it wasn't anything she wanted to share. Her heart, soul, and mind knew what she would marry for. She left, leaving her mother and that question in the bright room at the back of the house. As she walked up the stairs, Roman said, "Good morning, Hummingbird."

"It is morning. As for good..."

"You doing okay?" When she looked down at him, he was smiling—warm and welcoming, a gladiator with the heart of the sun inside.

For him, Jude returned a smile, though it was small. She sighed, "I don't know anymore."

"You're stronger than you realize." He nodded.

Wanting to believe him, she said, "Sometimes I forget."

"Remember who you are on the inside. You're strong and fast. Smart and brave. Never forget who you are."

When Ryan died, Roman had been there for her when her family had mentally checked out. When they returned to their day-to-day, like he had never existed, they blamed her, her stepfather leading the charge...

"If you hadn't convinced him to go to California, he wouldn't have been going to the luggage store."

"You preyed on his kindness by convincing him of your lies. He could have gone to college here in the city. But no, you were always trying to get his attention and when he believed you, you wrote his death sentence."

Her friend, her only friend other than Hazel, touched her shoulder. Her eyes flicked up to his and he said, "Be brave, Hummingbird."

She nodded, taking his words to heart. In her room, she went to the back of her closet, dug into a pair of Prada heels, and pulled out Hazel's phone number. She wanted to talk to him, to see him, to hold him, to cry for him, to marry him. But she wouldn't call him. It would show on the bill. And she had to protect him from them, from her parents. She had to protect him for herself.

She tucked the number into her pocket, slipped on a pair of flats, and grabbed a light sweater, then waited on the edge of her bed for eleven o'clock. At ten fifty-eight she ran downstairs and out the front door. She had no time to waste, so she hailed a cab and went to Hazel's apartment. She twisted the ring around her finger the whole ride over. Everything she felt for him hung in the balance of her heart, teetering between love and devastation. She needed to know how he was. She needed to see him, to touch him, to love him.

Entering his building made her feet lighter. She was being carried on the wings of euphoria, each step easier than the last. She wasn't walking to her future. She was running toward it. Taking a breath, she held it, and knocked on his door.

The door opened and he stood there with his lips parted and confusion furrowing his brow. "Jude?"

Throwing herself forward, she jumped up and wrapped her body around his and kissed him. Then, again. He kicked the door closed and held her against it. When they parted, they remained close enough to share their panting breaths. He said, "You're here." When he pressed his abs against her center her head knocked hard on the wood and he kissed the exposed skin of her neck where it met her shoulder.

He was strong. He was virile. He was not sick. That much was obvious to her eyes, but she had to know for sure. "Hey," she said, bringing his face up to see hers.

Lowering her down until her feet touched, he said, "I thought we were meeting at the park?"

"I couldn't wait."

His glorious smile chose to shine on her. "I'm glad you didn't. Do you want to go to the bedroom?"

Giggling, she replied, "Yes, so much, but I need to talk to you first."

"Okay." He walked to the couch and she stared at him, stunned. Jeans that hung low. No shirt. Boxers peeking out the top, and a V that directed her eyes below the waistband. He was an alluring tease as he stood there waiting for her to join him. Sitting on the couch, he patted it. "C'mere."

She started walking on shaky legs. As she passed the bar, she debated if she should stay there to preserve clarity. That seat next to him was tempting, but she knew she'd be flat on her back within seconds. So she hurried to his side and sat down. His hands were instantly on her. "You know how much I love this dress on you, but man, I want it off so badly."

He lowered her straps, but she stopped him. "We need to talk first, then we can get to the action." She backed up a bit and put her hands out. "Wait on that side of the couch or we'll never get to talk."

Chuckling, he moved. "I'll be good. What do you want to talk about?"

"I want to marry you."

Taylor automatically started moving closer to her again when she said that. "I'm glad to hear that. I want to marry you."

"What were you thinking about for the ceremony? Because I was thinking we elope. Just do it."

His eyes flashed with an excitement. "You want to go to City Hall? No ceremony? No white dress? No pomp and circumstance?"

"None of it. Just you and me, Hazel. That's all I need."

Suspicion crossed his face. "Has something happened with your family?"

"No, everything is fine." She moved closer to him and touched his leg. Looking him in the eyes, she said, "I just want to be your wife for as long as we both shall live." *Testing him.* Seeing if he would tell her.

He didn't flinch. He only smiled bigger. "I want you to be my wife for as long as we both shall live too." Looking down, he said, "I like that you're still wearing the ring."

"I'll wear it the rest of my life."

Touching her leg, he leaned in and kissed her. "So you really want to elope today?"

"I do."

"You stole my line."

"I think we can share it."

"Fifty-fifty from here on out. Do you want to go shopping?"

"No," she said, confidently. "It's the dress I met you in. It's the dress you tell me I'm beautiful in, so it's the dress I want to marry you in."

"To be fair, I tell you you look beautiful in everything you wear."

"I can give you that," she said, then laughed.

Standing up, he said, "Give me ten minutes and we can go."

"I'll give you a lifetime, if you give me yours."

"Deal, baby." He walked into the bedroom.

Jude sat on his couch, waiting, debating if she should tell him she knows.

Pro – If she tells him, he'll know she married him despite his illness.

Con – If she tells him, he may change his mind about marrying her.

Pro – If she doesn't tell him, one day he'll know she married him despite his illness.

Con – If she doesn't tell him, he may change his mind about marrying her.

Ugh! This was getting her nowhere. She would have to go with her gut.

Hazel came out and spun for her with some fancy footwork added for special effect. Smiling she said, "That's my favorite suit on you."

"It's now my marrying suit." He stuck his arm out for her. "You ready to go?"

"Ready."

They spent three hours getting a birth certificate for Jude and then headed to the bureau. After some research online, they applied for the license and left, but Taylor still felt like he should apologize. "It's only twenty-four hours."

"We can wait twenty-four hours."

They walked hand in hand down the street. "Hey, Jude?"

"Yeah?"

"What if you didn't return home tonight? What if we started our life together now? What will happen?"

She tugged him closer. "They'll be upset, but they'll have to deal with it. We'll be married when they see me again." Stopping, she faced him. "We can petition for my rights or if I can't get them, as my husband, you can."

The tips of his fingers ran from her temple down her neck. Goose bumps covered her skin. "We'll go to court and get your rights back. I promise. I'll do everything in my power to give you your freedom back. I'll do anything for you."

"And I you. Do you know that? Anything. In sickness and in health," she said quietly prodding for him to open up to her. She didn't understand why he wouldn't tell her about his disease or that Katherine was the one he was apparently supposed to marry at one point. But for some reason, he wouldn't open up about those two things. Jude felt like she knew him—knew everything that was important—and she would marry him based on that, despite his secrets.

His eyes began searching hers as if she was onto something. "Yes, in sickness and in health," he repeated then turned away, taking her hand and starting for home.

Chapter Eighteen

"I'M WARNING YOU, as your husband, beautiful. I'm going to want all of you. I want all your secrets and your soul."

She squirmed beneath him, forgiving him of his own sin of denying her his secrets, as he lowered himself. "Don't you know, Hazel? You've had all of me all along."

He kissed her just above where she really wanted him. Teasing her. "You're getting demanding." *Kiss.* "Is this how marriage is going to be?"

"I can't help it. You created a monster."

"You're lucky I find you so delectable."

She knew exactly how fortunate she was. "I am. I'm the luckiest girl in the—" She gasped when he kissed her exactly where she had wanted. "Oh God, Hazel. I'm *so* lucky." The tips of her fingers dragged slowly up her body as she murmured, "Lucky. Lucky. Luck! E."

Shortly after, the starburst whitened the insides of her lids, and she returned the favor. He was left helplessly at her mercy until his body was teetering on the edge of ecstasy and what felt like death. Jude got up and kissed his chest. "I want you, babe, inside me."

He sat up. "You want me? You get me on my terms. On your

hands and knees."

Her body clenched in anticipation. Even though they have had passionate sex, even some rough, play that was fun, he had never made demands of her. But she liked it. She liked feeling wanted sexually. Positioning herself, she felt his warm palms glide over her back and bottom before she felt a gentle pressure. Her breath was pushed out as he pushed in, holding her steady by the hips.

"God, Jude. You feel..." His words trailed off as he picked up his pace.

It didn't take long before he slowed down, out of breath, and reached around her leg. Touching her between the legs, she needed him to move. "Please, Hazel. Faster. Harder. Move. Please."

He stilled completely and chuckled. "I thought you said you never want it quick?"

"That was before you started torturing me with pleasure like this. God, please. I'm so close." She squeezed, tempting him into action.

"You are very bad, Jude. So bad, but feel so good." He grabbed her shoulders, and said, "Hold on."

Minutes of beautiful torture were shared until they collapsed together onto the mattress. He moved to her side and kissed her cheek, tasting her sweat. "It's almost tomorrow."

She turned to look at the clock. "It is." She smiled. "Are we going first thing?"

"We are."

"Then what?"

"Then we tell your family and get your stuff."

Rolling onto her back, she moved against his arm with her arm resting over him. "Can I go back to school?"

Watching her face as she kept her eyes lowered from his, he asked, "You want to finish your degree?"

"I have two years, but I missed too many days to get credit for the other courses."

"Yes, I think you should finish school. I think you should do everything you haven't gotten to do."

The silence engulfed her gulp and she kept her tears at bay. They were happy tears but she didn't want to cry again, not right now. "I don't spend much."

Kissing her cheek again, he leaned back on the pillow and stretched his arm behind his head. "I can afford it if you do."

"I don't know anything about your financials."

"If my financials concern you, we should talk about them."

Tilting her head down, she said, "I can't contribute. I've never had a job and I don't have my degree yet."

His fingers went to her chin and he lifted her up. "I have a solid job and a large stake in my family's company. We don't have to worry about money, Jude. You don't have to worry. You can leave your family behind, everything, and we can replace it all. You're twenty-two. I had friends who didn't graduate until they were twenty-six because they partied so hard in college. You can start this summer or fall and finish up. Then you can do what you want."

She smiled at the thought. "I used to want to be in publishing. I wanted to be an editor. But I might want to be a librarian now. I like the calm environment." His body tensed under her hand. "Oh my God, are you hard?"

"The librarian fantasy is a very real thing."

She burst out laughing. "Good to know. Maybe you can check out my books."

He rolled on top of her. Pushing her hair back from her face so he could look at her, really look at her. "I'd rather place my books in your slot."

Grinning bigger than the sun, she lifted up, and kissed him.

"You are a dirty, dirty boy." They rolled over and made love again.

Taylor woke up to sunshine staring in from the outside and Jude ironing inside. He rubbed his eyes, and with a groggy voice he asked, "What are you doing?"

She spread the skirt of the chartreuse dress out on the board the best she could and replied, "I want to look pretty."

"You're always pretty."

"I want to look extra pretty." She ran the iron over the dress a few more times. "I'm going to the store in a few minutes. I want to buy some makeup."

"I don't want you to wear makeup. You don't need it."

Her eyes met his sleepy ones. "I have dark circles."

"So do I."

"My lashes are lighter."

He shook his head. "I have no idea about my lashes."

"I have a pimple. I don't want a pimple in our wedding photo."

"Where? Where is this so-called pimple because I'm pretty sure I covered your entire body with my mouth at some point or another and didn't see one... or lick one."

"Ew."

He laughed and rolled onto his back, then yawned, closing his eyes and going back to sleep. When he woke up, he smelled food. Muffins to be precise. Lazily, he flipped the covers off and walked into the other room with a smile on his face. "Good morning."

Jude turned around and presented a platter of muffins. "Good morning."

"What kind of muffins did you bake?" he asked taking one, then taking a bite without waiting for a response.

"Blueberry. You had them in the fridge."

"It's really good. Thank you for making these."

"My pleasure, soon-to-be-husband." Her voice had an excited

lilt to it, which made him smile again despite his mouth full of food. "The courthouse opens soon. I'm going to shower if you're so inclined to join me." She swaggered past him, naked, and so very tempting.

He shoved the rest of the muffin in his mouth and followed her.

An hour and a half later they stood in line with the number fifty-five in their hand. Jude was nervous and starting to take her anxiety out on Hazel. "You're not allowed to take showers with me anymore."

Teasing her, he tapped her nose. "Was I a water hog or a Jude hog?"

"Both. We lost an hour to your antics."

"You didn't mind those antics when we were in there." His sexy arrogance was showing.

"That's my point, Hazel. It's like I have no self-control around you. Forget about saying no. I have no desire to turn you down, like ever. I could lose myself to you if I'm not careful." She stated this as if it were of real concern.

"Nothing wrong with losing yourself in something you love." He nudged her. "Anyway, that will just put us on an even playing field."

She rested her head on his shoulder and her hand on his thigh. "They are up to twenty-four."

Thirty minutes later...

"What's that?" Jude pointed to the small leather-bound notebook Taylor carried.

His hand stilled with the small pencil in it. "That's the sunroom."

"Ohh. I like that."

He watched her smile over his blueprints, and felt happy she liked the plans.

She pointed to another rectangle room on the pad. "What about this room?"

"That's your library."

She sat back with her mouth open and looked at him in disbelief. "I get a library?"

With an easygoing grin on his face, he said, "Of course. I have the plans at home, but I like to work on it when I'm out."

"I can't believe you're creating our house."

"So you like it so far?"

She kissed his cheek. "I love it."

They both looked up when an announcement came out overhead. "Thirty-one."

Forty-five minutes later...

Jude slid down in her chair, her arms hanging over and her legs straight out. "They sure do know how to suck the fun out of getting married."

Taylor tapped her leg, then bent over and rested his forearms on his knees. "Not much longer. I can feel it." With his body stationed, he lifted his gaze up to the number board. Forty-seven.

Thirty-eight minutes later...

"Fifty-five," Taylor said, shaking Jude. "That us."

"Thank God!"

"I thank God every day," he added, taking her hand.

They turned in their number and were escorted down a short hall to a small room and told to wait.

In that moment, they looked at each other but the moment seemed to have stolen their voices.

Three minutes ticked by, the clock on the wall loud. Jude finally said, "I have no doubts, just in case you were wondering."

"I wasn't wondering, but is this like reverse psychology where you're really reassuring yourself?"

She laughed, and it felt so good in the moment. "No, I really meant I have no doubts. We haven't known each other that long, but I think you said it best when we first met. It feels like we've known each other our whole lives."

Just as he leaned down to kiss her, the door opened and they stepped apart, not used to sharing what they mean to each other in public.

A man in a black robe stopped as if he was walking in on something he shouldn't, but then he continued and said, "It's okay to kiss her. She's about to be your wife, son." He set a book down on the table in the corner and introduced himself. Looking at the young couple, he went through his standard protocol. "So you want to get married?"

Taylor answered, "Yes, Sir. We do."

He smiled, then looked at Jude. She returned a sweet smile, and squeezed his hand. "Yes. I very much want to marry him."

"Very good. I reviewed your papers. Are you ready, Taylor and Judith?"

"We are," they answered together.

"Repeat after me." He went through the civil ceremony vows they had chosen.

Facing each other with their hands held tightly together, Jude looked into the eyes she fell in love with, the ones that held hope and possibility, an impossible sexiness. "I, Judith Ann Boehler, take you, Taylor Hazel Barrett, to be my husband, to have and to hold, from this day forward through sorrow and joy, richer or poorer, in sickness *and* in health, to love and to cherish as long as we both shall live."

The justice reassured her with a nod, then turned his attention to Taylor and repeated the vows that Taylor had memorized already. He faced Jude. "I, Taylor Davis Barrett, take you, Judith

Jude Boehler, to be my wife, to have and to hold, from this day forward though sorrow and joy, richer or poorer, in sickness and in health, to love and to cherish as long as we both shall live."

"By the power granted me by the state of New York, I now pronounce you husband and wife. Now's a good time to kiss her, again."

Jude stared into her own forever, her heart racing, and her chest swelling with love. Taylor cupped Jude's face and leaned down to her. When their lips were almost touching, her eyes closed, and he whispered, "I will always love you, Jude, and I will always protect you," and he kissed her.

Chapter Nineteen

"YOU'RE A BARRETT now."

"Shh. I'm not sure what to make of that yet."

Taylor's pursed lips slid to the side, and then he said, "So it's not a good thing?"

"It's a wonderful thing, but now there are two of us we have to save from a certain fate."

"Ohh, like attending charity events to be seen, instead of for the cause?"

"Precisely. And as a Barrett, *I* will never abandon the love for my husband to make an impression on strangers to gain social standing."

Taylor added, "As a Barrett, you will not only make the world a better place, but my world a better place."

She smiled, her happiness brighter than the sun. She touched him, not able to not touch him. "I will always be here for you. I promise, as a Barrett."

He took her hand and kissed each finger. "You already did that as a Boehler."

"Maybe Barrett is just Boehler 2.0, a better version."

"I think you were pretty spectacular already."

"Charmer."

"You know it."

An hour later, Taylor was sitting at the bar, watching Jude as she made omelets. "Why do you have to go today?"

"I don't. But I want to get it over with." With the spatula pressing down on the eggs in the pan, she turned to look at him. "I'm nervous and my stomach's upset over this. I just want to get it over with." Focusing on the food, she turned off the stove, plated their lunch, and joined him.

His hand rubbed her back and brought her closer for a kiss. "You know you don't have to cook for me all the time."

"I like to cook for you."

"I appreciate it. I just want you to know—"

"Eat before it gets cold."

He took a bite and chewed, savoring the taste. After he swallowed, he asked, "You're not going to eat?"

"I've lost my appetite."

Taylor set his fork down and rubbed his hands through his hair, then turned his body toward her. "Look, I'll go with you. It will be easier with both of us there."

Picking up her fork and knife, she cut a small bite, but right before she ate it, she paused to think through her plans. She needed him safe and if that meant staying here, she would make sure he stayed. "It's our wedding day. Let's not ruin it with talk about this. I'll go tomorrow or the next. There's no hurry. We're married now. There's nothing they can do to hurt me anymore."

They spent the afternoon between the sheets, marrying their bodies. As they lay on their backs, trying to catch their breath, Jude rolled over and smiled. "I feel like I've been let in on a great secret and now I want to tell everyone."

Taylor smiled despite how exhausted he was. Peeking over at

her, he asked, "Are you going to share your secret with me?"

"You're the one who shared it with me, my love."

Reaching over, he rubbed her thigh, his fingertips dipping between her legs. "And what's that?"

She closed her eyes, her body relaxing under his touch. "Sex." She wriggled so his fingers were closer to where she wanted them. "It's the greatest secret of all. I can't believe I waited so long to feel this good."

His hand stopped moving and his brow furrowed. "Hey, hey now. Let's not go that far."

Touching his cheek, she laughed. "I don't mean it like that. I just mean it feels so amazing. You feel amazing and you will be the only one I will ever feel this way with. That's even more powerful than the orgasms you give me. And those are pretty damn amazing."

He made her feel so good that she wanted more of every sensation, every kiss they shared, and every touch that bonded them in ways a piece of paper never could. Soon she was astride him seeking more of everything this secret revealed. And with each round of love they made, they felt even more sure of their decision to wed..

By evening, they were dressed in their wedding clothes again. After stopping to kiss and grope twice in the apartment, once in the hall, in the elevator, and twice in the small lobby, they almost threw their plans out the window completely, wanting to go back upstairs. If not for Taylor's insistence, they would have. "I've definitely created a sex monster."

"Are you complaining?" she teased, poking him in the side.

"Nope. Not one bit."

"What about regrets? Got any?"

"Nope," he said again. "Not one."

She slipped under his arm and said, "Good, because we've consummated our marriage, so there's no backing out now."

"When I make a promise. I keep it."

"I never had a doubt."

With his arm over her shoulders, he walked proudly through the lobby, introducing Jude as his wife to the doorman. Many congrats were had as he hailed them a cab.

In the cab, she practically sat on his lap. She just couldn't bear any distance. "This is what cloud nine feels like," she said cheerfully.

"I've always wondered what clouds one through eight were like. They get the shaft."

"I reckon a lot like the nine circles of Hell. But now we're rewarded for surviving our pasts."

Taylor kissed her on the head, and nodded. "Rewarded for surviving."

Over dinner, as they sat at a table for two in the corner of a chic restaurant, they admired the beauty of Central Park. When turning back to Hazel, she noted that the park held nothing in comparison to his eyes. It's what first drew her to him. That and how handsome he was.

"Sometimes the way you look at me," he started, "you look at me like I'm special."

"You are. You're special. You're kind. You're loving." She lowered her voice so the neighboring patrons couldn't hear her. "You're sexy and so giving in bed. I may not have been with others, but I know that you wanting to please me is special."

"Pleasing you, dear Jude, is a completely selfish act."

She blushed and sighed dreamily to herself. *Lucky.* She was very lucky. The waiter came to the table and said, "Congratulations on your wedding. Compliments of the chef." He set down a mini chocolate cake and refilled their champagne glasses.

Taylor said, "Thank you."

Then the waiter set a box down in front of Jude, and smiled. "This is compliments of your husband."

Now she really blushed. Looking at her husband in awe with love and all of cloud nine in her eyes, she felt amazed this was real. He smiled. The waiter left and she took the box and opened it, not shy at all anymore. "You're very sneaky, Mr. Barrett."

"In our rush down the aisle, we skipped a step. I thought we could make up for it."

A quiet gasp stole her words, but gave him the best reaction possible. Inside the box she stared at two gleaming bands. One for him and one for her. "When did you have time to do this?" A smile crossed her lips and before his secret was revealed, she took his ring out, and said, "This has some weight to it."

"It's solid like us."

She reached for his hand. "Hazel Barrett, will you marry me and let me take care of you for the rest of our lives?"

"I will."

She put the ring on him.

Taking the box from her, he slipped the other ring out and took her hand in his. "Jude Barrett, will you marry me and let me love you for the rest of our lives?"

"I will. Again and again."

He slid the ring on her finger right against the other ring that sealed a promise months earlier. When she looked at the ring, with the large diamond surrounded by smaller ones, she tilted her head in disbelief. "You spent too much."

"You've promised me your life. No price can be put on that. So accept this token as a show of my dedication to you and as a thank you for saying yes."

"Okay, Romeo. You already got the yes. You don't have to try so hard."

He laughed but didn't say anything. The tears in her eyes were evidence of her happiness. And for the smile on her face, he would have paid a lot more. Tapping his glass against hers, he said, "To a lifetime filled with happiness."

"To a lifetime filled with happiness."

After dinner, they stayed to finish off the champagne. They had become quiet, the weight of the day tiring them. Hazel finally suggested, "Home?"

"I'd love to."

The rush they'd felt earlier, to feel everything all at once, had gone, and peace settled in. In front of the living room windows, with the city they fell in love in as their backdrop, they had their first dance as a married couple. Bryan Ferry's "These Foolish Things" was playing and she spun around until he caught her. Swaying back and forth, she rested her head on his shoulder, and he held her tight.

She didn't leave his arms for two weeks. He called into work and organized some time off, using some of his saved vacation time. The lavender sundress and the floral dress were pulled from his closest. She'd loved them at the store. She loved them even more now because he had bought them for her. He watched her dance around their living room, jump on their bed, and admire herself in them. Her happiness meant everything to him and when he saw her laughing, he knew he was the luckiest man alive.

Their days were filled with walks in the park, shopping the farmer's market, or exploring Chelsea Market. They hung out at cafes and bookstores. Jude started drinking coffee for him and Taylor embraced her faltering storms. A visit to her family was looming, clouding her eyes. Those times, he would work to bring her back to the present, back to him, where she belonged. He loved her and everything about her.

No one else he'd ever met was more aware of who they were than she was of herself. Marriage turned this stunning girl into a striking woman. He encouraged her stardust dreams and let her soar through the moonlight.

He admired her optimism and enjoyed the freedom to be his true self when he was with her. With Jude, everything felt new. He felt new. He felt invigorated and excited for life, for their life together, and he could tell she felt the same. Perhaps he gave her this same feeling of freedom, of a new start without her damaged past weighing her down, inhibiting her.

Taylor also held steadfast in their future, protecting her from the bad of the world so she could capture the world in her pocket. So her carefree view of her surroundings was never tainted. Her past held enough of that for a lifetime or three.

Taylor didn't realize she was only like that with him, that being with him gave her the strength to be who she really was, the woman she was meant to be.

The last day before he would return to work, Taylor was organizing his drafting table and Jude was napping. He straightened the blueprints of their future house and put the last of his pencils in a holder. The apartment was quiet until a demanding knock on the door intruded into their peaceful world. Rushing to answer it before the annoyance woke Jude, he was irritated before he even opened it.

Rufus and Isla stood there. Rufus, with a smarmy smirk on his face, and Isla, looking less convinced this unannounced visit was a good idea, shifted uncomfortably. Rufus lead the charge. "What? No hello?"

"What do you want?"

He wrapped his arm around Isla, looking relaxed. "We're looking for Judith. Her family is worried. Right, Isla?"

"Yes," she said, nervously. "She's been gone for over two weeks now and we're all worried that something bad has happened. Have you seen her?"

With the worst timing in history, Jude opened the bedroom door and stepped out. Two sets of eyes, both looking shocked, peered over Hazel's shoulders, and he dropped his head down. A million lies crossed his mind.

Isla ran around Taylor to her cousin and hugged her. "Jude! Oh my God, you had us all so worried."

When Taylor looked back, Rufus walked past him, letting himself in. "Guess we found her. What'd I tell ya, Isla? I knew she'd be he—"

Taylor's gaze shifted to Rufus when he stopped suddenly, then volleyed back to the girls. He saw the moment of recognition on Rufus's face—wide eyes, mouth open—and Taylor's stomach sank.

"Holy shit! Is that a wedding ring?" Rufus's gaze went from Jude to Taylor, searching his hand.

It happened too fast for Taylor to hide the evidence, and he didn't want to anyway. He would never hide their relationship again. "It is. What of it?"

Rufus laughed manically. "Oh fuck. Taylor 'Golden Boy' Barrett has married the crazy girl."

Taylor was prepared to be mocked. That was Rufus's style. What he wasn't prepared for was hearing his wife be mocked. "What the fuck did you just say?"

Rufus was still laughing, but he was more than happy to repeat it. "Talk about irony." He looked at Taylor. "Your body is all messed up," he said, then redirected his attention to Jude, "and her mind is all messed up. Together you guys actually make one fucked-up person."

Taylor swung before his senses caught up with him. He landed a cross punch on Rufus's jaw sending him to the floor and eradicating his grin. Jude sprang between them, pressing her hands against Taylor's chest to stop him from hitting Rufus again. With Taylor's eyes locked on Rufus, Isla dropped to her knees to help him while Jude began whispering to her husband, "Stop! Please. Stop! He doesn't matter, babe. He doesn't matter."

When their eyes met, a calm washed through him, his better senses returning.

Isla barked, "You'll pay for this, Judith. Wait until your parents hear about this."

Jude sighed heavily and leaned the top of her head to Hazel's chest. "I guess the honeymoon is over."

Maybe it was the rush of adrenaline still coursing through his veins. Or maybe that was just damn funny, but Taylor burst out laughing. "Guess so." He looked down at her, glancing every couple of seconds at Rufus to make sure there'd be no retaliation through cheap shots. "The silver lining is that we now get to start the rest of our lives together."

She smiled. "That is a silver lining."

He moved her behind him while Isla helped Rufus up from the floor. Rufus's nose was bleeding, so he held his head back. Jude went to get napkins, passing them across the bar to Isla who helped Rufus.

Slightly muted from the bloody nose, Rufus threatened, "Fucker! You'll pay for this."

Taylor took a step closer. "Don't come into my home and fucking threaten me and don't *ever* talk shit about my wife."

Isla looked dumbstruck and her hand dropped away from

Rufus. She glared at Judith skeptically, and asked, "So it's true? You two are married?"

Nodding, Jude responded, "We are married."

Isla turned to Taylor and said, "Really?" She was wise enough to stop before saying anything more, but her furrowing brow and mouth hanging open was enough.

Rufus glared at her. "What? You disappointed there, Princess? Guess you're stuck with me," he spat in annoyance.

Isla huffed. "You're an asshole, Rufus." She walked to the door, but stopped to say one last thing. "Judith, you should really think about someone other than yourself and come home. Their worry has turned to anger and your mom's been crying the whole time." She pushed past Taylor and left, leaving Rufus there to help himself.

Jude and Taylor turned to him. The arrogant rich boy stood in contrast to the one who waltzed in unannounced five minutes ago. Even with napkins to his nose, Jude found it hard to feel sorry for him. After her experiences with him, that punch was probably a long time coming.

"You know what?" he asked. "I don't give a shit about your life anymore. Just go ahead and die already." Taylor stepped to the side and watched as he walked out, slamming the door closed behind him. Jude took the liberty of locking it.

The laughter they shared moments earlier had evaporated and uncertainty filled their love nest.

Walking around the bar, Jude took Hazel's hurt hand and gently pressed the large Ziploc bag of ice to his swelling and slightly shaking knuckles. He flinched, trying to pull away from her, but she held strong and asked, "Can we finally talk about your Parkinson's?"

Chapter Twenty

"YOU KNOW?" TAYLOR asked, standing in front of her, his heart shivering as she held his body still.

"I know."

"For how long?"

"I found out the day before we got married."

The subject seemed to hit every one of his nerve endings, making him feel vulnerable to the exposure. He pulled his hand away from her and the ice. He'd risk the swelling. "You married me knowing I would die?"

"We'll all die one day," she replied so matter-of-factly.

"I'll die in years, Jude. Decades aren't guaranteed."

She moved closer, not liking his distance. "No one gets guarantees, my love. We just have to live the best life we can while we have a life to live." Running her fingertips down his arm, she said, "Why didn't you tell me?"

Worry creased his forehead as he stared at her. "Because I thought you would leave me."

She touched the skirt of her dress, attempting to flatten a major wrinkle, then took his hand again, placing the ice on it. "I stand before you full of flaws. I'm Jude. Remember? I'm in no position to judge you. I can only judge who the man is *to me* and that man is the one I will love until *my* dying day." Her eyes, like her smile, were soft, filled with understanding. With the gentle way she touched his cheek, it felt like she was caressing the rough waters of his soul. "Why did you marry me if you thought you wouldn't be around to spend our lives together?"

"I married you because whatever days I have on this earth, I want them spent on you."

"Your life isn't currency, Hazel. It's worth more than any value you think you can place on it."

"Life is all about bartering, trading, or spending," he snapped. "That's what I do every day. I wake up and figure out how I'm getting through that day. It always comes down to the negotiation."

"Don't bargain with your life."

"I bargained for you. Don't you see that?"

"I know you want to save me, but save me because you intend to be with me. Not because you need a lost cause to give *your* life meaning."

"Oh Jude," he said, leaning against the bar, frustration invading his happiness. "My life before you can be summed up in three steps: I got up. I went to work. I came home. Now my life is an incredible maze of unpredictability. We have these days where we do such mundane things, but I see them in a way I never did before and they're not mundane. They're amazing. That's because of you." He took her arm and pulled her close. "I can't lose the only thing that gives my life meaning, so if I have to bargain with God every morning for an extra day, I will. If I have to trade my life for yours, I will. If I have to spend my days to have time with you, I will. I can't lose you."

"You won't. You have me. I'm not going anywhere, even when it gets hard. You'll have me. When I made that vow to you, it included in sickness and in health. I meant it. Then and now, always." She hugged him and his arms came around her. "Please don't hide it from me anymore. Teach me. Show me how I can help you."

It was hard to talk to her when he was so used to hiding that part of his life from everyone. He never wanted to be seen as weak or garner sympathy because of the disease that existed inside him. He wanted people to only see his strength. But he realized Jude and he were a team now. Unlike anything he had felt before, her love was immeasurable, as was his for her. She never gave him stipulations or contracts, tried to make deals, or sell a charade of perfection. Jude was the opposite of Katherine in every way, and being with her was healing the damage of his past. He'd never known love without conditions before her. She was his Barrett and he was hers. And that was forever.

Despite the humiliation he felt from his weakness, he felt more when holding out his hand for her to see. No level of comfort she could give would take his shame away. But he showed her anyway. "It's not shaking right now, but if you watch really closely, a tremor will shoot through one of my fingers."

She took his hand between hers, warming it with her love, then brought it to her cheek and held it there. "So when this happens, does it hurt?"

"No."

"That's good." Taking his hand, he brought it to her chest and put it over her thumping heart. The heartbeats were strong, stronger than any tremors he had experienced. "Do you need medication to help?"

"Only when it's bad. It's not been bad except when I was in the hospital. But yes, I'll need daily medication and treatments as it progresses." He kept his eyes on his splayed hand across her chest. "Jude?"

"Yes?"

"Do you think less of me now that you know?"

He loved that she didn't hesitate to answer. "I think more of you now that I know."

He moved his hand back to her cheek, cupping it this time. "Why?"

"Because," she said, "you had all of this happening to you, but you were only ever concerned about what was happening to me. You're brave. You know that?"

"I don't feel it sometimes."

After kissing the palm of his hand, she leaned into it. "It's not just about the outside, but also the inside that makes us who we are. And to me, you'll always be strong."

"Please remember that when I'm weak."

"I will be your strength when you are weak. Just as you have been for me."

"You don't owe me anything, Jude." His hand dropped down.

Taylor started to turn away, but she stopped him. "Payback has nothing to do with it. It's love. That's what you do for the people you love."

"You have been shown so little love in your life and yet, you give it selflessly to others. How did I get so lucky?"

Grinning, she said, "It's not luck, my dear Hazel, but good fortune. I was always told that good fortune comes to those who wait. Well, I've been waiting for you my whole life and I'm going to appreciate every day we have together."

How could he walk away after that? He couldn't, so he leaned against her, her back to the bar and kissed her temple, then the other. "My medical file is on my laptop. When you're ready, you can look through it. I won't keep any more secrets from you. I promise."

"I love you." She rested her head against him and listened to his heart.

As his arms wrapped around her, he said, "I love you more."

Jude spent the afternoon sitting at the drafting table, clicking on his laptop between his medical file and the browser tab with the medical terms defined. When she closed it, she sighed heavily and looked out the window. "That's heavy."

"You're telling me."

When she glanced over to the couch, two books were stacked next to him, but remained unopened. She felt confident. "It's not insurmountable though."

"What are you suggesting?"

Getting up, she made her way over to him and sat square on his lap. She wrapped her arms around him and said, "That we live each day to the fullest."

"Carpe diem."

"Carpe diem."

Taylor flipped her onto her back and began tickling her, loving to hear her laugh. Squirming beneath him, he stopped the pleasurable torture and giggles turned to moans when he started to kiss her. One moan led to more and they made love on the couch in the middle of the afternoon.

As the afternoon chased the evening, Jude paced the living room, internally debating. Hazel had asked her to sit down or talk to him, but she never heard him. The fear building inside her was overpowering any outside noise. At five o'clock, she announced. "I need to go. I need to deal with my family. If I leave now, I can be home for dinner. I'm in the mood for Chinese. Can we order delivery?"

"Of course," he replied, watching her move around the kitchen searching for something he believed was a distraction to the issue.

"I'm going with you." Her stress had become his and stress gave him tremors. He tucked his hand in his pocket and walked into the bedroom.

When she joined him, she said, "No. I'm going alone. It will be better. If I can smooth things over, we'll set up a dinner for all of us. If it doesn't go as hoped, I don't want you dragged into that mess or to witness it."

"I'm already a part of this mess. You can't protect me from them. They either approve or not, but I don't actually give a fuck if they do. I just care about you."

"That's why it's best if I break this to them alone. I'm going into a battle and I want to win without starting a war."

She was good. Very good, *and* she made sense. So he sat on the bed and watched her style her hair, and as if on autopilot, she pinned it back and up. She never bothered with makeup while here, which he liked, but he knew she would feel better while wearing her armor for this confrontation. Instead, she walked out of the bathroom with what he identified as her bravest expression of indifference, and said, "I want the Honey Chicken and an eggroll."

"Hey, Jude." When she came and sat next to him, he handed her his phone. "Call the home number if you need me or need anything. It's the most recent number, so it's easy to find. We'll get you one of your own tomorrow."

She took the phone and smiled while looking at it. "Thank you."

"I mean it. I want you to call me the second you leave. I can meet you."

"No, just stay here and order the food. I want a night of good food, maybe a movie, and my handsome, extremely sexy husband all to myself."

He conceded, realizing she wasn't going to change her mind. "You got it." He rubbed her thigh, then whispered, "I love you."

"I love you, too." She kissed him and stood up.

Grabbing her hand, he pulled her back to his lap. "Call me."

"The second I leave," she responded with an easy smile, then kissed his head.

Jude left Hazel and his worried expression in the apartment. As soon as she closed the door, her fears escalated. She had no idea how her parents would react to the news of her marriage or if Isla had already told them. But she found some consolation in the fact she would be able to make her own decisions soon. Her marriage gave her strength and confidence, but more than that it gave her comfort knowing she would be emancipated from her stepfather soon.

Thirty minutes later, she stood on the large stoop in her prettiest dress with the phone tucked into her pocket. She tried to fix her hair, but it was a windy day, so flyaway hair was inevitable. She rang the bell, not something she had ever done before, but this place no longer felt like home to her. She stood as an outsider to the place she'd called home for years, and she liked that.

Roman answered, and her heart started beating again. He stepped out, closing the door a bit behind him. "Hummingbird, you're back." Happiness to see her had overcome him. He stepped forward to hug her, but stopped.

She knew he halted because he felt he should, not that he wanted to. She ignored that invisible line that seemed to separate the two of them, not caring what her family would think. She hugged him because she cared about him. "I missed you too."

"Are you okay?"

"Better than okay." She stepped back and showed him her hand with the rings.

"You're married?" he asked stunned.

"I am. He's wonderful, Roman. I'm going back to him tonight."

Roman's eyes got glassy and gave her the response she so deeply needed. "Who is the lucky man? Is it Taylor Barrett?"

His concern for her, his care over her made her want to tell him everything. "It is," she replied surprised he knew. "How'd you know?"

"Nadia. She told me about him leaving that morning."

"Oh God! Did she tell my parents?"

"No. Only the two of us know."

Jude relaxed knowing she wouldn't have to explain that as well. "Thank you." Maybe Nadia wasn't as bad as she once thought, or perhaps she was changing. Either way, she felt grateful. "Thank her for me."

"I will. Now, you should probably go inside. Your parents are wrapping up their tea. Good luck, Hummingbird."

She nodded. Whether she was ready to face them didn't matter. It was going to happen whether she was or not. She followed Roman inside and walked to the wooden archway that led to the living room.

The tray of sandwiches and pastries, cookies, and biscuits was empty, only crumbs remaining. The teapot was discarded to the side, the warm brew now cold. The four of them—her mother, stepfather, aunt, and cousin—talked idly as if nothing had changed at all. It didn't look like her mother had been crying for two weeks. The house of opulence they wanted everyone to see stood strong before her as if she had never disappeared. Jude's loyalties had long been betrayed, so standing before them now, she felt nothing of the love that one should for her family.

Suddenly her aunt's mouth dropped open when she saw her. "Judith?"

The other three followed in succession gawking at the girl in the lavender dress like she was an ugly duckling among swans. Isla smiled, but Jude struggled to distinguish where her alliances lay. Isla sat back in her chair, as if getting comfortable for the ensuing fireworks.

Aunt Leslie broke the silence. "Well. Well. *Welllll*."

Jude's feet moved back, the attention overbearing. Then her thumb felt the metal bands on her finger, which enabled her to gather strength. "I guess we should talk."

Isla tutted and said, "You think?"

Guess she's on their side. "Isla, I know you're upset and I'm sorry. But I'm not sorry for anything that happened today."

Her family turned to Isla. Jude's stepfather asked her, "What is she talking about? You saw her and didn't tell us?"

Standing up, Isla declared, "She's here. Judith is back. That's all that matters. That's all that has ever mattered to you people."

Isla's mother stood. "Isla, shut your mouth."

Isla's arms went wide. "I can't do this anymore. I'm tired of her getting everything. She's crazy. You all said so yourselves. It's always about Judith."

Her mother went to her daughter and gritted her teeth. "Get hold of yourself, dear daughter, before you ruin everything."

Jude stood there, flabbergasted. "Ruin what?"

Isla shook free from her mother and asked the same, "Yeah, ruin what exactly?"

Her aunt smiled, but it wasn't authentic. "Nothing, Judith. Everything is fine. Isla's not feeling well. That happens to spoiled brats when they don't get everything they want."

Isla didn't calm down. She got more riled. "I don't know what is going on with you, but Judith has something to tell you. Tell them, Judith."

Jude didn't have to. Aunt Leslie grabbed at her chest and stumbled back to the chair. Jude's mother jumped up to help her.

"Leslie, are you okay?"

Leslie pointed at Jude and Jude covered her mouth to avoid screaming. She had no idea what was happening, but she started fearing for her life. Her feet stayed in place as her eyes went wide. Isla stormed passed her, barely missing her shoulder.

The other three were staring at her in horror. Her stepfather said, "What have you done?"

Her mother burst into tears, lowering her head into her lap. Jude took a step back, and then another.

Her aunt growled, "What have you done, child?"

Jude had tried to prepare herself for any reaction they would have upon hearing the news of her marriage, but she hadn't expected this. She felt like a lamb standing in a den of lions. She backed up again, but her stepfather rushed her, grabbing her, and shaking her as he yelled, "What did you do? Judith. Judith. What have you done?"

Tears streaked down her cheeks as her hair fell free around her face. "What?" she cried. "What are you talking about?"

He let her go with a devastating push and she fell. She had never seen her stepfather break down but that was what he was doing. He was covering his face in agony as he walked to the couch and sat down next to his sobbing wife. "Shut up, woman!" he shouted at her mother.

Confused, Jude continued to cry, and asked, "What is wrong?"

Her aunt glared with no feeling left to give. "You got married. We know what you're doing, you manipulative little bitch."

The rings were turned over deftly, the diamond sticking into her palm as she fisted her hand. "I did. I got married." She found herself *bartering* the best part of her life—Hazel—for their forgiveness. "He's wonderful and so good. So, so good. He's—"

Leslie stood up again, her composure back in place. "How could you do this without asking us?"

"Because it had nothing to do with you."

"You didn't tell us, Judith, because you knew we would say no. Now you've gone and ruined your life on a whim and we are left to clean up your mess. As usual." She turned to Jude's stepfather and said, "Handle this." She walked out with regained poise without looking twice at Jude.

"What is ruined? Nothing is ruined. I'm in love. He loves me. This is good. This is good for me. I'm happy."

"Judith, go to your room." Any affection he'd felt for the girl he'd help raise had disappeared years ago, but judging by his antipathy now, she wasn't even worthy of his anger, much less his approval.

"Don't you want to know who I marr—"

He stood, meaning business. "Go to your room. We need to talk. I'll be with you shortly."

Remaining where she was, she wondered if they would ever treat her as the adult she was. "I don't understand."

"I don't either," he added. Her mother still sobbed at his side.

Jude would go because she needed to resolve this tonight. Lowering her head, she turned and went to the foyer. She caught a glimpse of Roman and Nadia down the hall and their expression spoke of defeat, similar to how she felt. Taking the stairs one at a time, she retraced her tracks, each step representing another time she had disappointed her family.

When Ryan died, her saving grace died with him. Until she met a hazel-eyed man who made her breath stop short while she basked in the glow of his kindness and beauty. She stuck her hand in her pocket and her fingers settled around his phone. She wanted to call him. But when she walked into her room, she decided it was best if she didn't. There was no need to upset him needlessly. *I'll be quick and get out of here even faster.*

Setting the phone on her vanity next to the photo of her brother, she went to her closet and grabbed a suitcase. This would no longer be her life. She refused to remain in this room any longer. It was time. Time to pack up her life from and leave this pink-walled prison. Opening it on the floor, she started gathering her clothes.

She had filled the suitcase, but the rest of her stuff didn't matter. There wasn't much she wanted from this room, this house, this life. Not much she wanted to take into her new life really. After tucking the photo of her brother between some clothes, she shut the suitcase and stood it up, placing it by the door.

Going back for the phone, the door opened and she looked back, stilling.

Her mother stood there, her face red and her eyes swollen, making her blue eyes even icier. She quietly closed the door behind her, seeming to question the act. This was not the composed woman she knew her mother to be. This version of her mother's voice shook like her trembling body. "I love you, Judith. Remember that. Okay?" Jude didn't reply. Instead she stared at her mother, watching her like one would watch a caged tiger. "I didn't want to do it, but I understood the need. I'm a victim like you. Blackmailed into sacrifice."

"What are you talking about?" Jude spoke with strength, but her knees felt weak. "Mother?"

Her hands twisted round and round each other and Jude was mesmerized by the action. Her mother started mumbling, "I tried to talk some sense into them. I tried to stop this. But you don't understand. They're very convincing. I'd lost my son already. They promised I would get to keep you…"

Jude's brow grew heavy as her fate dawned on her. Spinning

around, she went for the phone—her saving grace in the moment.

The door burst open, slamming against the wall and puncturing the plaster. Just as she picked up the phone, two men grabbed her. It fell to the floor as she was thrown to the bed. Facedown, she turned to the side gasping for air. *Trading* her fate for her destiny, she begged, "No. No. No. Please. I'm married now."

The needle went in while she fought and screamed against the tight hold on her arms and legs. When released, she immediately rolled onto her back. "Why?" she cried, pushing against the mattress to move her body toward the headboard. *How? How do they get here so fast? It should take hours.*

Tears streamed over her temples and into her hair, but she lay there, knowing there was no point in fighting the drug. She wouldn't make it to the door before collapsing. She wouldn't even make it off the mattress. She knew this part too well. Her soul started to detach itself from her body and she began floating.

The men left and her aunt appeared, standing over her, staring down at her. "Just one more visit and we'll have all we need. Then you can kill yourself and succeed at one thing in life."

Paralyzed in place, her mind began obscuring the details. Jude whispered, "He'll come for me. You'll see."

"Who, dear?" she asked, leaning over her.

"Hazel..."

Chapter Twenty-One

TAYLOR SAT AT his drafting table, but was unable to focus on the project in front of him. He looked at his watch for what felt like the millionth time. It was after seven, the sun had set and he still hadn't heard from Jude. *Finally*. A knock on the door sent him to his feet, rushing to open it.

When he saw the food delivery guy, logic returned reluctantly. Jude wouldn't knock. She'd come in. He paid the guy and took the food to the kitchen to unpack it. He struggled to care about dinner with his mind on his wife. He picked up his home phone to call her. He should have gotten her a phone number long before now. Before it started ringing, he hung up. He reasoned. *She said she'd call, so she'll call.*

By nine o'clock, he stood at the window staring down, not focusing on anything in particular except where his Jude was. He finally gave in and called. It went to voicemail after four rings, so he hung up and grabbed his jacket. Within minutes he was in a cab heading to the Boehler's.

The lack of plan didn't hit him until he was paying the driver. He should have thought this through better, but what if they were happy, accepting, celebrating even? What if they've caused her to cry, caused Jude pain? He didn't know what he was walking into but as he stood on the sidewalk in front of the Boehler's brownstone, the unease that had been smoldering inside him grew.

From the sidewalk there was nothing out of the ordinary, nothing to see. The lights were on, but there were no shadows, nor silhouettes, no life to be spied at all.

He trudged up the stairs, rejoining his heart that had already leaped. There was nothing that would keep him away at this stage, but he still had no idea what to expect. Expecting the worst and hoping for the best gave too much credit to how he felt. He was anxious and irritated, his breathing slightly labored as he tried to calm his growing distress.

Knocking on the door, he was solid, composed, but ready to see Jude, hoping he had misread the confusing signs that led to this moment. The housekeeper who caught him that one morning as he snuck out answered. There was no greeting and her expression fell as she grabbed hold of the door, appearing to need the support. Taylor said, "I'm here for Jude."

"She's not here, Mr. Barrett."

"Where is she?"

She looked down and away from him. "I should get Mr. Boehler."

"Why?" he asked, as she walked away leaving the door wide open. Taylor entered and shut the door. He didn't wait in the foyer. He ran up the stairs taking them by two and straight into Jude's room. His feet came to a sudden halt and panic seized him as he took in the scene—suitcase by the door, hole in the wall, phone on the floor. "Jude?" It only took him seconds to piece together what had happened.

Running back out, he started yelling, "Jude? Jude?" He called for her all the way downstairs. "Jude? Answer me. Jude?" Two men were waiting for him. One he recognized as her stepfather. The other, he didn't.

"Where is she?" Taylor shouted, staring down her stepfather.

With his hands clasped in front of his belly, Brewster Boehler, said, "Get out of my house before I call the police."

Taylor stopped in front of him, not intimidated, but furious. "Where's my wife?"

"*My* daughter is a sick young woman that you have clearly taken advantage of. We have sent her away to get the help she needs."

"She's not sick. You're medicating her to make her sick."

"Mr. Barrett, our Judith is a bit on the insane side. This will be news to you, but she's tried to commit suicide twice. She can't be trusted with her own life. Your marriage is a sham. I'm sorry to tell you this as it seems you care for her, but she's not in her right mind." He stepped aside. "Roman, please show him out."

Taylor rubbed his forehead. "Bullshit. All of this is the same bullshit you tell her. I know about all of this. I know about her uncle and her brother and Bleekman's. I know everything and you know why I know everything? Because when she was with me, she wasn't drugged or out of her right mind. She was thoughtful and insightful, open and free. You'll pay for what you've done. I'll make sure of it."

He stormed out, but before he reached the sidewalk, the man he didn't know called him, "You're Hazel?"

Taylor stopped and looked over his shoulder, taking one step back up. He was surprised to hear that name from anyone other than Jude. "Yeah?"

"One moment." He disappeared, but a few minutes later, just as Taylor was starting to lose patience, he returned with her suitcase and his phone. "Bleekman's won't be open tonight. You won't be able to get on the property until after nine in the morning."

Taylor took the phone and the suitcase. "Thank you," he said, somberly. "When was she taken?"

"Around six."

Around six, Taylor thought. *Forty minutes after she'd left our home.* He wondered how that was possible. *Had Isla given them forewarning?* As if Roman could read Taylor's thoughts, he added, "Bleekman's has a location here in the city, a satellite office. As if he's ordering a pizza, Mr. Boehler calls and they deliver two men to your door within thirty minutes."

Taylor pondered the lost hours—wasted—where he could have saved her. He didn't understand completely what that meant, but felt fueled with anger. "I saw the hole in the wall. Did they hurt her?"

"She felt nothing once they injected the shot."

His phone was almost crushed as Taylor imagined how it played out. "What's your name?"

"Roman. Say hello to Hummingbird for me."

"Hummingbird?"

It was slight, but Roman smiled. "She's small, but fast, a good escape artist—usually. She's strong. She'll be okay tonight. She won't wake until morning."

"I'll be there when she does."

"I have no doubt." Roman stepped back inside, and said conspiratorially, "Good luck."

"Thank you." Taylor watched as the man shut the door and was left with a small shred of hope that maybe Roman had helped Jude as he had helped him. That maybe when Jude was here, she had him. No one could truly help her in the past, but hopefully she had someone on her side to listen, to be there, to comfort her when she'd needed it most.

On the ride home, he saw his missed call on the phone, but there were no other signs of use. Setting it down, he researched Bleekman's and noted it was three hours northeast of the city, close to the Berkshires. He would get a plan together as soon as he got home. There was no way he would leave Jude in there.

When he arrived home, the suitcase tipped over just inside the apartment and Taylor bent down in the middle of the entry to open it. He felt around the edges, searching for anything besides clothes and shoes, a clue to something, anything that would give him an answer, a lead, something to pursue. Or to solve the mystery that was Jude. As he patted the clothes that looked as though they had been thrown in the case in haste, the fact that she had been packing to come home to him hit hard. He became desperate to find something of her, needing a piece of her to hold on to before he lost his mind.

Rifling under a soft blue sweater, he felt something hard and pulled the photo frame. The eyes staring back were familiar, the same coloring as Jude's but maybe more green than blue. Ryan. He flipped it over needing the reprieve from her brother's piercing eyes. When he looked at the photo again, guilt engulfed him. He hadn't just let Jude down, but he had failed her brother. Taylor was supposed to take care of her. *How could he let them take her away? Why had he let her go in the first place?*

Remorse ravaged his soul and the tremors appeared. Fisting his hand, he pounded the hardwood floors trying to make it stop, trying to gain control over his weakness. When his hand was sore, leaning toward bruised, he stopped. He stretched his fingers. They ached, but it was better than the shakes. Getting up, he looked around his apartment, looking for her presence that was lacking in her suitcase where her life once touched. Reaching down, he took the frame and put it on the kitchen bar and went to his computer.

Taylor stayed up until midnight contacting his lawyer and making arrangements.

Since he couldn't sleep, he showered and changed clothes, packed his overnight bag, and put some of Jude's clothes in along with some of her toiletries from the bathroom. The GPS was set on his phone, and he sat, waiting. Five o'clock couldn't come soon enough. Eager to see his wife, he was standing curbside when a taxi pulled up to take him to the rental car company. The sooner he could get there, the better. With his charger, snacks, bottled water, and overnight bag in hand, he got in, ready to retrieve his wife, ready to have her home again.

The drive was long and uneventful. Taylor's eyes were on the road, but his mind was on other things. Things like was Jude hurt—physically. He knew she was already hurt emotionally, but if they touched her... He tried not to let himself go down that path or he'd kill every doctor there. He redirected his attention to the plan. He would first try playing by the rules. If that didn't work, he couldn't guarantee people's safety and something about that welling emotion even scared him. He just hoped that playing by the rules worked first.

He found the "center" at half past eight and sat in the parking lot. Scoping out the dreary cream-colored building and the fence that wrapped around it, he looked for entry and exit points. He'd seen enough movies to know this information would be useful if everything went to shit once he was inside.

At nine a.m. sharp, he watched a nurse help a patient out through the front doors to a bench in a little garden area. He got out, stretched his legs and back, and grabbed his wallet before heading to the front gate. His body was stiff, but he could fight an army if he had to. He would for her. He would do anything for Jude.

He pushed the call button on the speaker.

"Good morning. How may I help you?" a scratchy voice answered.

"I'm here to see Judith Boehler." *Barrett.*

"One moment please." The intercom buzzed, then went quiet.

The sound was blown out when it came back on. "You may come to reception."

The gate unlocked and Taylor headed for the desk just inside two glass double doors. Putting his most charming smile on for the two women stationed there, he tapped the counter lightly when he reached it. They both glanced his way, then did a double take. One said, "Good morning."

"Good morning. I'm here to see Judith Boehler."

He saw a flash of recognition in her eyes when he mentioned Jude's name, but she quickly looked down at her computer. "When was she admitted?"

"Last night. Maybe overnight."

She hummed as she typed. The other receptionist told her to stop because it was driving her nuts. Then they laughed. "Nuts. Crazy."

Taylor was not amused, but he tried to hide his disdain for their poor taste in jokes. The second lady looked up at Taylor and said, "She's not been processed yet."

"What does that mean? Checked in?"

"Correct. So she can't have visitors until she's been checked in and resided at least twenty-four hours inside the center."

"Reside? That sounds like she'll be here for a while." He kept his voice light, inquisitive, but not on the offensive. *Yet.*

"Yes, it says she'll be here for a month this time. So she'll be placed in the residency hall when she's processed."

Processed? Like an animal. What the fuck? Covertly he took a deep breath, trying to keep his temper even. "Does it say when she'll start this processing?"

The first lady looked up and smiled. Her lashes fluttered and her intentions were clear when she started to flirt. Flipping her short hair out, she leaned closer to him. "They've started. She's been in holding since she hasn't woken up yet."

Leaning closer to her, he read her nametag, then returned her smile. "Woken up?"

"Yes," she said, then giggled as if the people admitted here don't mean anything to her at all. "Patients are given a light sedative to help make the transition easier."

Easier on the patients or the doctors? He didn't ask that though.

She asked, "Are you family *or* medical?"

He lowered his body so he would be closer to her and whispered, "I drove such a long way. What would it take to get back there for just a few minutes to visit with her? Is that a possibility, Maxine? Is there *anything* I can do to make that happen?"

"Sir—"

The other receptionist cut her off and said, "I would just about do anything for an extra large peppermint mocha from the coffee shop in town."

Maxine stared at her, then turned back to Taylor. "I do like the ice they use in the large pear-berry teas."

Taylor stood up smiling. "I'm gonna go on a quick coffee run. Would anyone like breakfast, you know, since I'm going?"

They both giggled and said they would love some donuts. Taylor was out the door and in his car within a minute. He found the coffee shop easily off the main road that ran through town. He placed the order, stressed while he waited. Every minute that ticked by felt like an eternity.

With drinks and donuts in hand, he was promptly buzzed back into the facility. The ladies oohed and ahhed over the service, the kindness, and how attractive Taylor was as they tucked away the monetary bonuses they conveniently found under their coffees. Maxine walked him to a hallway and instructed, "She'll most likely be asleep, but she's down this hall at the other end, second door from the emergency exit, on the right. You've got ten minutes."

Taylor had rarely relied on his charms or good looks for gain, but he would use whatever it took to get to Jude. "Thank you, Maxine."

"Don't get me fired. Now go."

Taylor kept his head lowered as he walked down the hall. Orderlies were cleaning and nurses were helping patients in their rooms along the way. The other doors were closed. Locked, from what he could tell. He was conflicted. He didn't know if he wanted her room to be locked for safety or open for him.

Grabbing the handle of her door, he turned and prayed it would open. And it did. The door opened and he stealthily slipped in. His breathing changed when he saw her on the bed, her hands and legs strapped to the bedrails. He sucked in an angry breath as he rushed for her.

Jude's eyes were closed, her breathing even. She was sound asleep, but he went to work unfastening the straps at her wrists and then her ankles. Sitting down next to her, he brushed her hair away from her face and admired the beauty that lay beneath the dark circles under her eyes. Leaning down slowly, he kissed her just as she exhaled, her breath replacing his. "Jude? Jude, can you hear me? Wake up, baby. Wake up."

She didn't move. Her skin was pale and her lips dry. He knew she was alive, but he needed more, so he put his ear to her mouth. Her breathing was faint. Lifting up, he started gently shaking her.

"Jude, wake up!" Each time he got more demanding. They were running out of time and he needed her awake. "Jude! Can you hear me? It's me, Hazel."

"Hazel." He heard it, but it was so feeble he wondered if he was imagining it.

"Jude. Jude. Please wake up. It's me. Hazel."

The door opened and a doctor stopped, obviously startled by the presence of someone other than his patient. He backed out and shut the door quickly. Taylor was done for, but he needed to see her awake, so he shook her a bit harder. "Jude, please wake up. Wake up!"

The door crashed open and two large orderlies came in. "Sir, you are not allowed in here."

Taylor stood next to his wife's bed, and took her hand, squeezing it. "I'm her husband. I go where she goes and I stay where she stays."

One of them came forward just as the doctor reentered the room. "Not this time, Sir. Now, please come with us peacefully."

"Fuck you."

The doctor stepped in from the doorway. "Mr. Barrett, we were warned about you and that you might show up. We're prepared to call the police if you don't leave on your own accord."

"I'm her husband. You can't deny my right to be with my wife."

"Your wife is under strict care of not only this facility, but the state has granted conservatorship to her parents. So actually, you have no rights when it comes to Ms. Boehler."

What the fuck? The hospital has a say over her? "Barrett. It's *Mrs.* Barrett to you. She's my wife and will be addressed and referred to as such."

"Not until it's recognized by the court and rights are granted to you. This is a private facility, so I suggest you leave and take care of the legalities before your next return or face the consequences of trespassing." He stepped around her bed to the opposite side of Taylor and said, "Please excuse us while I conduct an evaluation on my patient."

The word evaluation sent flashbacks of Jude telling him what happened during these "evaluations" and his fists clenched as he stepped to the end of the bed, trapping the doctor in the corner. "You touch her and I will kill you."

The doctor held up his clipboard as if that could save him. With his already beady eyes, he narrowed them even more, and said, "I'll make sure to take good care of *Mrs.* Barrett for yo—"

He never saw the punch coming. The doctor's smug smirk was knocked right off. The blow would cause quick swelling and soon it would be tightly shut.

The orderlies were on him, grabbing each of Taylor's arms and pulling him backward. Taylor fought the best he could but he knew they were trained for worse. He yelled, "Don't you dare touch her."

Antagonizing Taylor, the doctor took one of his fingers and poked Jude's leg. Taylor went ballistic, freeing himself just to be tackled to the hard linoleum. A two-hundred-fifty-pound man had him pinned as the other put a cable tie around his wrists and pulled hard. Despite Taylor's best efforts to escape, the tie cut into his skin and he continued swearing as he was dragged to his feet and yanked backward to the door. "Jude? Jude!" he shouted. Just before he was taken around the corner, her eyes opened and connected with his.

She mouthed, "Hazel," then the door was slammed shut and locked, keeping him out and the doctor in.

Chapter Twenty-Two

"SIGN THIS." THE doctor stood over Jude with a pen. "Sign this," he demanded, much more forcefully. He had never spoken to her like that before, but she was groggy and couldn't land her thoughts on reality.

Striving to focus, the form in front of her was blurring as well as the pen. Her arms felt heavy as they lay at her sides, but she reached for the pen anyway, and missed. Reached again and missed. The doctor took her hand and wrapped her fingers around it, then brought the ink to the document. "What is it?" she asked, too tired and closed her eyes.

"Just sign it!"

His angry words penetrated her foggy brain and she opened her eyes again, this time in fear. The doctor stood over her, the green of his irises intimidating. Her gaze went from the doctor to the pen, and back to the doctor again, noticing his swollen face. He held an icepack to his upper cheek with one hand and with the other he pushed the pen on her again. "Sign. I have rounds to make."

She took the pen in hand this time and tried to work out the words that jumbled through her blurry vision.

"You got married, Judith. That has caused a lot of problems for us."

Married. She moved her thumb to touch the underside of her rings. When she didn't feel them, panic rose, and she held her hand above her to visually verify. "Where are my rings?"

"You know hospital policy. No jewelry. Nothing of any kind can be brought in."

"Give them back," she said, attempting and failing to sit up.

"You *might* get them back if you're a good girl over the coming month."

She stilled. Her vision may not be focused, but her mind understood the ramifications of his words perfectly clear. "Month? What are you talking about?"

"Yes," he said, smiling while flipping through her chart. "You'll be spending the next month with us. Isn't that good news?" His dark gaze hit her, penetrating her heart. "Even better news. That means we'll get to spend *lots* of time together."

Everything was clear now, including her vision. "I want to see my husband."

"I've added that you'll not be allowed any visitors during this time of recovery. But you'll be able to see him once you're returned to the care and custody of your parents. Now sign this and let's start our month off right."

She flailed up, but was easily pushed back down, her body weak compared to his. "You'll pay for that!"

"Actually," he said, "you'll be paying that."

Her body shuddered under the fear. "I won't sign until I see him. What is this anyway? And how does my marriage affect you?"

"Do you really think we're going to share this with your new husband? After all the planning we've done?" The clipboard was taken from her and slammed down on the bed. Through a clenching jaw, he gritted out, "Are you going to sign?"

Her heart began thumping in her chest, her fear echoed with each dense beat. There was no out. He wasn't leaving until she signed, so when he shoved the pen back into her hand and placed it on the clipboard, she scribbled her name across the wiggling line.

Dr. Conroy ripped the pen from her hand and then the papers, leaving a deep cut in her finger. He had her wrists secured in the straps before she could think to struggle.

"He'll come for me." She looked at him, really looked at him, eyeing the bruising, and whispered, "Or has he already been here?"

"I can see we have a lot of work ahead of us. Your delusions have gotten worse." He laughed without humor. "I'll note your worsening condition in the chart for the guardianship review coming up."

Jude had rarely cursed, but it flew out in anger and frustration. "You can go fuck yourself!"

"Marriage has made you bold when you should be scared, little girl."

Her body went limp from the threat and tears filled her eyes. With all of her strength, she willed them back in, and grinded her teeth. "I hate you."

"That makes two of us because I hate myself too, but it changes nothing. We're still stuck in this shitty world trying to improve our remaining days."

Jude turned away from him. The doctor left her strapped to the bed and shut the door. She heard the bolt and she was stuck in this holding cell, locked away from the world once again.

Yanking a few times, she knew it was pointless. She would be here as long as they wanted her to be here, or until she was released, whichever came first and right then, she had no idea when that would be.

She despised every aspect of this place, all the different stages they dragged each patient through, but lying in this room "waiting" to be moved to her usual room had to be the worst. Her arms hurt from being stretched out and she wanted her legs together. "They" liked how vulnerable patients were in this position, and took advantage of the hospital gown barely covering her.

Focusing on the box breathing technique she learned after her first suicide attempt, she tried to settle the outrage that pinpricked every awakened nerve.

Inhale. One. Two. Three. Four.

Hold. One Two. Three. Four.

Exhale. One. Two. Three. Four.

Hold. One. Two. Three. Four.

It didn't work. She was in full-blown fight mode, and knew they wouldn't put her in another room until she was subdued. The problem with subdued meant that she was giving in and she had no intention of giving in. She never did. She just eventually got moved.

In Bleekman's, time was irrelevant. It moved over the hours like a snail, every minute escalated to more importance than it should be given, the day disappearing beneath her. There was no beginning or end. Just the sun rising, the daylight, the sun setting, and the nighttime. Four distinct times.

Hold. One. Two. Three. Four.

She watched the sun steal the day as it crossed the room in light and shadows. Maybe the last four months of her life were all in her head. Maybe she had been here the whole time.

No breakfast.

No lunch.

Exhale. One. Two. Three. Four.

When a nurse arrived with dinner, she set the tray down on a table in the far corner. One Jude couldn't reach and the nurse walked closer. "Why do you fight this so much? You know how this goes, Judith."

Jude rolled her eyes. "Oh, I don't know. Maybe because I'm not crazy."

"I don't know if you remember me, but I'm Nurse Lacy. I've been your nurse once before," she said quietly, looking over her shoulder to make sure no one else was listening. She moved the strap higher on Jude's arm and then pulled some lotion from her pocket. Dabbing a little on Jude's wrist, she smiled. "They say you're married."

"I am," Jude replied even quieter.

"Congratulations. Is he wonderful?"

Through the haze of past visits, Jude remembered Nurse Lacy. She believed the young nurse was doing the best job she could and actually cared about her patients. She was just naïve to what was really happening at the hospital. "He's wonderful."

She leaned down, and whispered, "Dr. Conroy was hit by a very angry husband today, a husband wanting his wife released. Do you think...?" She left her question open-ended.

I hadn't imagined him. He was real. She smiled. *My Hazel came for me.* "I do think, but more than think, I hope."

"That's good," Lacy replied. "Always hold onto hope." Backing away, she grabbed the tray and sat back on the side of the bed. "I need to feed you. Are you going to cooperate for me?"

Jude was famished and thirsty. Eating didn't mean giving up or giving in. Eating was for survival and to keep her strong. And in her current predicament, she wanted an ally, someone who had shown her compassion, so she replied, "I will."

The sun disappeared just after the nurse left her room. Jude stared out the small window, having stopped pulling on her straps before the sun was above the facility.

She lay in the dark, her weaker thoughts starting to get the best of her. *Was Hazel here? Was he not? Was she imagining things when she saw him?* Maybe she was crazy.

Jude wanted sleep. She wanted to go to sleep and wake up to Hazel next to her in bed with his eyes open like when he watched her sleep. She wanted to wake up and see the sun rising outside his high-rise as she lay in his arms. She wanted to sneak out of bed and make him comfort food to give him the same feeling he gave her. She wanted to believe that her life with him was real, that he was real, and not a figment of her imagination, not a side character to her crazy.

Even though Nurse Lacy had confirmed Taylor was alive, she struggled to believe when locked in this oppressive room. "Dear God, please let Hazel exist in the world. Please." She closed her eyes and eventually, after much discomfort, fell asleep.

The sun didn't wake her. The doctor didn't wake her. The kind nurse who had sympathetic brown eyes didn't wake her.

An orderly did.

Flicking the overhead fluorescent light on, he said, "Wake up, sunshine! Time to move."

Jude groaned, her body stiff from the tight bonds and her heart aching for Hazel. "I need the bathroom."

"You're getting moved first."

"Please."

"No."

She looked him in the eyes. "Please. Don't make me wet myself."

"I'll clean it. I'm used to it."

Traitorous tears pricked her eyes. They made her show how weak she felt and she hated appearing weak. But she'd wet herself once before when she was isolated for a day and she swore she would never let that happen again. "I'm asking nicely. Please let me use the bathroom."

"How bad do you want to use it?"

Everybody wanted something... "Is Nurse Lacy still on duty?"

"She's gone. You're stuck with me." He licked his lips as he looked her over.

"Who is having me moved then?"

"Dr. Conroy. Do you want him? Or me?"

Pulling herself toward the wall as much as she could, she backed away from him. "Neither." There was no good option out of those two.

"Well, there's your answer." He unfastened one ankle and then the other, but her legs felt too limp to fight. Her muscles had betrayed her and she glared down at them while pulling on her arms to test them. "Don't hit or kick me or I'll leave you in here."

The smell of corn chips and coffee on his breath churned her stomach, so she turned her head away from him while he worked on her wrists. One arm. Then the other. They fell to her sides, her shoulders screaming in pain from the new position. "Can you walk?" he asked.

"I don't think so," she replied with her head still turned, now embarrassed. This is what they wanted. They wanted their patients at their weakest.

He scooped her up as if she weighed nothing and set her in a wheelchair waiting in the hallway. Jude looked around as she was pushed. It was the middle of the night by the vibe of the place. Empty of medical staff. The patients locked in their rooms. The center eerily quiet. She saw the abandoned reception desk and the front doors just beyond. A red light was lit up in the corner—either a camera or an alarm. He turned and took her down a green hallway. "Where are we going?" she asked, starting to feel uneasy.

"To your room."

"I've never been in this hall before. I usually stay in the blue hall."

"Not this time. You're here for a longer stay and apparently need the extra security."

Squirming in her chair, her voice got louder. "Can you double-check? I'm always in the blue hallway."

"What's the big deal? They're all the same."

"Maybe I do need to speak with Conroy."

He stopped in front of a restroom. "Stop your complaining and I'll let you use it."

She sat back and nodded. "Thank you."

He helped her out of the chair and she used the railings to go inside, shutting the door for privacy. She wished she could stay in there forever, but she knew her fate was sealed while she was drugged out.

When they walked into her room next door, she instantly saw what the big deal was—there was no window. There was a bare mattress in the corner and nothing else. Shaking her head, she repeated, "No, this can't be right. I need a window. I need a pillow and sheets and a bedframe."

"You do realize this isn't the Four Seasons, right?"

Jude didn't reply. She just stared ahead as he nudged her forward, the chair hitting the back of her legs. When she was in the room, he pulled the wheelchair out and said, "Sweet dreams."

Turning and moving, she shouted, "No! Don't leave me in here!"

The door shut and the overhead light was left on. Looking at the walls, she didn't see a switch. Her hands were trembling, remembering she would be here for a month. *They're trying to make me crazy.* She recalled telling Hazel that and here she was in a room with no window, no way of telling the time, the day, which way was up or down. She was facing her biggest fear—complete and terrifying isolation—in a place she feared more than death itself.

Standing over the mattress, she dropped to her knees and curled onto her side. Images of her usual cell, the one with chipping paint and metal bars on her window, came to mind. She always hated that room, but it was luxurious compared to this one. It had given her an isolated form of safety. It wasn't trying to be perfect or prim or proper. It was what is was and she valued that room's honesty. But here... she had none of that. It was a room covered in treachery with people *selling* her to the highest bidder. Closing her eyes, she pushed all the bad to the back of her mind and pulled the good forward—*Hazel. Hazel. Hazel. Hazel. Hazel.*

Chapter Twenty-Three

WHEN JUDE WOKE, the doctor was sitting in a chair nearby. He looked up and she scrambled to the corner of the room, half on the mattress and half off, but away from him.

"Good Morning, Judith."

"Leave me alone."

"Now. Now," Dr. Conroy said condescendingly. He tapped his pen against a clipboard. "Don't be upset. We have some business to discuss and then you can be moved to a nicer room."

"What business?"

"Money. Yours to be precise."

"I have nothing, not a dollar to my name."

He stood and set his clipboard down on the seat with the pen on top. She had visions of flipping into action and stabbing him with the pen... but she would never do such things. She may be in an asylum, but she wasn't crazy. And by the way the doctor left the pen unguarded, he didn't believe she was crazy either. "That's where you're wrong, Ms. Boehler. You have more than a few million dollars to your name in fact and I want a lot of them."

"I'm not following. I have no money," she insisted.

He rubbed his face, and grunted in what sounded like frustration.

"Have you really not been paying attention? What do you think you do when you're here?"

"I'm supposed to be recovering, but this place makes me crazy."

He sighed heavily and sat down again, his intense stare aimed at her. "This is about money. It's always been about money. You were just dumb enough to drag someone else into this mess."

"What money?"

Leaning forward, he said, "Listen up because I won't be repeating myself. Here's how it's gonna go. You are going to sign this, which will allow a transfer of two million dollars into an account. When I see it's there safe and sound, I'll let you see your husband."

Thinking of Hazel, she sat up, feeling ashamed of how she looked and ran her hand down her hair to keep it in place. "What two million? How am I going to make two million magically appear?"

"See, this is the story. Pretty little Judith was being molested by her big bad uncle. She tries to commit suicide. When she doesn't die, life goes on just as if nothing had changed at all. Am I on the right track?"

Rolling her eyes, she says, "Just go on." This has been talked to death every time she'd come in for an evaluation.

The doctor smiled. "Uncle picks up right where he left off, but after your brother died, you had nothing to lose at that point and told his little girl—your cousin—all about it. Did she believe you?" He sounded bored with the story. "Not only did she believe you, but she blamed you. The family did. Uncle commits suicide. At the reading of the will, Little Judith—tempting, beautiful Judith—hits the mother lode or what we like to call a payday."

Bringing her knees to her chest, she stared at him, holding a steady expression of disinterest despite the shock she felt inside. She had no idea what he was talking about with the will. *Hold it all in*, she reminded herself. *Give him nothing.*

"Yes, Judith, I've been doing my homework, have talked to you, to your family, and since we've kind of masterminded this whole thing, I want my cut now. As for this unfortunate husband, what's his name?"

Silence and a hard glare were her only response. The doctor stood and started to walk away, but Judith said, "Is he still here?"

He mocked her with a hardy laugh. "I know his name, where he lives, his age, all about his disease, and who his parents are. What I don't get is where you fit into his life or why you call him Hazel."

Her eyes glinted with anger hearing Hazel's name roll off the doctor's tongue as if he has a right to even utter it.

"I don't understand what you want from me? How you expect me to produce two million dollars when I can't access a single dollar?"

"I'm sure he's nearby. You're wasting my time, Judith. For all I've done, for my time and my overdue compensation, I want my cut now. So think long and hard about your choices here. Husband or money? I'll be back in twenty." The door closed and the light went off, leaving her alone in the pitch-black room. She couldn't even see her hand in front of her face. *They're trying to make me crazy.*

Fight.

Fight.

Fight.

She felt for the mattress and climbed onto it. Lying on her side, she stared in the direction she thought the door was. Struggling to tell if her eyelids were open or closed, she tucked her head down and tried for sleep instead. This was going to be a very long month.

TAYLOR SAT IN the small town police station, waiting for someone to help him. When he was finally called in, he was led to a young deputy's desk. They shook hands and the deputy asked, "What can I do for you, Mr. Barrett?"

"My wife is being held against her will at Bleekman's."

As soon as he mentioned Bleekman's, the deputy sighed and leaned back in his chair. "There's nothing we can do about that facility. They have regular inspections and pass code. If you'd like to file a complaint, Lucille can help you do that, but I have to warn you. It's not a fast route."

Taylor's palms were sweating. "I have my lawyers looking into options, but I need to get her out today. They have her strapped down and drugged."

The deputy picked up his pen and said, "Not to offend you, but if she doesn't belong there, how did she end up in there?"

"Her parents admitted her."

His chair squeaked as he leveraged back. "Why would her parents do that?"

"She's not crazy, if that's what you're thinking."

His impassive face wavered. "Look, when it comes to Bleekman's it's complicated."

"You're telling me," Taylor added.

"I can't just go in there and take people out free Willy. If you truly believe she's not crazy, you can get a court order and send in an agent."

Taylor stood up. "How do I do that?"

Eyeing Taylor, he said, "Get those big city lawyers of yours on it."

As soon as Taylor got in his car, he called Caleb. "I want her out of there right now!"

"I'm working on it, Taylor," Caleb Monroe said after a heavy sigh. "Nothing in the legal system moves fast. You know this."

"What I know is what I fucking witnessed, and that's my wife passed out, looking like she's on the verge of death while they have her spread out on that fucking torture device. So don't tell me what I know. Just help me get her out of there."

"Give me an hour."

"You've got thirty minutes."

"Don't go back there without a court order. Do you hear me, Taylor? I understand you're upset, but don't make this harder for me to get her out. Get something to eat and save your energy. You're going to need it."

"What have you found out about the conservatorship?"

"Her parents have full right and the hospital has some say in what is required for recovery. Look, you should have told me you got married and about her situation. I could have had a head start on this. We're working against time now. And it's not looking good."

"Why?"

"Because she's sitting in an asylum that her guardian and doctor think is necessary. On top of that, we're going to have to fight the expert opinion that she wasn't capable of making the decision to marry you."

Sucker-punched in the heart. Suddenly terrified that he might lose Jude, Taylor couldn't breathe. His only air worth inhaling was shackled to a hospital bed. "We love each other."

"I understand that." Taylor didn't like his lawyer's tone. "But it's not up to us and this is not about emotions. It's about what's best for her. The courts will have to decide that. Listen, I need an hour. Go eat. Take care of yourself. I'll call you back."

Taylor started retracing their days after they got married. There was so much he should have done. He should have taken her to his lawyer so she could have filed to gain her rights back. He would have gotten her a phone of her own. He would have never let her go back to that hell again, much less alone. He failed her time and time again. So much he would do differently in hindsight.

He was determined to make things right for her, even though he sat in his car now, gutted by the fact he may have no rights at all, that he may not be able to help her, much less save her. He had great lawyers. This was their time to prove it. Starting the car, he looked down at his phone. He couldn't just sit here any longer, so he backed out and drove to Bleekman's to wait on his lawyer to call him back.

Fortunately he didn't have to wait long. Caleb called, and said, "I've got a judge who will make a call for us. Since this will turn into a legal matter, he'll request she be released into your custody. Be aware. They do not have to comply since her parents still hold legal guardianship over her. The marriage blurs lines in this case. I'm going to file on your behalf for an immediate transfer of guardianship based on not only the marriage license being legal, but on your clean record and upstanding citizenship in the state of New York."

"How long do I have to wait?"

"Get to Bleekman's—"

"I'm already here."

"Then hang tight. I'll call you when I hear back from the judge's office."

"Thank you." Taylor hung up the call, but held on to the phone.

He watched the building like a hawk. When she was released, he wanted a quick getaway, so he moved his car up a row closer and into the end parking spot. The phone rang and he answered immediately, hearing what he wanted. "You're clear. Go get her."

Taylor hung up and tossed the phone into the cup holder. Running to the gate, he stopped when he saw the doctor coming out of the building. "Mr. Barrett, you do not understand the damage you are doing. We got off on the wrong foot, but I'm asking you now to leave her."

"Get my wife!" He pressed the button and the receptionist didn't answer. She just buzzed him in. Thank goodness for earlier charms.

Dr. Conroy looked annoyed when he heard the gate buzzed open without his permission. Turning back, he had his hands up as Taylor came toward him. "I'm begging you to let her stay another day or two. She's a very sick woman."

Taylor ignored him and continued walking straight inside. Maxine, the receptionist, stood up and smiled. "Down hall three. Room six."

He never paused and started to run. The doctor was calling after him, but he didn't care. Jude was his only goal. Until the doctor said, "Judith is confused. She kissed me. She begged me for more. Are you willing to be responsible for a woman who can't even tell the difference between you and me?"

With his hand on the door, he looked back. It took all his willpower to stay focused on getting Jude out of here. How dare he talk about Jude as if she means nothing, as if she wasn't Taylor's every waking thought. He wanted to end him, but kept his mission on Jude. "She would never confuse us. You have done nothing but hurt her and I will do nothing but protect her. She knows me not by sight, but by heart."

Nothing prepared him for seeing the room cradled in blackness. His heart started beating and he felt for a light switch. When he didn't find one, he leaned back and saw it just outside the door. "Jude," he called softly before flipping it on.

Her body was in a tight ball on the mattress in the corner. She didn't move.

Walking in, he heard the doctor behind him. "This is unorthodox and can ruin her treatment."

"Back away from us."

"I don't have to allow this."

Taylor turned, his body heaving, his hands fisted. "Get away from me. Get away from her. That is your final warning." His anger steamrolled the doctor making him take three steps back.

Even with the shouting, Jude didn't move. Taylor bent down, his anger morphing into heartbreak, and whispered, "Jude? Baby, it's me. Hazel. Can you hear me?" *No covering on her. No sheets on the mattress.* Hostility mixed with unease in his stomach. Hate for the man behind him mixed with sadness for the woman in front of him. *How could they treat my Jude like this? How could they treat anyone like this?* He touched her shoulder lightly and could feel her body shivering. His hand moved slowly over her shoulder and to her head. "I'm going to pick you up. Okay, Jude?"

Still no response.

Taylor scooped her into his arms. Her breath hit his neck as he held her close. He got up and walked toward the door with no fear of the doctor or the two orderlies standing by. Taylor walked right past them and to the desk. "Where are her things?"

Maxine put a large clear Ziploc bag on the counter that contained her lavender dress, her shoes, and her two rings. With a sympathetic smile, she said, "That's all she had."

He nodded, unable to speak. The tragedy of their love gripped his heart and strangled his words. As he walked to the front doors, a nurse ran up and opened it.

The nurse seemed to understand his silence, and whispered, "She's going to be okay. I checked on her vitals less than an hour ago."

Taylor didn't trust any of them. Their *care* seemed to be to torture the patients and see who survives. Walking ahead of him, the nurse opened the gate for them as if this somehow made a difference. How could she leave Jude in a place like that and feel pride in her job. *For fuck's sake.* That room would haunt him, so he could only imagine the fear Jude felt. He turned sideways. Jude, with her eyes closed, had stopped shaking, and whispered, "I told them you would come for me."

His lips pressed to her head, and he said, "Always."

The nurse opened the passenger door when Taylor unlocked the car with the key remote. He set Jude carefully inside. When he stood up, the nurse handed him a bottle of water. "Make sure she drinks lots of liquids and she needs to eat in the next hour or so. If you need anything, my name is Lacy."

"I won't need anything from this place," he bit, a warning in his tone. He left her standing there with the bottle still in her hand. His hand began to shake as he went through the motions of buckling in his half-conscious wife. He could tell it was from anger this time, not his illness.

While he buckled himself, he glanced over at her—frail, lifeless, pale—not his Jude at all, and yet, this is what her family preferred? Ordered up for her destiny? How could they do this to their own daughter? How could they do this to anyone and sleep in their ivory tower so peacefully?

He started the engine and backed out of the space. He wanted his wife back and he would do whatever it took to bring back her smile. Getting the hell away from the hospital was a good start, and he floored it, speeding away as fast as he could.

When the sign for the hospital was long gone, Taylor touched her gently and whispered, "We'll be home soon, my love."

Chapter Twenty-Four

THE CAR CAME to a stop on a dirt road concealed beneath tall trees on both sides. Jude slumped to the side before righting herself. She looked over at Hazel in the driver's seat next to her and smiled. It was feeble, but it represented her whole heart.

He put the car into park and turned to her. "Hey there."

"Hi."

Her voice was slightly hoarse either from dehydration or shouting. He wasn't sure and didn't want to ask. Handing her his water, he said, "Drink. I can tell you're dehydrated."

She took a few small sips, then looked out her window. "I'm gonna go... out there."

"I can take you somewhere else. I just thought—"

"This is fine." She reached for the bag of clothes in the back seat and Taylor ran around to open the door for her. Jude took his hand and stood up. Their bodies came together, and she fell into his arms. "Thank you," she whispered.

He held her. He held her so tight he didn't know if he was holding her up or if she was holding him. It didn't matter either way. They were together again.

Jude stepped away with her head lowered. When she looked up

into his eyes, she requested, "Don't look at me like that anymore, okay? I can survive anything they do to me at Bleekman's. I can survive anything my family puts me through. But I cannot survive knowing I've dulled your impossible eyes."

Putting on a smile just for her, he said, "Okay." He wasn't sure what else to say. He was worried he wouldn't be able to always hide his inner turmoil from her, but he would hide it from her today.

He added, "I packed clothes for you."

"The dress will do," she replied, holding up the bag.

Leaning against the car, he watched as she walked into the woods, just behind some large trunked trees. He looked away, giving her privacy, though the thought of her needing privacy from him stung.

Minutes later, she returned looking more herself already. She lifted up on her tiptoes and kissed him lightly, then said, "It's amazing what a pretty dress can do for your attitude." She twirled, not as fast as usual, but enough to make her smile, and more than enough to make him.

"We'll fill the closet. You'll have dresses in every color."

She rubbed her hand over his chest. "And where will your clothes go?"

"I don't care. I just want to fill your life with dresses that make you smile like this one does."

Tilting her head, she blushed. "I missed you."

Guilt bombarded his heart, landing each and every regret. "I'm sorry. So sorry. Will you ever be able to forgive me?"

"You've done nothing to apologize for. I'm here, only because of you. Thank you for loving me."

The architect and the double dipper embraced, but now as bonded lovers—no past, no future, just them right in that very moment. "I do," he said, "I love you so much."

"I love you too, Hazel."

He breathed her in, her natural scent muted by the dark past of the last twenty-four hours. He wanted her light back. He wanted his Jude back. She was there, but he would have to unearth the woman beneath the stench of deceit. "We should go. Get you home."

She pulled herself away from him begrudgingly, but she knew he was right. "I'm ready."

Jude spent the trip back to Manhattan mostly quiet. She felt the drugs altering her on the inside, and through her peaks of lucidity, she fought the crazy thoughts desperate to surface. She just needed to wait them out. Tomorrow. Tomorrow she could think clearer.

Taylor alternated between watching the road and watching her. He had a ton of questions, but it didn't seem the right time for deep conversation. By the way she leaned against the door with her head on her hand, she looked too tired. Determined to help her the best he could, he pulled over and they ate lunch at a roadside diner.

She leaned her head on him now, the two of them sharing one side of the vinyl booth. With his hand on her leg, and while waiting on their order to arrive, she asked, "Do you love me like you did before?"

Rubbing her thigh, he kept his trembling heart out of his voice. "I love you more."

"You're all I saw when my mind tried to play tricks on me, you grounded me to something real, something pure. You gave me a reason to fight." Sitting up, she looked at him, then to the rings on her finger. "I'm sorry you saw me like that. I'm sorry about everything."

"You don't have any reason to say sorry, but I have a million." *The call to the lawyer he should have made. The phone he should have bought. Stopping her from going back...* A million regrets that burdened his heart.

"You keep saying that, but you'll never convince me." After a heavy sigh, she let her shoulders and her guard down. "I don't want to relive it. I never want to think about it again."

He understood, so he nodded. They could talk tomorrow about the legal stuff, but Bleekman's got benched for good.

Taylor's eyes were wide in astonishment as he watched her finish a half-pound burger, French fries, and a piece of apple pie a la mode. Then he felt bad for her on the car ride home watching her rub her belly in pain. "Why did you let me eat so much?"

"I was afraid if I tried to stop you, I'd lose a hand." He chuckled.

She didn't at first, feigning offense, but gave in and laughed. "You might have. I was starving." Groaning again, she said, "I can't wait to be home."

When they walked into the apartment, Taylor dropped his bag on the bedroom floor and Jude went straight to the bathroom and started the shower. He gave her space and waited for her in the living room. After texting his lawyer that they made it home, his lawyer replied.

Come in tomorrow at ten, so we can sign the papers to start the process.

He would talk to her later if she was up for it. If not, in the morning. Passing the time, he sat at his drafting table and sketched out a larger closet just for her in their future home, until his hand trembled. The difference this time was it was his other hand. He watched his left hand on the white surface moving just enough for the eye to catch what his body knew.

"I feel so much better after that shower," Jude said from the kitchen.

Taylor wrapped his right hand over the other, hiding it from her. He just hoped he hid the fear he felt as well. "What?" he asked, looking over. She was the vision of the beauty he fell in love with. Her hair shone under the light, her happiness too bright to hide in her blue-green eyes. She wore his boxer shorts and college T-shirt, giving him flashbacks of the first time they were together.

She repeated herself, "I needed a shower. I smelled." She shook her head. "So embarrassing."

Staring at her, he said, "Nothing to be embarrassed about."

"Are you okay?" She quirked her head to the side and stared at him. "You seem distant?"

Turning back to his table and the house rendering, he tried to ignore the disease that wouldn't give up on him. "I'm fine. I'm tired. I'm sure you are, too."

"Exhausted," she replied dramatically, but when he didn't respond to her antics, she walked to him and placed her hands on his shoulders. "What's wrong? *For real.* What's going on?"

Her hands were warmth and strength, reassurance, and patience. He wanted to give her the same in return, so he secured his voice and covered what he should be telling her with what he needed to tell her. "We have an appointment with my lawyer at ten tomorrow. We'll get your rights back whether they're granted to you or me, your family will no longer have access or control over you."

She squeezed and gently rubbed. "That's great news. Thank you. You're very tense. Maybe you should take a hot shower too."

He took a deep breath and straightened his face, holding steady. Taking her by the hips, he said, "Yeah, that might help."

Leaning down, she took his face between her hands and kissed him. There was more than passion exchanged. There was a promise of a happy life. And Jude felt safe once again. Sitting on his lap, she wrapped her arms around his neck. "Is it bad that I'm still craving Chinese food?"

Now that made him laugh. "I can't believe you're hungry after that big meal, but if you want Chinese food, you've got. I'll order it now."

She kissed his head. "I knew you loved me."

"You're right. I do."

Pausing, they let a quaint silence surround them as they spun to look out the window at the city beyond. "When did you start loving me, Hazel?"

"The first time I saw you." *Chartreuse dress. Red snow boots. Wrapped in chaos and breathing life into a party that was stale, and a heart that had gone cold.*

"So was it the double dipping that won you over?"

"No. Although that was quite the turn-on," he said sarcastically. "It was watching you dance to the music all by yourself."

Her head tilted back and she laughed. "That makes me sound weird."

"Not weird at all. Quirky, yes. But you were the most magnificent sight I'd ever seen. You were touchy and completely invading everyone's space—"

"Especially yours."

"You didn't have to invade mine. I happily surrendered the moment you looked into my eyes."

"Hazel."

He held her and kissed her shoulder. "You smell sweet. I'm glad to have you back."

"Not more glad than I am to be back." She bent down to kiss his lips, then pressed them to his ear instead, and whispered, "I'll spend my life trying to repay you, but let me start by saying thank you."

Turning, he closed his eyes as his cheek rubbed against hers. "I'd rather you spend your life happy, free to be who you are, and with me."

"Me too. With you. Everything with you." She released him and stood up. "I'm going to rest until the food gets here."

Tugging on her shirt, he agreed. "I'll wake you when it arrives."

Her finger traced his jaw, then tapped his lips. "I love you."

"I love you more."

With a smirk, she replied, "Impossible," and disappeared into the bedroom, leaving the door cracked open.

Taylor ordered the food and then sat on the couch with his head in his hands. Bitterness was seeping into his heart, the disease attempting to steal his future out from under him.

Money, power, talent, connections. None of it mattered. The disease he fought against couldn't be bought, sold, or traded. Bartered or deterred. His disease was set to destroy all that was good in him, all that was worth having, worth living. He would leave this earth one day too soon, but more than this world, he didn't want to leave Jude.

Chapter Twenty-Five

THE FOOD WAS delivered and from the bedroom, Jude heard the rustle of the plastic coming from the kitchen. She didn't hear Hazel though. He was eerily quiet and it bothered her, twisting her stomach in knots.

With her eyes open, she watched as he opened the bedroom door slowly and paused, his dark body silhouetted by the light from the kitchen. Her words got stuck in her throat. She so desperately wanted him to speak first, to tell her everything's going to be okay. But as the bed dipped and she felt Hazel's body against hers, she also felt more than his weight. She felt his burden. In the dark room, he sat there, not moving, not attempting to wake her. He sat there next to her drowning in his pain.

"Hazel?" She rubbed his lower back, but he didn't turn. "Let me in. Please."

"You have so much shit to deal with. You don't need mine."

"I want your... shit." She laughed softly. "That sounds bad, but you know what I mean."

He didn't laugh, but whispered, "I do."

Her hand continued to touch him. "Don't hide things from me. Everyone hides things from me. To me, you're honesty and trust.

Please let me be the same for you."

"I don't want to hurt you."

She sat up. "You can't. You won't. Don't you see? You heal me." She had felt his pain before but when their eyes connected, she *saw* his pain for the first time.

"I'm going to die, Jude. It could be ten years from now."

She could feel the weight of the universe through the tense muscles of his shoulders and she rubbed to ease them. A silence hung between them and she started to wonder if he would ever fully share his burdens with her. He had given himself so selflessly to her, to be the strong one for her. What he didn't realize was that she could be that for him. She would be his comfort, his lover, his companion, and his wife for life. "It could be seventy."

Sliding around, she was across his lap and caressing his neck when he said, "Tell me you'll love me no matter what?"

"I'll show you." She kissed him as she pushed him back on the bed.

"I thought you were hungry?"

"I am," she said, straddling him. "Ravenous." And kissed him.

The Chinese food was room temperature when they wandered into the kitchen an hour later. They ate at the bar as the sun set. The apartment was peacefully quiet, both of them content for the time being.

With full bellies, they got up and cleaned, put the extra food in the fridge, and went into the living room. She sat on the couch, he at the drafting table. After picking up a ruler, he watched his hand as he pressed it to the paper, waiting to see if it would shake or not. It didn't, so with a pencil in his right, he completed a line since his hands were cooperating.

Jude opened a book from the case and pretended to read, but when he wasn't looking, her eyes were on Hazel. His glasses were on, his hair a mess, shirtless, boxer shorts, and like a god from ancient histories past, he was too good for this world. A cruel fate would reclaim him and one day she would be alone again. Alone didn't bother her as much as his death did.

"Do you love what you do? Creating? Architecting?" she asked with a smile as she lay down lengthwise.

With a smile already on his face, he said, "I love what I do. It's one of the few professions that uses both sides of your brain—the creative and the analytical. I can feed my moods."

"What mood are you in right now?"

"Analytical." Turning back to his house on paper. "I need order, logic."

"How bad is it, Hazel? Tell me."

He knew what she was asking, but it wasn't that easy to answer. "Telling you means I've come to accept it and I haven't. So I'm just going to keep working on this project." He peeked over at her. "I'm sorry."

Their conversations had been full of words like sorry and I love you. But she realized that sorry only came to be because the I love yous existed. She preferred the latter though she understood they must grieve through a process of guilt and gratefulness.

"You don't have to be." Jude, of all people, understood the power of denial. She just hoped his denial didn't end in his death. She opened her book and picked up where she had left off a few days earlier.

The day had been exhausting for both of them, but they lay in bed together after midnight wide awake. They tried for sleep, but it was hard sought and restlessly eluded them. Finally Jude gave into reality. "I can't sleep."

"I can't either. What are you thinking about?"

"What am I not thinking about?" She rolled toward him and

asked, "Make me forget."

"If one day you'll help me remember." He wrapped his arm under her neck and she moved closer. "I'm scared I'll forget how to control my hands and draw, or sketch, or touch you the way I want, the way you like."

"You'll not forget, my love. If you do, I'll be your hands. I will. You can teach me."

"How to touch you?" he asked.

Jude moved on top of him, took his hand, and placed it on her breast. "Teach me everything."

His hand squeezed and she closed her eyes, her body stimulated awake from his touch. Sitting up, he kissed her collarbone and felt her—the dip of her waist right before it meets her hips, the roundness of her bottom, and then back up to her firm breasts. Her body was a compass to his life's journey and he planned to explore and conquer.

With his mouth on her skin, he tasted her sweetest valley and hills. His hands rolled over her stomach and between her legs, which opened for him like the petals of a flower. "You like this," he whispered, then kissed the top of one of her breasts.

"I do." She shivered under his words.

He lifted up until her eyes met his, holding her gaze while he moved down her body. He kissed her where the secrets she only shared with him were hidden, like treasures.

She smiled and let her mind and body relax back. Rain started hitting the windows and she turned just to catch the beginning of the storm outside. While her body was revered into its own brewing storm, she let her thoughts thunder toward tomorrow. Taylor straightened over her and thrust inside her, no patience for the weather inside or out.

The temperature rose in the room, their bodies melting from

the heat. She reached above her, her fingers grappling for leverage. When she kissed his shoulder, she fell back, lightning striking. "Taylor!" she cried out as his own tornado ripped through him. "Jude!"

They watched the raindrops hit the window until they fell asleep in the early hours of a new day.

The storm got louder throughout the night, the sky lighting up from booming lightning. Jude woke up just before when sunrise should have happened. She moved to the chair and watched the weather taunt her as if it could predict her future.

When Taylor stirred, his arm reached out, feeling for her. She said, "Is it a sign?"

He opened his eyes and she was the first thing he saw, making him smile his sexiest, most peaceful smile. "We don't need signs. We have love and truth on our side."

"I was told by the doctors I can't have children." She just said it. Like his disease, this fact picked at her bones, eating her alive.

Taylor sat up slowly not sure if he should go to her or give her space. "Which doctors?"

"Bleekman's. They said the drugs have done damage to my insides. Do you think you can heal my body like you've healed my soul?"

Afraid to look at her, to let her see his sadness, he stared out the window at the rain. "I don't think you should have kids with a man who won't be there to help you raise them anyway."

His tone was flat and she hated it. "You can't be consumed with death when we have so much life to live. A baby of yours..." she looked away from him, "would be a gift."

Anger surged over his grim reality of a future. "Those doctors would tell you anything to hurt you."

"We've never used birth control and I've not gotten pregnant. I think they were right."

"Jude," he started, shaking his head ever so slightly. "I'll do this if you need me to, but I don't think we need to talk about something we can't control before our appointment this morning. We can pick it up later tonight if you want."

She pulled out a cigarette and lit it while staring out at the city on the other side of their glass refuge. "I started smoking because my uncle hated cigarette smoke."

Another piece of the puzzle clicked into place, the rounded edges of her confession sharp with pain on his already beaten heart. "What if I asked you not to?"

Exhaling smoke, she then replied, "I'd quit for you."

"I want you to stop smoking. I don't ask much of you, but this I ask because I love you and even if I can't live a long life, I want you to."

Jude dropped it in a glass of water on the floor. "For you, anything." Standing up, she said, "I'll make breakfast."

With all the talk of what they couldn't do, he wanted to focus on what they could. Tucking his hands behind his head, he watched her naked body walk by and into the kitchen. He just hoped the shades were drawn in the living room. Getting up, he went to take a shower. He wrapped a towel around his waist before joining her in the kitchen.

He formed around her back, encompassing her. She stopped scrambling the eggs and leaned her cheek against his. He whispered, "It's going to be okay."

"You're not mad at me about the birth control?"

"How can I be mad when I didn't use any either."

She moved the spatula around the skillet, then turned off the flame. "Living dangerously, Mr. Barrett?"

"Is there any other way to live these days?"

"Yes! Safely."

"I guess I didn't mind being tied to you before we tied the knot."

Jude's body stilled and she turned in his arms. "What are you saying, you crazy man?"

"Don't call me crazy," he teased.

Her fist lightly pounded his chest. "Never," she replied with a smile. "But you're saying you would have had a baby with me?"

"I still will if you play your cards right." He waggled his eyebrows for extra emphasis.

"But I can't."

"I don't think you should believe anything those doctors told you. You can find a doctor here in the city. We can do tests to see, but I'm not going to believe you can't just because those psychos said it."

She kissed his chin and then his lips. "Thank you. Now let's get you fed and we'll start getting ready."

Taylor settled on the barstool with a plate and fork in front of him. Jude poured two glasses of juice and set one down for him. "Thank you for taking care of me."

"I will always take care of you."

Just before he had a chance to take a bite, a knock on the door surprised them. Their eyes met, panic setting in. Taylor stood and whispered, "Don't worry. I'll answer it. Go to the bedroom and get dressed. He watched her hurry into the bedroom and checked the time. 8:08. Too early for company. He tightened his towel around him and looked through the peephole. Two police officers stood on the other side of the door. "Hello?" Taylor called.

"Mr. Barrett, please open the door."

"What's this regarding?"

"Again, please open the door so we don't have to disturb your neighbors."

Red flags were firing with every receiving synapse, but he had no choice. One way or the other, the police had rights as much as he did. He slowly unbolted the main locks and opened the door just enough to see each other's faces. The cop closest said, "We have a court order for Ms. Boehler to be returned to her guardians."

"It's Mrs. Barrett. We're married. She's twenty-two. Legally old enough to make her own choices. She's choosing not to return to them."

"She doesn't have that right, legally," he stated firmly, but the softening around the edges of his eyes belied the sternness of his words.

"We're married."

"But her guardians are still her parents and they have filed for her return."

"They're abusive. She can't go back. We have a meeting with our lawyer at ten. He's filing. Just pretend we weren't here and let us go to that appointment."

The officer sighed and looked down. When he looked up again, Taylor saw the sympathy in his eyes. "Hey, Mac. I may not understand the details of this case, but I have to follow orders. Ramirez here has to follow orders as well. We'll have to arrest you if you keep us from our job."

Taylor was not going to let her go without a fight, again. "Officers, let me ask you this: if someone had been drugging your wife, emotionally torturing her, physically abusing her, would you just step aside for her to be taken back to those people?"

They stared at Taylor a good, hard thirty seconds, then the cop said, "You're in a towel. I have no idea how she's dressed, but here's what I'm going to do. We're gonna step back, a few feet down this hall and pretend we haven't had this conversation. You're gonna get dressed, make sure she's dressed, and open this door in five minutes when we knock. You seem like a nice enough guy, so we'll extend you that courtesy, but we can't walk away without Ms. Boe... Barrett in our custody. If you fail to open this door in five minutes, we'll bust it open and arrest you and your wife for obstructing justice."

Like rats—they were trapped. He started to shut the door, but the police officer added, "I'd also spend that time calling your lawyer, Mr. Barrett."

The door shut and he locked one of the bolts. When he turned around, he saw Jude standing there in a pair of pants, a sweater, and sneakers. Her gaze lowered to the floor and she said, "Call your lawyer and go into the bedroom and wait until I'm gone."

"No." His eyes, like his tone, were defiant. "I'm not letting them take you."

"You have no choice, Hazel. *Please.* You can't help me if you're in jail."

He went to her, taking her by the arms, his eyes pleaded as his hands squeezed. "I'm not giving up. Don't you give up either!"

"I'm not giving up. I'm playing by their rules. It's poker and they have a better hand this round. We'll have the better hand next deal. I'm going with them. You're not going to stop this. You can't. All you can do is help me through the legal system. Please, Hazel, I beg of you. Go into the bedroom, get dressed, and call the lawyer."

He shook his head. "I can't just let them take you."

"Then come with me. Follow them to the station. They can't just deliver me back home. There's a paper trail they have to deal with. Go get dressed."

They stole seconds together and stared into each other's eyes. He touched her face and said, "Don't open the door yet. I'll follow you to the station." Taylor wasn't going to give up this time. He had failed her two days ago. Never again. She was his, and he will defend her from those determined to make her powerless.

Jude had accepted her fate this early morning and went to the door while her destiny stayed firmly wrapped up in the man in the bedroom. One bolt. Her hand shook, but unlocked it. When she opened the door, the two officers straightened themselves after having been leaning on the wall. She stepped out, and whispered, "Please don't hurt him."

They nodded. The deception of what was happening might not have been understood by the cops, but the gravity of ripping two people in love apart was. "I've got a wife at home. So does Ramirez."

Jude nodded this time and lowered her head as she shut the door. The three of them walked to the elevator and were safely on it when she heard Hazel calling for her.

Inches remained when he caught sight of her while he pushed the button erratically to stop the door from closing. "Jude! Don't go! Fight!"

An inch left before the door closed, blocking him. She said, "I love you. Always." She heard the slam of his fists on the outside of the elevator as they started to descend. With her back to the officers, she glanced at them in the reflection of the doors. "We need to hurry. He'll fight for me."

The tall man standing directly behind her said, "I'd do the same for my wife."

She found some comfort in the fact that he shared that with her, and she smiled.

Chapter Twenty-Six

TAYLOR JUMPED TO his feet when his lawyer, Caleb Monroe, walked into the police precinct. "Are you getting her out?"

"She's not in jail, Taylor." He walked with purpose to the counter, but added, "We'll find out where she is, but right now, you need to calm down or they won't tell us shit. Now go sit down and let me handle this."

"Caleb—"

"Go."

Taylor's hands fisted and his teeth were grinding together, but he did what Caleb told him to do because he wanted to know where Jude was and everything, other than going to her family's home—which he was threatened by Caleb not to do—he had tried had failed so far. From his chair he saw his lawyer discussing what seemed like the weather from the way they laughed and were so relaxed. After a few minutes, Caleb came over to Taylor, and said, "Let's go."

"Where is she?"

"We'll discuss it outside."

They walked out onto the busy sidewalk and down half a block before Caleb stopped and said, "She's with her parents. We could have assumed that since she wasn't under arrest. That leaves us to file papers on her behalf if you feel she still wants to pursue her rights at this point."

"What are you talking about?" Taylor asked, crossing his arms over his chest. "Why wouldn't she?"

"Because she went willingly. She returned to these apparent monsters on her own."

"No, she didn't. They were going to arrest me. I would have fought for her. She knows that. She went to protect me."

"But right now, we don't have a statement from her saying that or to back that as her claim. We only have that she returned to their home willingly."

"We need to go. They'll send her right back to Bleekman's."

"As your lawyer, I'm advising you once again to stay away from the Boehler residence until we have the law on our side. They can have you arrested on a number of charges, Taylor, and those arrests will make it more difficult to change the guardianship." He sighed. "I know this is har—"

"No, you fucking don't know. You don't know what it's like to live with the knowledge they're abusing her emotionally and physically. When I saw her strapped to that damn bed at the hospital, she was so drugged she was unconscious, her face was pale, and her lips were dry, which means they hadn't given her anything to eat or drink in about sixteen hours at that point. Look me in the eyes and tell me you could see someone you love like that and just sit around and wait."

He looked away, and then down the street, anywhere but at him. When he turned to face Taylor again, his voice was lower. "Work. Within. The. System. We'll get her freed, but in the meantime, you have to use the law against them. Vigilante actions only hurt our case and ultimately, her."

"I'll give you two hours."

"Three."

"Fine. Three. You better fucking get the paperwork sorted out by then."

Two hours later Taylor got the call he didn't see coming. Caleb said, "They've filed for a restraining order against you. It was approved until we can prove otherwise. I've already sent in the request for an expedited hearing on the case. I'm waiting to hear back."

Taylor sat there on the couch, numb. His emotions seeped into his voice, which were disillusioned and stunned. "A fucking restraining order? Against me? Are you kidding?"

"Unfortunately, I'm not."

He was grappling for anything that would keep him afloat from the despair that waited to devour him. "Is her name on it?"

"You can't go near her, but no, she didn't file it. Her stepfather did, and in the court's eyes, that's all that matters."

"They should have the restraining order against them." Now Taylor was pissed.

"We're getting hit. It's been brutal, but we have legal rights, we have plans in place. Let's just continue on with the plan we've agreed to and when I get word on the hearing, I'll call you back. In the meantime, don't go over there. Don't go near Judith."

The hearing was set for four that afternoon after Caleb pulled strings and once the judge was assigned. He'd played cards with him twice and used that relationship to benefit his client.

Seven hours later, Caleb and Taylor stood there in his chambers across the table from the Boehler's family lawyer. Jude was not there, neither was any family member. That was probably safer for them considering Taylor's contempt.

When the judge sat down, he looked tired. Taylor didn't feel this would bode well for them, but Caleb seemed confident. The judge said, "I've read the arguments on both sides and I'm curious how this case even came to be. You have Mr. Barrett on one side that has shown exemplary behavior and is from a prominent family in our fine community. They've raised millions through charity work over the years. He's well educated and a hard worker with a respected architecture track record." He paused to look at Taylor as if to verify his findings from the file. Then he pushed his glasses up the bridge of his nose, and added, "Then you have the Boehlers, who have filed this order against Mr. Barrett in protection of their daughter who is currently under their care—legally." He glanced at the Boehler lawyer but didn't seem impressed. "So what's this really about?"

Caleb spoke up. "Judge Matthews, the Boehler family is not protecting their daughter, but are putting her in harm's way. Mr. Barrett can testify to the conditions she is put under as well as recall the gruesome details of what she has told him privately regarding her treatment under the 'care' of her family and doctors at Bleekman's. But beyond that, Mr. Barrett is Judith Boehler's husband. They were married two weeks ago—"

The other lawyer interrupted, "I'd like to speak to that so-called marriage."

"It's not a so-called marriage," Caleb interjected. "It's a legal, binding agreement between two people who love each other."

The judge's attention was volleying between the two lawyers.

The Boehler lawyer said, "Judge Matthews, the Boehler family feels their daughter Judith was coerced under stress and medication to go along with this marriage plot."

"Fuck you!" Taylor stood and shouted, slamming his hands on the shiny wooden table between them. "I love her and she loves me. There was no coercion."

Caleb grabbed Taylor's arm and Taylor sat. "Please let me handle this, Taylor."

Caleb questioned the other lawyer. "What is this coercion based on? She wasn't on drugs at the time because she was with my client. She's only drugged when she's with your clients. So she got married on her own accord—"

"Like she left him of her own accord this morning."

"She left because the police said they would arrest my client if she didn't go with them."

The other lawyer smiled. "You're really reaching. The family, with consent from their daughter, filed this restraining order against your client." He opened his file. "Besides, he's abusive and is trying to brainwash her against her own parents." Scoffing, he glanced to the judge for what appeared to be extra drama. Setting three photos of Jude in front of the judge, he said, "The photos speak for themselves. This is the current state of her body—bruises on her upper spine, collarbone area, and around her ribs. All places distinctly chosen by your client so they couldn't be seen by her family."

Taylor gulped, knowing each and every one of those bruises by heart. He knew them by taste and feel. His heart sank seeing the photos, seeing Jude in distress and covering herself, clearly photographed against her will. Taylor cleared his throat and nudged Caleb, who was starting to lose ground on the case. "I need a minute with my client."

Judge Matthews said, "I'll give you two and it better be good."

Caleb and Taylor walked to the far corner of the room and Taylor whispered, "I would never hit her. I would never hurt her."

"What are the marks?"

Taylor hated exposing their intimacy so publicly but he had no choice. "I gave them to her when we made love the other day.

They're hickeys."

Caleb looked him square in the eyes, and asked, "Are you sure?"

Annoyed, Taylor responded, "Of course I'm sure. I knew what I was doing and..." Taking a deep breath, he added, "and she liked it."

Shaking his head, he sighed. "I can't go back there and debate that she liked it. We've got to stick to our side of the story and the facts."

"I would never intentionally hurt her."

"Listen to me. Do not say another word in here. I mean it. Not one damn word no matter what he says. He's trying to get another rise out of you to prove you're violent. So sit there and don't give him shit. Got it?"

"Got it." Taylor felt like he was starting to drown under the accusations coupled with the warrant. That he couldn't talk to Jude had added another level of stress to their already fucked-up situation. He sat back down and his shoulders hunched forward as he had clear visions of his defeat sitting on his horizon.

Caleb cleared his throat, and stated, "Those are love marks given and happily received during lovemaking. My client would not hurt the woman he loves and is trying to protect." He pushed the photos back to the other lawyer. "If he is being accused of domestic violence that is something we will not tolerate and will fight wholeheartedly."

Judge Matthews was losing his patience. "This case is getting off track. Since we don't have the petitioners here to verify one way or the other, we cannot prove if those bruises at this time were made through abuse or other means. With that said, for the sake of our time and the petitioner's protection, I'm granting the restraining order to be upheld for a total of three days, reducing it from six months. We can reconvene with the two parties and witnesses at that time to determine how this will extend beyond the three days." He stood and said, "Good day, gentleman."

Taylor was left speechless. Caleb was fuming but held his poker face. The Boehler lawyer chuckled under his breath as he gathered the photos and file together. "Better luck next time," he said, gloating.

There was so much Taylor wanted to say, but listening to Caleb, he remained silent. His hands, both at the same time, started trembling and he looked down at them in his lap as if they were detached from his own body. Stress incited the disease and he was feeling the effects.

Caleb instructed him to leave and not to say anything until they were out of the courthouse. Taylor followed him out and the two men walked in silence side by side down the sidewalk. "That went to shit," Caleb announced, looking down the street once they stopped. "But it's not over. We've just been given three days to gather our evidence and get our case together. That's a good thing."

"How is it good again? Is it the part that I don't get to see her for three more days or that I was just accused of beating my wife? Or is the good part that I apparently coerced Jude into marrying me against her will? I'm lost, so feel free to help me out here."

"Other than the coercion, those accusations are not cited on the restraining order. They spared you that, so we can deal with it now. We know what we're up against. We will be more prepared when we reconvene." Looking Taylor in the eyes, he said, "Don't do anything stupid. Don't go over there. Don't call them. Don't contact them in any form. Everything you do or say will be used against you in this case. For us to win, we need to keep you squeaky clean. If we can, I have no doubt she'll walk out of here with you on Friday."

"She'll be here?"

"Yes, he wants them present. She'll have to look you in the eyes and accuse you of coercion for this order to stay in place. Is there any chance she'll do that?" He searched Taylor's eyes for any tick that might let him know if he's lying.

Staring him unflinchingly in the eyes, he replied. "No. None."

Caleb nodded, pleased. "Good. Let's keep it that way." The two men started walking toward the corner. Caleb put his arm out and hailed a cab. As he was getting in, he said, "Hang tight. We'll take them down on Friday. In the meantime, I'll do my due diligence. Keep your phone handy and yourself out of trouble." The door slammed closed and the taxi drove off.

Taylor stood on that corner for minutes... at least five disorienting minutes before his feet started moving. He didn't know where he was going but he knew there was nothing at his apartment worth hurrying back for.

When he looked up at the cloudy day, his life seemed to play on a projector before his eyes, for a brief second worrying him that maybe he was dying. As he walked down the street, he recalled so many of the times Taylor had been called a "Golden Boy." With a nickname like that to live up to, he was always doomed to fail in some way.

Parkinson's.

Katherine.

His parents.

Rufus.

And now, Jude's family.

The world seemed determined to right the wrong it made when the boy was born too smart, too handsome, too kindhearted, too talented, too much of everything. Karma wanted her penance and she was taking it threefold.

But what none of them counted on, and what Karma couldn't predict was that the "Golden Boy" was also too determined to let fate destroy his happiness. Jude was not in a power position. She was at the mercy of the courts, the hospital, and her family. She may not be able to fight, but he could, and he would. He'd fight not just for her, but for him. His whole heart and soul were wrapped up in the woman he was just forced to leave behind.

All the depressing shit that had happened to him, fine. Whatever. But this, he refused to accept it, refused to let anyone else dictate his future.

Taylor would get Jude back. There would be a way to prove them wrong and he was determined to find it.

Chapter Twenty-Seven

THERE WAS NO way to properly prepare to have your life shoved under a microscope, dissected, and left to defend the mutilated pieces that were pulled apart out of context under examination. But Taylor tried his best. He wore his wedding suit to court that morning, hoping the threads that bound her to him would hold strong today. It had been three days since he'd seen Jude. He was ready to defend his love and get his wife back.

June twelfth. Caleb was waiting for him outside the courthouse at a coffee stand on the corner, and wasted no time with his client. "Do not talk unless you are on the stand. Got it?"

"Yes."

"Do not make eye contact with anyone other than the judge. Got it?"

"Not even Jude?"

"She's different. We need her sympathies on our side."

"Sympathies? We're married."

Caleb didn't respond to that. He just raised a perplexed brow. "Do not make eye contact, Taylor, with anyone else. Not her parents or any member of her family or her legal team. They'll read it as aggressive and use it against you. Remember they will try to goad you as proof that the order should be kept intact. Don't give them that reason. Got it?"

"Got it."

He stopped and looked at Taylor. Caleb Monroe was very serious in tone for eight in the morning, but Taylor liked that. Caleb warned, "Speak to no one but the judge. No one. Got it?"

"Yes."

They walked inside the courthouse and went through the metal detectors. Once they were alone again, they continued walking, and Caleb continued talking, "We're lucky to have this hearing so fast. Damn lucky that Judge Matthews is open to hearing the case after the other day. Let's not blow it. No matter what they throw at us, we've got to keep our cool. Understand?"

"I do, but we can't lose."

Caleb was focused ahead. "I fight to win."

Taylor liked the confidence in his voice and nodded because he related. He fought to win too.

They walked inside the courtroom and took their seats. Taylor hadn't bothered to tell his parents for many reasons, but foremost, he couldn't deal with their disappointment that this was even happening to a Barrett. He hadn't even told them about being married, so bringing up a restraining order wasn't something he really wanted to do. So he was going at it alone. There were a few unrecognizable faces behind him, a few on the other side, and Jude and her legal entourage had yet to arrive.

The large wooden doors that needed oiling opened and the squeak of the hinges made Taylor glance back. That's when he saw them: the lawyers, the stepfather, the aunt, Isla, and Jude at the back. Today, she was a mixture of the woman he knew. She was part Judith, with her hair pinned back tightly, and part Jude in the dress she'd been wearing when he'd fallen in love with her. It was the one he had married her in, too. Chartreuse with little pink flowers embroidered around the bottom. A matching pink sweater covered her shoulders. Even with the overwhelming sadness on her face that left only traces of the laughter they had shared, she was stunning, and Taylor's breath was taken away.

Isla saw Taylor and a small smile appeared, a silent apology of sorts it seemed, but he didn't care about her. He only wanted Jude to look at him, but she kept her eyes down as low as her head hung. *This was not good.*

"Let me guess," Caleb whispered. "The one in green and pink?"

"Yep."

"Shit," he muttered under his breath. "They've gotten to her."

At first sight he thought the dress was a sign for him. But she wouldn't look at him and that sign shouted louder than the sundress. The thought of how they had *gotten to her* made his blood boil. "I told you they would hurt her."

"Calm down, Taylor. We have the facts on our side."

"The facts don't matter if she argues them, if she is being forced to side with them."

Caleb turned to Taylor. "Tell me again. Is there *any* way she'll turn against you?"

"She won't speak a word against me. I know it," he replied, not hesitating. "She would be tortured first, but probably has been. She won't hurt me if she can help it."

"The question remains, can she help it?"

Taylor stood as Jude passed by, but she still didn't look at him. Her lawyer stepped between them and led her to the far side of the table. Taylor had never been a violent man. He was too sensible for that. But once he met Jude, once he felt real love, he suddenly understood the desire to lay down one's life for someone else, to offer to take a hit to protect someone you love. He turned away from the lawyer's back, wanting to pummel him for being a wall that kept him from her. He sat, trying to swim to reason and catch his breath again.

Thirty minutes into the proceeding, Taylor looked to the opposition and saw big blue-green eyes stealing a glance at him. She looked away, but it was as if her eyes were drawn to him because she soon looked back again.

Jude saw Hazel. Jude saw Hazel in his "marrying suit" as he had so playfully called it. Her heart was on the other side of the courtroom, tucked firmly in that front pocket of his, but when she looked at him, and their eyes met, she felt the faint ghost of a heartbeat in her chest again. The beat grew stronger the longer she sat there.

She snapped to when her lawyer pounded on the table in front of her, and said, "It's not love you're feeling. It's obsession. The medication. It confuses the mind. You fell for his smooth pickup lines and the flash of wealth. Mr. Barrett made it so attractive to marry him when all along he had ill-intentions for your inheritance and your well-being."

She wanted to run, to take flight from the hate that consumed the air around her. Her lawyer's words were acid as they pierced her ears. She couldn't look at Hazel having finally *bartered* her life for his. They said they would go easy on him. They said they would drop the charges if she just agreed to another year. One year of her life in exchange for his... which meant letting him go. She gulped and looked down, wanting to escape this room. This courtroom may be covered in shiny wooden walls and plush seats, but it was no better than the "holding cell" at Bleekman's. Just less obvious of the torture it inflicted.

The photos were introduced to the judge again and she wished she didn't have to hear the horrors they concocted. As the judge examined them, she stole a peek down the long line of people that kept her heart apart from her body. Hazel's head was lowered and his eyes closed as he rubbed his temples. But he looked up as a woman sat down behind him. *Her mother?*

When the officers escorted her home, Jude's stepfather and aunt were in the formal living room. Jude dropped to the hard, marble tiles of the foyer wishing she would shatter to the point of nonexistence. "You got what you wanted."

Her aunt smiled and said, "Not quite yet, darling. But soon."

What more can they take? Jude had nothing left, nothing that mattered to her.

She found out soon enough. The deal had been made. One year. One year and all that remained of the inheritance. One year in exchange for her life. Enough time to get the money transferred into offshore accounts with no suspicious activity attached. And for that, she was promised no more Bleekman's in the meantime. They would give her everything she wanted back—her freedom, her happiness, her husband—if she just gave them one year and the money.

After Jude sold her soul to the devil himself, she went upstairs, then realized her mother had been missing from the witch-hunt. She had looked back once, for any sign of her, but she remained absent.

Isla stood up and joined Jude's mother on Hazel's side of the courtroom. She had no idea what she was up to or if she should even trust her, but when she saw the sympathy that laid heavy in Isla's face, she wondered if maybe she suddenly had an ally. Nothing in her life made sense anymore and it was wearing her down. Seeing two of what she considered former foes supporting the good side made her smile. And Isla softly smiled in return.

Until her lawyer spoke of Parkinson's and how it cuts a young life even shorter. Hazel was right. Everything about them had been *sold* in exchange for money. *Could this really only be about money?* She couldn't take it anymore.

"Stop."

At her demand, the entire courtroom looked her way.

The judge asked, "What was that?"

Jude's eyes blinked rapidly as the imaginary interrogation lamp was spotlighting her. She slid down in her a chair and in the softest voice repeated herself, "Please stop attacking him."

She didn't dare venture a glimpse at Hazel. She would break and right now she was fighting to be strong.

The judge eyed her. "Ms. Boehler, please remain quiet during the proceedings. You've hired a lawyer to represent you. Let him do his job."

"Don't talk to her like that."

The gavel came slamming down as everyone's attention turned to Taylor, who had just spoken. The judge demanded, "Mr. Barrett. Sit down or I'll have you removed."

Caleb pulled Taylor by the arm until he was sitting next to him again. "Shut it," he insisted under his breath.

The Boehler's lawyer went for the jugular. "This is the type of behavior we have listed in the order. He's unpredictable and lets his emotions get the better of him. Ms. Boehler is a sick woman who needs care around the clock, supervision that doesn't involve someone else's agenda. Their marriage is a sham. He coerced her into marrying him when she was medicated without clear thoughts. She was in no position to make that kind of judgment about her future."

"I object!" Caleb said, standing up. "What did he have to gain from coercing her? He has his own money."

Taylor was shell-shocked, bombed in the middle of Manhattan

by this turn in focus. He turned to the only one who gave him comfort, but she wouldn't look his way. His heart thudded on as it soldiered through this field of mines.

"Overruled."

The lawyer went into deep documentation to point out all attempts that Taylor had forced her to spend time with him. Every gallery brochure, business card from a restaurant, and flower he had given her was being used against him.

Jude felt sick. All of her memorabilia was on display, the truth twisted. Every last thing she had taken to remember their time together was now tainted and manipulated into something bad. Tears started to fill her eyes as the lies replaced her life. *Her. Life. For. His.* Sold to the tune of seven million dollars. She didn't let her tears fall, needing to put on her bravest face. It would soon be over and by how things sounded like they were going, she would start serving her one-year sentence soon enough.

As soon as Caleb started into his own argument, the other lawyer pulled his biggest hit. He slammed down a file and said, "Let's not overlook the details that Mr. Monroe does not want you to see."

Judge Matthews had a reputation of shutting down antics in his courtroom, but even he seemed intrigued enough to want to know, despite Caleb's objection.

To the horror and humiliation of Jude, the photos were shown for all to see, along with a medical report showing that she had indeed been prescribed medication two days prior to marrying Taylor. She shook her head in disgust. Prescribed didn't mean taking. She was so frustrated by the accusations. She had never agreed to this. She would have never agreed to attacking his character or their love. But she had to let it go because she had to let *him* go.

But as Jude's lawyer continued, no charges had yet to be filed against Dr. Conroy, so his word sealed their fate. "She is not of sound mind."

Three hours later, Caleb walked Taylor out of the courtroom and down to the lobby. Taylor caught in a daze.

"What just happened?"

"I'll file an appeal as soon as I get back to the office."

Still shocked by the outcome, Taylor pointed in the direction of the courtroom. "Caleb, what the fuck just happened in there?"

Caleb shook his head.

Taylor ran his hands through his hair. "So the restraining order got dropped. But he just annulled my marriage?"

"He did."

"On what grounds? Make it clear for me. Layman's terms."

Caleb knew better than to get into details this close to the courthouse, but by looking at Taylor, he had no choice. "Bottom line—she was coerced while medicated."

"We were in there for an unjustified restraining order. How did our marriage come into play?"

"It's all intertwined, Taylor. They filed the paperwork this morning. I don't know why Matthews accepted it. To save time? The marriage. The conservatorship. And the medical records. A doctor went on record to say she suffers from insanity and needs her parents' care."

His world was crumbling around him, and his right hand began to tremble. "What am I supposed to do?"

Caleb sighed. "Go home. Get some rest. We'll try again another day. We'll fight this until we win, but right now I need to get to my office and find out how we were fucking blindsided in there."

"In the meantime, she'll die. They'll kill her one way or the other. Didn't you hear? She has seven million dollars on the line.

Wonder how much they've made her sign away."

"That's a good idea. We can try to find out how much is left of it when we're waiting on the appeal. That can prove motive."

Taylor felt numb and physically beaten. He struggled to hold onto hope when he lost his whole reason for being. Unable to find reason in this insanity, he asked, "How long will the appeal take?"

"I don't know. I'll file for a new judge to hear the case."

"Caleb, tell me there's a possibility. That there's a chance of winning here."

"I'm not even sure what we're fighting anymore."

Fuck!

Chapter Twenty-Eight

JUDE'S MOTHER APPROACHED Taylor and Caleb around the corner outside the courthouse. Taylor, surprised to see her coming his way, stopped. He saw sadness in her eyes, and he watched as she took a deep breath.

"My daughter would like to speak with you a moment."

He didn't know why she was speaking for Jude. Why could Jude not just come over to him? But like what his lawyer would advise, he knew she was told not to. He shook his head, disappointed and hurt that they now required a messenger between them. Looking over her shoulder for any sign of Jude, he asked, "Why were you on my side of the courtroom?"

"Because..." she glanced at Caleb, shifting uncomfortably, and whispered, "love should win." She walked away, leaving that sentiment lingering long after.

Caleb warned, "I don't think this is a good idea."

"I don't care anymore."

When Jude's mother returned, Jude was on her arm arguing with her. As soon as she saw Hazel, she went silent, then broke down. Jude stood there in her wrinkled sundress with her face buried in her hands, her shoulders shaking from the devastation.

When she looked up at him, she knew they weren't going to have their happy ending. *Too much pain.* Too much slanderous torment had divided them.

But despite all the water that had passed under their decaying bridge, they stood there, their hearts still beating only for the other.

"Why aren't you looking at me, Jude?" When she closed her eyes and put her hands over her face again, he demanded, "Look at me!"

"I can't."

"Yes, you can."

"No," she cried. "I can't. Please."

"Please what? What are you doing? Are you siding with them?"

"I'm not siding with them. I'm not. I just can't do this."

"This? And by 'this,' you mean be with me?" Tilting his head back, he closed his eyes, and took a deep breath.

"Taylor, pleas—"

"Don't call me that. Don't you fucking call me that!" He pointed his finger at her in anger. "You're giving up. You're giving up on us. Giving up on us is the same as you giving up on yourself. I can afford to fight this for as long as we need to fight. But I can't do it without you." He felt frantic and took her hands in his. She was warm, recalling a million other gentle touches from their past. "Jude, listen, I'm here, however you need me, but don't think for a minute that us being apart is going to solve anything. We will always be stronger together. I'll take care of it, Jude. I promise."

She wished he would repeat that promise and make it come true, but she knew he couldn't. And more importantly, she knew what she had to do to prevent any further damage, namely his. The deal she had made shrouded her heart and blocked her faith—*her life for his.*

Pulling her hands back, she turned her back to him. She

couldn't handle her own tears, so his tears would do her in completely. She cleared her throat and barely above a whisper, said, "I can't be with you. I can't handle my own problems, so I can't take on yours." He tore down the invisible wall she had built and took hold of her arm, spinning her around to face him again. "Go, Hazel. A better life awaits."

"No." He lifted her chin. "Look at me. You're not going to fight? You're just going to walk away from me?"

"I'm doing the best I can. You won't understand, but it's how things have to be."

"Why? I know you. I know you think what you're doing is right, but setting me free, telling me to go live my life without you is not what's right. What have they done to you?"

Her tears slowed as she looked at him, really looked at him. "Did I ever tell you that you're the most beautiful man I've ever seen, even on the saddest day I've ever known?"

"Jude, don't do this. I need you here. Don't close yourself off to me."

"Please, Hazel." She slipped when she called him the name she swore she wouldn't anymore. That name held all her feelings in it and pain shot through her heart. "Please, just go with it."

As he studied her face, her tears drying against her porcelain skin, he saw the wall firmly in place—whether for his protection or hers, he wasn't sure, but he knew he wasn't going to get her back on a busy street corner in New York City. So he gave in, knowing this was not the time for arguments, knowing she needed him to, and lightened their last moments together. "Not handsome?"

Jude touched his cheek, unable to stop herself. "One doesn't stand before the ocean and call it handsome. We didn't stare at the stars last April and say it was a handsome night. Love knows only the beauty of its power, not the intricacies of verses. So no, Hazel, you're not handsome. You're beautiful like the stars. You're beautiful like the ocean. You're beautiful like the love I feel for you."

"This feels final," he said, his fingers running up her arm until he was cupping her hand on his cheek. He had to try one last time despite the passersby. "I've designed a closet for you. It's huge, the size of a bedroom. Just for you. For all the dresses you'll own."

"I'll always live in that beautiful home, but it will be in my dreams." Her hand dropped to her side and her heart finally stopped beating as she uttered the most painful six words she would ever speak, "This is where our story ends."

Her ache was visceral. The sound of her heart breaking rang in her ears as shards filled her blood stream. She backed away, her chest barren of beats or purpose. Turning away from him and his impossible eyes, she needed to block him out as his tears welled like hers.

"Jude, no. Please," he said, his words rushed, "I'm begging you. Choose me. Choose us."

"You deserve a better life. You deserve the *best* life." She stopped speaking, not wanting to say it. Jude knew she should, her own maddening reasoning that brought her here needing to be buried for him, for his happiness. "Everything about our lives dictates that maybe, maybe you should give Katherine a second chance."

Sideswiped by her words, he stepped back from her. "What? What are you talking about?"

She would use anything to walk away from him, leaving him as unscathed as she could. "When you're sick, she'll hire the best nurses to care for you."

Jude's head dropped down as tears flooded her eyes again.

Too much pain.

The thought of him sick, the thought of a nurse caring for him, the thought of him spending his final days without her broke her.

Her mother touched Jude's arm. "We've got to go. They're looking for you."

The harsh ticking of time chimed in their ears, rushing the last few seconds they had together. Jude said, "I tried to kill myself after Ryan died because I had nothing to live for any longer."

Taylor knew she was pushing him away. He didn't know why, but he knew she would only do this if she had to. So even if he couldn't have her, he still wanted her to be safe. Grabbing her by the shoulders, he held her firmly, needing her attention. "You have to live for you." He demanded, "Promise me, Jude, when you feel alone, you'll live." His voice faltered. "I can't live knowing you no longer breathe, that you no longer walk this world with your love, with your life."

She pressed herself against him, needing to hear his heartbeat one last time. "I never had a reason to live before. But now, I can live because I've loved and I've been loved." She looked up at him, her eyes pink from crying, and smiled. "Our love was spectacularly wonderful."

"And reckless." He breathed her in.

"The most reckless of love affairs."

Touching her neck gently, he always loved the delicate angle. "Jude?"

"I'll never forget you, Hazel." She slipped from his arms and took several steps away.

"I'll never forget you," he added. "I'll never forget the first time I saw you. I'll never forget eating ice cream in the middle of winter. I'll never crave breakfast like I do for dinner."

"Don't do this, Hazel."

"What am I doing, Jude?"

Backing even farther, she said, "You think you're convincing me of a future that can be when really, you're convincing yourself." Sighing, she tilted her head while watching him pull at his tie. "Go now, before you say something that I can't say no to. Go back to your beautiful life. You're free to start over without the problems I bring. Go, Taylor." She started walking, but stopped and said, "But occasionally, think of me."

"I don't believe you, Jude Barrett." He let her go this time, but made sure to say, "You can't hide your love away forever. And when you're ready, I'll be here and we'll be together again."

Jude had no doubt.

Suddenly she was grabbed and embraced. Her eyes fell closed and this was everything. Everything that mattered. He felt so good, too good—warmth and safety, like ice cream on a hot day, and hot cocoa on a cold night. He was made of the best things in life.

"We can leave together. Go right now. Anywhere. Anywhere in the world, Jude. They will never find us. They will *never* find you. They won't be able to hurt you anymore."

She turned her back to him again, but heard shuffling behind her. Almost to herself, she said, "I'm not as strong as you think I am."

"You're stronger," he said, his voice echoing his persistence. "You've just forgotten."

"I need peace in my life. That means life without you." The silence behind her grew as she continued, "I will always love you, Hazel." She wanted to keep distancing herself but she loved him too much to ignore the name she loved the most.

As she walked away, she thought about the year ahead. She was right to set him free. She couldn't hold him back from living the life he deserved. Staring at the long sidewalk ahead of her, she knew she had to let him go. *For now.* And if he found happiness, found a better life without her, she would let him go forever.

Legally, her aunt and stepfather owned her again. With her heavy, miserable and broken heart she travelled back to her incarceration.

One more year.

Taylor stood there, watching her, watching his soul leave his body, choosing to reside in another. The battle today was over. Defeat was never easily accepted. Heartbreak even harder. Caleb stood beside him and watched Jude go, and then asked, "Do you believe her?"

Looking over at him, he said, "No. She's not a selfish person. They know this."

"What are you going to do?"

Taylor needed to think this through, to figure out what was really going on, but deep down he knew any conclusion he came to wouldn't make a difference to the outcome.

She was convinced what she was doing was right. He'd seen the conviction in her eyes. "I have my wife taken away because I'm sick. I have my life taken away because she's sick. The legal system has failed me. I have no idea what I'm going to do."

JUDE WALKED INTO the pink bedroom and found documents on the vanity where her brother's photo used to be. She sat down and looked at them.

Her back stiffened when she heard her stepfather's voice behind her, "Sign the document."

She looked at him in the mirror. "I don't care about the money. You can have it all. If I sign it all away, can I go free today?"

"Judith, how would that look to the courts. I can't just have you going around, *of sound mind*, and telling all our secrets. The deal stands as is. One year. No one will be the wiser." He sat down on the bed as if they were friends. "You know, Judith, I didn't plan any of this. My brother was weak—of mind. He promised he would stop... He promised, but he didn't. Guilt got to him before I could have. You were never meant to be a pawn, but when he killed himself, an opportunity was presented. Your aunt and I had plans. We loved each other back then."

A shudder of shock rolled through her. An image of her mother behind Hazel in court came to mind. *Is this why she chose the better side?* "You don't love my mother?"

"I love her, but she's soft. We didn't plan this. Leslie came to me—"

"Leslie? You're blaming her? *You* sent me away to be tortured. *You* sent me away for money—blood money, guilt money, dirty, hate-filled money." She held up the papers and said, "I would have given you this money years ago if I had known about it. I would have rather had my life."

"You tried to kill yourself twice. Now you say you wanted life? I spared your life. I saved your life."

"You saved me to get the money. You've played this all wrong. Don't you see?"

Standing up, he said, "I see a spoiled little girl who wants a shiny new toy. But Taylor Barrett will never be yours until every last cent is mine and safely in my bank account." He walked to the door that had no lock. "Sign the papers, Judith. This game is exhausting, so do us both a favor and sign."

"I don't trust you."

"Sign the damn contract!" His harsh glare softened though not friendly in any way. "I'll keep my word, but in the meantime, the Barrett boy is off limits."

His name is Hazel. She gulped.

Too much pain.

"Your word has no value to me."

"Don't push me." He walked out and slammed the door behind him.

Jude looked down at the contract again. They had been very clever, different names up top, varying amounts transferred. But she had no way to fight back, nothing and no one truly in her corner to help, so she picked up the pen and signed, taking her trust and handing it over to the people she hated most.

One year.

Her life for his.

But what if he would no longer be hers?

Chapter Twenty-Nine

JUDE WORE JEANS. She never wore jeans, but then again, she had never set out to break someone's heart before. *Again. Break his heart again.* Looking in the mirror, her face was sallow and her cheeks sunken in. She had not been eating much and it was wearing on her physically. Emotionally she could have cared less about food.

Hazel was the only sustenance she needed and he was no longer there. She knew she had to let him go. She just needed to hear his voice one last time.

Walking downstairs, she saw Roman in the foyer. He turned and gave her the gloomiest look, one that kind of summed up her predicament. She sat on the bottom step and he sat down next to her. "Where you going, Hummingbird?"

"To appease the court. As of this morning, I've been granted some freedoms. To appease my family, I will only be gone for a short time."

"And to appease you?"

"I'll break my heart to spare Hazel any more pain."

"Won't that break his?"

It would. And she knew it, but selfishly, *she* needed one last time to say goodbye. And it couldn't be here. Not in her prison. It had to be where she had felt free. Alive. Herself. Jude. *His* Jude.

Jude dropped her head down in shame, her weakness exposed to one of the few people who believed her to be stronger. She wiped at her eyes before the tears could build. She was tired of crying. When she looked back up, she asked, "Why do you work here? Why do you work for people that I can tell you despise? Why do you stay?"

As if the answer was obvious, he said, "For you. If I'm not here, who will you have?"

"Kind of says it all." She stood up, using the railing to lean on. When he stood, she said, "I free you, my friend. The burden of myself will no longer be. Leave. Find a good family with happy children and loving parents who are just too busy to have dinner ready on time. Take care of people who will be grateful for you and your loyalty."

"You're grateful."

"I am, but I'm the only one." She walked to the door. "I'll be seeing you."

"You're coming back, right, Hummingbird?"

"The bird always returns to its cage." The door opened and the bright June day was too yellow for how blue she felt. She went anyway.

Taking the long way, she headed toward the park. She thought about going to his apartment, but knew that would be too cruel. Too many beautiful memories there, a blaring reminder of the happy life she *almost* had. Instead she headed for their favorite bench by walking around the park instead of through. When she finally sat down, she pulled the phone from her pocket and made the first call on the phone she had never used before.

Her heart hurt when he answered, "Hello?"

She seemed to choke on her breath as it stopped and all words disappeared from her head. But her heart knew... her heart knew she couldn't do this to him. She couldn't give him hope when there was none. She couldn't give him a way of reaching her, even if her heart desperately wanted that. It wasn't fair to him.

"Hello?" he repeated, sounding less patient.

This was going to be the hardest thing she had ever done and she couldn't have his soothing voice seeping into her veins any longer. Two weeks had been painful enough, but it was a start and she owed him that much, if not more, to get his life back on track.

She hung up.

Why was she even here? Why did she call? Was she so adrift in her addiction to him that she needed just one more hit of his human kindness? Just one more taste? One more touch? Would she really have asked him to come find her only to turn him away again? No. She couldn't. Wouldn't. She couldn't drag him through this, opening the same wounds again. And hers. When all she thought she needed to say had already been said. When her phone rang back, she looked at the screen and the number that appeared. Her heart wrestled with what the right thing to do was and she ghosted her finger over the screen, careful not to answer it.

"Goodbye, my love," she whispered and the phone stopped ringing.

Breathing turned difficult as her heart collapsed in on itself. She wished she could be swallowed up with it. That would be less painful than the loneliness she now felt.

Maybe he'd only been a dream. That was easier to imagine. He was a part of her, inside her, a man that only existed to exist inside her.

But the severed organ that fought for survival in her chest said otherwise. He existed. He had to. He was her light. *Had been.* And how could there be dark if there was no light, even if it didn't exist in her world any longer.

As she walked, there was no doubt in her mind that she had hurt him outside the courthouse. *What a mess I've made.* And now, even honesty couldn't get them any closer than they were right this moment.

The marriage had been annulled. He could now find someone who didn't have to live in fear of retaliation, in a state of distress looking for peace, someone who could give him the family he deserved.

But for her, she wanted something simpler. She looked up at the puffy clouds in the blue sky and wished she could go to that place that doesn't exist, the one Hazel spoke of as if it were real. Daydreaming had been her life for so long that she couldn't believe she no longer had the ability. It had been lost somewhere in the last two weeks. Daydreaming had become a dangerous pastime once her dreams were realized. She didn't know how fragile those dreams really were until they were twisted and destroyed while she held them in her hands. She took the remains and sprinkled them over her heart, hoping to feed the delicate seeds and maybe one day her dreams could bloom again.

But not today.

When she walked out of the park she made a right. Taking a left would lead to her house, but she needed more time before returning to her personal prison.

Three blocks up she waited on the corner to cross the street. Her mind was on other things when someone called, "Judith."

She cowered and scanned her immediate surroundings, flinching her first reaction. A woman waved her hand from the other corner. At first she checked behind her, then when she saw the woman walking toward her it clicked. "Nurse Lacy? I didn't recognize you out of uniform."

Lacy laughed. "I get that sometimes. But yeah," she said, shrugging, "they let me out of that place every once in a while." As soon as the words left her mouth, she clasped her hand over it. Lowering it again, she took hold of Jude's arm gently. "I'm so sorry. I didn't mean—"

"Don't worry. I knew what you meant."

Lacy looked concern. "Have you been crying?"

"Feels like my whole life." The words reminded her of Hazel and how he told his parents that very same thing the day they met.

When Jude's eyes started to water, Lacy wrapped her arm in Jude's and declared, "You look like you can use a friend. We're going for coffee."

"You don't know the half of it."

"Then tell me. Coffee is on me."

Jude didn't know what to think of this young nurse. On one hand, she instantly liked her and was drawn to her joy. On the other hand, she was suppressing the fear bubbling inside her from seeing someone from Bleekman's. "I'm not sure that's allowed. Patients and nurses hanging out? Sure-fire way to get in trouble."

She put her finger to her mouth, and said, "I won't tell if you won't." She continued with pep in her step and practically dragged Jude down the street until they came to a French bistro that opened to a patio out back. They were seated at a small round table. Lacy continued to smile at Jude while she placed her napkin in her lap. "How are you? I know that's a broad question, but I've been worried ever since you left the center."

"I was more worried being there, personally."

"I'm sorry you had such a bad experience." She leaned in and whispered, "I shouldn't be telling you this, but I've wanted to for a long time—"

"What shouldn't you tell me?" Jude was direct, the hair on her arms rising as her nerves started twisting in her stomach.

"I've researched your case and tried to talk to Dr. Conroy on your behalf. But they seem set on the early tests they did years ago on you." Her eyes shifted left, then right, before centering back on Jude. "I think there was a misdiagnosis when you were first admitted."

Jude smiled. "If their tests are wrong, what do *you* think is wrong with me?"

The waiter walked up and took their drink order as well as handed them menus. They quickly looked it over and Jude ordered a chocolate croissant. Lacy ordered the bread pudding, then when they were alone again, she said, "I don't think you're insane, or unstable, or crazy, like they say, like your chart says."

"Then what am I?"

"You tell me, Judith."

The ladies held their gaze until the waiter returned with their drinks, setting them down in front of them. "I'm not crazy. The drugs make me crazy. They fog my brain." Lacy nodded in understanding as Jude continued, "Sometimes I wish I was crazy so I didn't care so much, so I could escape this reality once and for all."

Reaching across the table, Lacy covered Jude's hand with her own. The gesture was reassuring and Jude felt more and more comfortable with her. Lacy confessed, "I can find another job, but I feel like my patients need me there. For some, I'm their only advocate. I can be one for you as well if you tell me what's wrong."

She hesitated, not used to opening up, much less to someone who worked at her own personal hell, but something in Lacy's eyes—maybe the sympathetic kindness she saw—made her trust the nurse. "My marriage was annulled and we're no longer together."

"What?" she asked, dropping back. "How can that be? That's not possible. I thought—"

"You thought what?" Jude asked, curious to hear her thoughts.

"I could tell how much you loved each other. I could tell how much *he* loved you."

"My family didn't agree."

"Who cares about them? You can't lose love like that."

"I didn't lose it. I was backed into a corner and had to sign it away."

"I don't understand." The waiter walked by and set down their food.

"Lacy..." she started, but stopped, not knowing if she could tell the lies anymore. She wasn't numb. Every last emotion was clogging her arteries and making her heart throb all at once. "My family has been blackmailing me for years for my inheritance."

Lacy's mouth dropped open and she gasped.

Jude said, "Dr. Conroy is being paid to keep me insane."

She double blinked at Jude, and then again. Her hand was back over her mouth as she stared at the woman in front of her. When her hand came down, Lacy took a sip of coffee as she processed the accusations laid before her. But then did something surprising.

Her finger flew straight up, her elbow stationed on the table. "I knew it!" A thrill flashed through her eyes. "My gut instinct knew it, but no one would listen to me."

She. Believed. Jude. *She believed me.*

"I'm very familiar with nobody listening. I've been shouting it for years, but somehow I've never been heard."

"I'm hearing you now. I became a nurse to help people. Maybe I can help you."

Chapter Thirty

TAYLOR SAT INSIDE a hotel ballroom at a round table for ten. August 18th. His parents were on one side and Katherine on the other. The band played as the two-thousand-dollar-a-person plate was taken away. He ate two bites, but had no appetite. Katherine smiled watching the band, then put her hand on his arm. "You're not hungry? You should eat. You need food to keep up your energy."

He didn't reply. Taylor had discovered weeks ago that conversation existed around him whether he participated or not. And ever since his parents found out about the marriage and the annulment, the court case, and restraining order, they were determined to help him get over the loss of his heart, but failed to notice he was dying a slow death without it. Without *her*. Some people were more persistent than others.

Like Katherine. "Did you hear me, honey?"

This time he did respond, "Yes."

"What's wrong? Do you want to dance or get another drink?"

Wordlessly, he stood up and started walking. Away from Katherine and his parents, away from the table and two-thousand-dollar-a-person plates of food, away from this fundraiser that besieged him—all the things that were smothering him with their laughter and happiness. It was all too much.

Too much pain.

The architect walked right through the double doors of the ballroom and down to the lobby. He made it out onto the sidewalk and took his first deep breath all night.

"Taylor? Wait."

And then his breath stopped, strangling his lungs.

His hands began to tremble. He took one step to get away and his legs gave out on him. Gasps were heard as he fell to his hands and knees to the concrete. Pandemonium surrounded him as two men righted him. Katherine was directing them to a nearby bench, and Taylor let them drag him, unable to make the move himself. When he was secured, they left, but Katherine remained until the ambulance arrived. Worry marked her face quite nicely. *Maybe she really does care about me.*

The chaos that engulfed him that night was not the chaos he craved. He was hooked to monitors. An IV was next to his bed, dripping straight into his veins. Nurses flitted about, as Katherine fluffed his pillow, and sat next to him gossiping about mutual friends of theirs, friends he didn't consider real friends.

He wanted ice cream in the middle of winter and jellybeans in baked goods that had no business being there. He missed the element of surprise. He missed the curve of *her* waist where it meets her hips. He missed those damn blue-green eyes that stayed the same when her clothes changed. He missed Jude. He missed her and that pain was far worse than any his body could inflict. As long as his mind was intact, the image of the girl in the chartreuse dress and snow boots would haunt his memories, his dreams, his waking hours, and his dying days.

Instead, he was offered blue gelatin as if he should be happy. Katherine said, "I told them you didn't eat much at dinner. That might be causing this. I told them. Just a sugar dip. They suggested you eat this."

He turned his head in anger, his voice tight. "This isn't a fucking sugar dip. I'm not a diabetic. I have Parkinson's." He paused to stare at her. "Isn't that your cue to leave?"

"Don't get snippy with me, Taylor. I'm only trying to help."

He huffed, wanting to throw something or punch a wall to get this pent-up aggression out somehow. Taking it out on a woman who was clueless wasn't satisfying his need. He turned away from her, blocking her out of his mind and getting her out of his sight.

She got the hint... finally, and went to the coffee shop down the street. Once the last nurse left the room, Taylor stared out the window. It was larger than the last hospital room's and it faced the city instead of the roof of a dilapidated structure. The lights were off except a small lamp on the wall near the bed, but he reached up and turned it off too. The buildings outside were the only lights he wanted to see. They reminded him of Jude sitting in the chair by the window at his place. She used sit there for hours staring out. And he used to sit nearby for hours staring at her. She once called herself broken. She was this small angel with huge wings wrapped around her. She wasn't broken. The world around her was.

His lids grew heavy and he let himself go...

The overhead light flicked on and Taylor was startled awake.

"Oops," Katherine announced unapologetically. "Sorry." She turned the light back off and walked to his bedside. "It's not even ten. I didn't expect you to be asleep. I brought you coffee." When he made no effort to take it from her, she set it on his hospital tray. "I'll leave it here so you can reach it."

He kept his eyes focused outside, outside where Jude lived, and asked, "Have you ever wondered what you would do if you had nothing?"

She laughed until she figured out he was serious. "Why do you think about such horrid things, honey? You should be thinking positively. That will help you heal."

This time he laughed, and turned to her as she sat in a chair by the window. She was beautiful. Any guy would find her attractive—on the outside. Vapid on the inside. But he preferred the unpredictable nature of the little brunette with wide beautiful eyes. He preferred Jude. His reality didn't include her though, so he was trying to make do with those who did want him. "Horrid? There are worse things in life, Katherine, than having a clean slate."

"No money. No job. No family or friends. That sounds horrid."

"You don't have a job now."

"I do too. I'm the head of three fundraisers this year. One of which is being held at the old theatre down in Soho. We'll be the first allowed in there since it closed twenty-six years ago."

"Oh," he said, withdrawn from this conversation already. "Sorry for assuming. I was thinking about how you would support yourself if your parents didn't."

Her eyes flashed at him. "Taylor, we both come from money. Can you stop acting like we're so different? You and I are alike in so many ways. A perfect match." She perked up. "Hey! There's one thing I would like a clean slate on."

Taylor actually perked up in response. Maybe there was hope yet. Maybe her soul ran deeper than a puddle after a light rain.

She said, "If I hadn't had my *dalliance*, we would be married right now and I'd have my first little one on the way." She rubbed her stomach.

Besides questioning if the baby would even be his, all he heard was "I. I. I." Not *we*. *I*. She will never change. It will always be about her.

How did he end up here, back with her? They were never good

together. It was an illusion that everyone had convinced him of. He was sold a bill of goods that was past its prime. He thought if Jude was gone for good that he could return to his old life like she hadn't rearranged all the pieces. The puzzle that was his life was missing corner pieces and important ones that made up his core. How could he foolishly think dating Katherine would fit... could fill in those gaps?

He had tried. But after three dates with her, the sight and sound of her made him cringe and his heart clenched, so he turned away from her. He turned away from the window he wanted to look out. And he turned away from the thought of Jude out there in that city somewhere. "I'm going to rest now."

She stood up. "I should go. The visiting hours are ending soon and I feel dirty being around so many sick people. I want a hot bath and a good night's sleep. I'll be back in the morning. I'll bring you fresh coffee." She walked to his bedside and leaned in to kiss his cheek. With a pat to his shoulder, she added, "I'll see you in the morning." She walked toward the door and he watched her go.

Thankful for the peace, he began to roll over and try for sleep, but an unwanted visitor walked in. Taylor took one look and said, "Go away, Rufus. I'm not in the mood to fight with you."

Rufus made himself more comfortable in the chair by the window, a regular hotspot tonight. Taylor decided he'd ask the nurse to remove the chair when Rufus leaves.

Rufus looked at Taylor, but his normal agitated expression wasn't there. He looked—humbled, as if that was even possible. "I came to apologize."

Now this Taylor wanted to hear and lay on his back to watch and listen. "Go on."

"I've been a real asshole to you. You know why, jealousy,

whatever the fuck with that, but that doesn't make it right. I'm sorry."

"How'd you know I was here?"

"Some friends of mine were at the fundraiser and you know how gossip gets around."

"So you're apologizing because you think I might die?"

"Something like that, but I owed you one or fifty, anyway. Just thought it was a good time to say it."

"To clear your conscience?"

"Hey, Taylor," Rufus sounded serious, "this is hard for me. I don't apologize. Ever. But I am to you."

"*Again*, this is hard *for you?* It's hard for me, Rufus. I understand you feel entitled to people and things, but you aren't entitled to be a martyr in this situation. I get to own the whole *I'm a victim* thing because when you go home tonight, I'll be stuck in this hospital bed for who knows how long. So as much as I can appreciate you apologizing for years of bullshit, don't do it to make yourself feel better. That's not a real apology. Say it because you mean it. And say it to make things right."

Rufus stood, his gaze out the window. Taylor hoped Rufus was absorbing what he just said. When Rufus turned back to him, he said, "I'm sorry, Taylor. I really am. You've lost a lot." Taylor realized Rufus had heard about Jude. "And have more on the line to lose. So I'm genuinely sorry for everything I've done to you that made your life more difficult."

Now that, Taylor could appreciate. "Thank you." It didn't mean he wanted to grab a beer with him anytime soon, but the effort he made was nice.

Rufus turned to leave and said, "Take care, man. I wish you the best."

"Thanks." He said the word, but he wanted to punch Rufus for the bastard he was. What was the point? *The. Ass.*

As soon as he left, he rolled completely over being careful not to agitate the IV. The hospital became quieter over the next few hours as all the visitors left and the night staff started their shifts.

His parents' brief visit earlier in the night still irked him. He wished he could start over with a clean slate and go far away from here. His values weren't aligned with the people who were aligned with him. When he thought about it, they never had been. Glancing down at his IV, he had images of escaping in the night, going to his place, packing a suitcase, and disappearing. He could start over. The money was nice, very nice, but he could make a living. He could make a life.

But that damned IV was a strong reminder that he didn't have the luxury of living a life on the run, a life without healthcare, or his trust fund. His body had betrayed him just like Jude.

He couldn't care about Jude anymore. Or where she was. What she was doing. She had betrayed their love by leaving him to drown in it. She had betrayed their future by abandoning it. She had betrayed him, his hope finally faded. Like the windows in the buildings across the way, his bright light for a life went out and he closed his eyes and went to sleep.

A nurse with gray hair pulled back in a bun tiptoed into the room. He opened his eyes and saw her checking the IV. "What time is it?" he asked, his voice still rough with sleep.

"Sorry. Did I wake you?"

Her voice was kind enough for him to want to reassure her. "It's okay."

"It's just after three in the morning. How are you feeling?" she whispered. Touching his head, she smiled at him. "I think you'll be released tomorrow if you're up for it."

"I'm up for it now." Taylor sat up.

"Slow down." She angled the bed up to support his back. "You're here for the night, so settle back in. I brought a fresh pitcher of water a little while ago." She pulled the tray closer. The coffee Katherine had brought him was gone. "Can I get you anything? Are you comfortable?"

"I'm fine," he said, returning her kind smile. "Do you know anything about my results?"

"You're not worse. That's good news. The doctor will be here in the morning to go over everything with you." She leaned against his bed and said, "You know, my mother has Parkinson's disease. There are many reasons to what causes severe symptoms, but with her, stress brings it on. Have you been stressed?"

He didn't lie. "I have." Something about her compassionate eyes made him confess, "I lost the love of my life. And even though my life may not be long compared to some, she made me believe we would be together forever."

He gulped. Suddenly feeling he shouldn't have admitted that to himself, much less to a stranger. He poured himself a cup of water and avoided the sadness he could see in her eyes.

When a few awkward moments passed, she covered his forearm with her hand, and said, "I don't think you've lost her. I saw her in here earlier. It's obvious she still cares about you, and deeply."

"Katherine doesn't care about anything that doesn't revolve around her salon-filled, socialite-anointed existence."

She sighed, but gave his arm a gentle squeeze. "I'm sorry."

Nodding, now he felt embarrassed.

The nurse moved to the other side of the bed. "Would you like me to close the blinds? When the sun rises, it will wake you if I don't."

"Leave them open. Thank you."

"Get some rest, Mr. Barrett. You've had an eventful night that

I'm sure you don't want to repeat in the new day." She walked to the door, but as if she had forgotten something, she returned to his bedside. "I shouldn't be doing this..." She looked over her shoulder, then back to him. She had his full attention, but his grief lingered. "I know you said she doesn't care about you, but she wanted to leave these for you. I checked your chart to make sure it was okay, to err on the side of caution. But it's fine. You can have them." She pulled a small bag from her pocket and placed it in his palm.

The nurse left, but Taylor's eyes never left the bag in his hand.

Jellybeans.

Chapter Thirty-One

TAYLOR FLIPPED THE sheet off him and stood up, slowly, making sure his legs were steady, ready to support his weight. They were, though his knees were damaged from the earlier fall. He grabbed his IV and wheeled it with him toward the door.

The gown was breezy in the back, but he had on his boxers so he didn't care. He only cared about finding that nurse again. Walking into the hall, he could hear the sound of monitors, coughing coming from a room nearby, and the soft voices of nurses discussing a file. He walked down a bit and saw a nurses' station. The same one who gave him the jellybeans looked up and was surprised to see him, but then worry creased her forehead. "Mr. Barrett, is everything all right?"

He held out the jellybeans. "Who gave these to you?"

When her gaze left his hand and reached his eyes again, she looked perplexed. "The young woman in your room earlier."

"Which woman? What color hair did she have?"

Her eyebrow rose. "How many women visitors have you had, Mr. Barrett?" she teased.

"That's what I'm trying to figure out. Was she blonde or brunette?"

She glanced at the other nurse, then laughed, very lightly. "Brunette." Her hand went to a spot on her arm. "About here. Very sweet girl. We spoke for a few minutes about how you were doing, but she couldn't stay since it was after visiting hours."

Taylor stared at her in disbelief. "Sundress?"

The nurse smiled. "Yes. Cream colored with tiny flowers all over. You do know her, right? She seemed to know you very well."

His fingers closed around the baggie. "Yes. I know her very well, too... or I thought I did. How long ago was she here?"

She checked her watch. "At least three hours ago. It was late."

Disappointment set in, and Taylor dropped his head forward, hoping the nurse couldn't hear the pounding of his heart.

"If it makes a difference," she started. When he looked up at her, she came closer. "She asked how long you would be here at the hospital and said if you were here tomorrow night, she would come again. I joked with her that next time she needed to come during visiting hours."

"What did she say?"

"She said she would try, but no promises." The nurse laughed as if that had been the most charming answer ever.

"That sounds like her."

"Who exactly is she? If you don't mind me asking."

"For too brief a time, she was the one who made forever seem possible."

The nurse's expression softened, and she gently patted his shoulder. "You need your rest, Taylor."

He agreed. His body was tired just from standing here. "Okay, but if she returns when I'm sleeping, will you wake me and please let her visit?"

"Of course, I will."

"Thank you."

When Taylor returned to bed, he ate the jellybeans. He always hated the popcorn ones, but tonight, they were the best things he'd tasted in a long time. Looking out the large picture window, he slowly chewed and savored each candy, then lay back.

Jude had been here.

She had left the candy for him. To Taylor, that meant Jude wanted him to know she'd been there. Out of the blue, like his forever, hope felt possible again. There was no way he was going to get any rest now. So he just lay there smiling.

Three hours earlier, in a large single-family brownstone ten blocks away from the hospital where hope was growing, Jude snuck back into her room. The door had been oiled and didn't make a sound. This was just the way she liked it. She would have to thank Roman in the morning.

After getting ready for sleep, she climbed into the posy-covered bed and rolled to her side. She smiled in the darkness of the room. She couldn't help it. Seeing Hazel made her happy, even if he wasn't hers to be happy over anymore. The nurse had been kind to ease Jude's worry, reassuring her that he would be fine, or at least not worse.

She probably shouldn't have left the jellybeans, but it was all she could give him to show she cared, would always care about him. She closed her eyes and snuggled into her covers. Tomorrow she might try to stay away... or she might try to see him again. Eight weeks and two days had been far too long. He might not want to see her, but either way, she knew at some point she would reach out to him again.

In the brightest morning hours, Jude had already dressed for the day and finished breakfast before leaving just after eleven for her eleven thirty appointment. Her mother was living in a different bedroom and if she wasn't there, she was out. Three weeks ago, she had asked her why she stayed. When she answered that she'd stayed for Jude, her heart had felt a little lighter. She would stay to serve her sentence alongside her. Jude hugged her that day. It was the first of many to come and she no longer felt so alone.

Isla had rented an apartment in Tribeca. She occasionally came over to take Jude to lunch or out for coffee, but she was trying to separate herself from the others. Jude understood. Distance often seemed the only way to survive.

Even Nadia had flown the coup. She took a job in Brooklyn, not even entertaining a counter offer from Brewster Boehler.

Jude rarely saw her aunt, which suited her just fine. And her stepfather worked longer hours, making the house a much more peaceful place to live. But Jude still had Roman. Her friend. Her confidant. He welcomed her with a smile and she hugged him. "Thank you for staying."

"I stay if you stay."

"I'd go if I could go."

He chuckled and walked to the door with her. "Busy day?" he asked with delight in his eyes.

Her confidant knew all.

"Very busy. I should get going."

He always looked at her as if it would be the last time he saw her. She rubbed his arm, and said, "I'll see you later."

"I'll see you soon, Hummingbird."

Twenty minutes later she entered the doctors' office and took a seat in the waiting room. Lacy walked in, the wind blowing her hair and covering her face until the door closed. The two ladies had become good friends, allies even, and Lacy spent her days off in the city visiting her. They hugged before Lacy sat down and asked, "Are you ready?"

"I'm ready," Jude replied, smiling so big. "So ready."

They were called into Dr. Robert's office and sat on the other side of the desk from him. He greeted them, happy as always. "Your system has been clear of the meds for two months now. We completed more than enough sessions together for me to give an assessment. I've typed my professional opinion and emailed your lawyer. As of today, there is no medical basis for your family to retain conservatorship over you." He sighed. "I'm afraid there probably never was, but we can't fight the past. I just hope you get the justice for your future." He stood up and held his hand out. When Jude took it, he clasped his other over it, and added, "If you need anything, a witness on your behalf, I'm here for you."

Jude was in shock. *Freedom.* The doctor had just confirmed what she knew already, but to hear the words come from his mouth... it hadn't sunk in, but she felt grateful. "Thank you so much."

Lacy picked up the letterhead and stood. "Thank you, Dr. Robert, for helping her. I know you don't normally take on cases free of charge, but I thought you'd understand once you met Jude."

From the moment Lacy had introduced Jude to Dr. Robert, Jude felt at ease in his presence. He was an older gentleman with gray hair and a clean-shaven face. He had always spoken to her with respect, compassion, and sensitivity. He restored her faith in doctors because he never treated her like a pawn to be used and manipulated. He came around the desk to open the door for the women, but stopped and said, "You're a remarkable young woman. Promise to do great things with this life of yours."

"I promise." She walked to him and hugged him. *Was it professional?* No. But she didn't care. This man was helping to get her life back. A hug of thanks felt necessary. "Thank you so much for believing me."

"I believe *in* you."

Lacy and Jude left the psychiatrist's office and walked with purpose a few blocks farther to a tall glass building. Lacy hugged Jude, and said, "I think you're ready for this."

"You're not coming with me?"

"Nope. You've got this!"

Jude had come to rely on Lacy for so much, but she was right. She needed to stand on her own by taking these final steps on her own. "Wish me luck."

"You don't need it. Call me later though and fill me in on the plan."

Jude hugged her once more, grateful for her support, but even more so for her friendship. "I will. Thank you for everything, but especially for being my friend."

Lacy embraced her just as tightly. "Thank you for being mine. Now go. I want to save my mushy tears for when you walk out of that courthouse. Then we'll go celebrate."

Nodding, Jude stepped toward the door. "I'll call you soon." She turned from her friend and walked inside the building. Excitement built as she took the elevator up. When she was led down the hall to her lawyer's office, her nerves kicked in.

Caleb Monroe had taken Jude Boehler on pro bono. He had worked with Taylor Barrett a few months back, and taken an interest in her case. After his client had previously lost and the appeal was denied, Caleb was determined to right things for the both of them. He and Jude sat at a small round table piled high with files. She set the letter down and he smiled. "This is a victory. You understand, Jude? Take everything else we're fighting for off the table, and this doctor's letter alone can get your rights back. Don't get me wrong. We're still going to take them for everything they own, but this will be enough to get your freedom back."

Music to Jude's ears. A sense of amazement came over her and her heart filled with joy. Jude sat on her hands to help contain her eagerness. "I don't care about the money. I just want..." She stopped to gather her emotions—happiness, hope, faith. She was just given a gift of all of those. But wanting to know his intention for her family, she asked, "What will the final petition say?"

He grabbed a thick file and set it in front of her. "I don't want to sound arrogant, but there's no way the Boehlers can fight against this much evidence. At the forefront, we want you to be able to make your own decisions regarding your well-being. We want no ties to them in any way—financially, medically, or emotionally. They will pay you all monies owed, in full, from your inheritance that they stole from you under duress from the estate of Merwyn Boehler, your step-uncle. Or all monies that remain in their accounts currently, if less than the overall inheritance."

Jude would normally feel sympathetic for purposely hurting others, but not them. She would hurt them where they would feel it the most—their bank accounts. If only she would have meant as much to them as money did, things would be so different. *Her life would have been so different.*

"Dr. Conroy will be charged with extortion of a patient as well as medical misconduct." He pulled another large file across the table. "The staff has been more than happy to help the case. He's a hated man. He'll lose his medical license, everything he has, and spend time in jail if we win."

"When are you filing?"

"I was only waiting on Doctor Robert's counsel and recommendation. Now that we have it, there's no reason to wait. I can start the paperwork today. It can be filed tomorrow morning."

"How long do you think it will take to get a court date?"

Caleb tilted his head in thought. "I wouldn't think more than two weeks. I'm listing that it's a concern to be under their care any longer. We could luck out and get something early next week. You have your private phone still?"

She pulled the phone that Lacy had bought her from her pocket and set it on the table. "I do."

"I'll call you as soon as I hear anything. Until then, you should be prepared to leave the premises of that home. Get anything you want to hang on to and get out before they're served. It won't be safe for you to stay there."

There was nothing left. Hazel had everything of hers that mattered—a picture of her brother, a smattering of clothes. The rest was replaceable.

Caleb dropped his shoulders and got personal. "I'm not sure if I should tell you or not, and that always means I should. I'm going to be straightforward with you. Taylor is in the hospital. I thought you should know."

"I probably shouldn't tell you this, but what's the worst that can happen anymore? I saw him last night."

The lawyer looked surprised. "You saw him?"

"I did, but I didn't speak to him. He was sleeping."

Caleb processed what she was saying, and added, "I got word he's okay and will be released today." He stacked the folders and then turned back to her. "How'd you know he was in the hospital?"

She didn't want to admit that she had done a bit—okay a lot—of stalking, but how else would she know? "I was at the same fundraiser."

He raised an eyebrow and asked, "By invitation *orrr*?" He stamped down the folders to align them. "You know what? Don't tell me."

Laughing, she replied, "Probably best."

He stood and she followed. His smile was comforting and gave her courage. "Prepare yourself. Once this is put into motion, there's no going back even if you do drop the case. Are you up for this?"

"I am," she said without hesitation. "I'm ready."

"Let's do this."

Chapter Thirty-Two

JUDE WALKED INTO the hospital shortly after leaving Caleb's office. It was only a detour, she convinced herself. Just a peek to make sure what Caleb said was true. She hoped Hazel was strong enough to leave today. One quick walk-by and then she would leave as well, her mind at ease. This was her plan—to make sure he hadn't relapsed since she checked on him the night before. It was a good plan. Solid. Hazel would never be the wiser.

She was fast approaching the door up ahead on the right, so she slowed her steps. Just as she walked by, she looked into the room, but then stopped. The room was empty. Her first reaction was relief. He'd gone home. Her second reaction was that dreaded what-if scenario that started playing on a loop in her head.

What if he relapsed?

What if he was rushed into emergency?

What if he was unconscious and they had moved him to another room?

What if...

What if...

What if...

She walked inside the room and touched the unmade bed,

hoping it would give her guidance, a clue to where he was or if he was returning. The door shut behind her and she whirled around. She came face to face with Hazel himself, who was particularly smirky at the moment. "Looking for someone?" he asked.

Jude's mouth opened, then closed, and opened again. "No. No one in particular." She followed her heart and started for him, momentarily forgetting they weren't together. Then detoured toward the door, but he leaned against it, blocking her from exiting.

"I think you were looking for me. I mean, why else would you be inside *my* hospital room?"

Yep, no getting out of it, so she confessed half-truths. She had no option but to face the man she let go months earlier because she loved him too much. She tried for casual. "I heard you were in the hospital and I was worried. So I was checking on you."

While he stared at the one woman he loved, the only woman he would love long after this life, guilt overwhelmed him. "Jude?" he started, but stopped. He took a deep breath. "I tried to do what you wanted, but I can't. I don't love her."

"I know."

His hazel eyes pierced her heart, letting the rest of her truths bleed. "How do you know?"

"Because I saw you last night. I see you every day. Sometimes twice, if I was lucky."

He restrained the huge grin that wanted to surface and gave her a smaller one instead, hoping to make her feel safe. "The whole time?"

"The whole time."

As much as he loved to hear this revelation, now he felt bad. "I'm sorry."

"For what? I just told you I've been stalking your every move and you're apologizing to me?"

"The stalking, I'm not complaining, but I'm sorry for dating her, for thinking I could."

"You don't have to be. You were free to do so. You were trying to rebuild your life after I destroyed it." She turned, putting her back to him and looked out the window with a heavy sigh. She didn't *love* that he'd dated someone else, but she couldn't blame him either. She'd practically set them up by pushing him away. And whether that was for his benefit or hers at the time, she refused to hold it against him. Anyway, she knew where his allegiance lay. Beyond what she felt deep inside, a bond that was never broken, she saw it with her own two eyes.

"But I know you don't love her." She turned around to face him again. "I know *because* I saw you together." She reached out and touched the front of his suit, then took the jacket in her hand and fisted, pulling him closer. "I saw. I saw everything, then and now."

His voice was but a whisper. "What do you see, Jude? Tell me."

"I see your love for me."

Abruptly moving forward, he grabbed her and kissed her. The stubble on his face grazed her skin, tickling and scratching. His warm, soft, but determined lips captured hers along with her heart and she kissed him just as eagerly.

A gasp broke the two apart and they twisted around toward the door. Katherine stood there with a hand over her mouth and shock in her eyes. "Taylor!" Fury took over her refined features and she spat, "Is this revenge?" When he didn't reply, her hands went to her hips. "Fine. You win. We're even. Now get away from her this instant."

He didn't move. He wouldn't. Not again. Not from Jude. Not ever. "No."

"What do you mean, 'no'?"

"Exactly what it sounds like. I'm in love with her. I was from the moment I saw her. I was forced to leave the battlefield before. I'm not leaving her again without a full-on war."

Katherine held her large purse in her hands and squeezed. "Taylor, what are you doing? Are you on drugs? Is the medicine messing with your head?"

"No," he replied, smiling. "I've never been more aware in my life. And that's because I'm with her."

"But she's crazy!"

In unison, Hazel gritted the words, "Don't call her crazy!" while Jude said, "Don't call me crazy!" They looked at each other and in that moment, when their true colors united once again, they both started to laugh. Maybe it was the kiss that had just tickled their lips, or the honesty that poured so freely from their hearts. Or maybe they were both just too tired to argue anymore. Taylor took Jude's hand and held it. He turned back to Katherine, and said, "I'll take her kind of crazy any day, over yours."

Taylor walked with purpose, his hand tightly around Jude's, and out the door. Katherine had stepped aside, too appalled to say another word. "But I brought you clothes."

"Keep them."

In the wide, sterile hospital hallway, Jude quick-stepped next to him and looked up. She had a million questions, but none of them seemed important right then. The man she loved was on a mission and she was the beneficiary of it. This is what she would take any day over the loveless days that had preceded it.

The sun hit their faces as they exited the building and Taylor didn't ask which way or if she wanted to come at all. He knew where he was going all along. And once they took two corners and three blocks, she did too. He stopped once, to ask, "Why did you come back?"

"Because they were changing who you were. And you were

perfect before."

He seemed okay with this answer and they continued on. Ten more minutes without either of them offering anything more had led them to this point, and her feet slowed until they stopped. "I can't go to your apartment, Hazel."

"You're not. You're going home."

"Semantics."

"Our hearts don't know the variances of words. Our hearts only know what they feel." He kissed her again, simply because he could. If it reassured her, all the better.

When their lips parted, she said, "I don't want to cause you harm or pain, or worry. Give it time, and I'll come back."

"I feel those things now," he insisted. "Time won't fix this. Time spends every second torturing me while we're apart. Do you not feel that already? It overrides everything in my life."

His hands were cupping her cheeks, so she covered them. The intense focus he had on her was felt like an explosion inside, reviving her latent heart. She relented, for him, for herself, and they started walking again.

Entering that apartment was like hugging an old friend—warm and comforting. The smell made her smile and the place made her happy. Hazel locked the door behind him and leaned against it. "I'm never letting you go." Then a smile appeared and he added, "That's not creepy in the least, is it?"

It wasn't. Not in the least. Not to Jude. She stood with nothing but herself to offer him and the way he looked at her, that was enough.

Looking around, she saw the photo of her brother on the bookcase and went to it. It had been a while since she'd seen him, and through her soon-to-be freedom found in her new eyes, she saw his happiness. The sadness she once felt looking at it was gone.

Hazel and Ryan were a lot alike. Both gentle souls with passionate sides for the things and people they loved. She set the frame on the shelf and sat down at Hazel's drafting table.

It felt like Christmas, and all the small memories wrapped in the apartment were like gifts to her soul. Sketches she thought he might not want her to see were scattered across the white surface. House plans mixed with familiar lips, eyes, a nose, hair, and a dress that when pieced together could have been a mirror. "These are beautiful."

"You're beautiful." He moved around her, giving her space though not much. Peering over her shoulder, he felt no shame in his pastime. "So tell me, Jude Barrett, why did you give up?"

"I didn't give up. I let you be by setting you free. Isn't that what the selfless do?"

"I didn't want to be set free. I'll happily be grounded to you forever."

"I know. That's why I had to do it." She spun around and faced him as he sat on the couch. "You were going to fight until your last breath, but we were losing. You heard them—my sickness for yours. Yours for mine. Nothing could have changed their minds. Hazel," she pleaded, "you have to start thinking of yourself. I loved that you were fighting for me, that I wasn't alone, but it would be no victory if it came at the expense of your health."

"I was fine until you 'set me free.' Because don't you see? It was never about you being sick or me fighting my disease. It was always about being together for as long as we both shall live."

He sat back, crossed his leg over his knee, and said, "You once told me you married me despite my illness. Now you're telling me you left me because of it. But I don't see it. I don't see it in your eyes. I don't hear it in your words. I don't feel it when we kiss. You *love* me. You love me no matter what my health because that's what love is. Love bends and folds, straightens and secures itself to the one it cares about." Sitting up, his enthusiasm was contagious and Jude smiled at his architectural references. "We're tied together, fastened, and bonded. They can take away that piece of governmental paper, but we remain married in the eyes of God and in my heart."

He was so easy to believe with his grand statements and flattering declarations. He was easy to believe because she agreed. "Our marriage can be annulled, but our love remains. Always."

"Our commitment is still there."

"You didn't have sex with her, did you?" Jude might have been smiling to control her jealousy, but she was still hoping for only one answer.

Taylor admired Jude's eyes that were persuasively blue today, against the backdrop of the light blue dress she wore. "No. But you know that already. You know what we have doesn't go away because you convinced yourself you had to set it free."

"I knew. I just thought maybe I should ask anyway. Isn't that what normal girls would do? Ask if you did?"

"There's nothing normal about you, Jude, which is exactly why I like you."

She got up and settled onto his lap, tired of fighting the inevitable, and just not wanting to anymore. She wrapped her arms around his neck as he rubbed her hip and back. "And I thought it was because I gave you my virginity."

With a big cocky grin, he popped an imaginary collar. "I will proudly carry that V card of yours right here in my wallet."

"Hazel?"

"Yeah?"

"We live in an impossible world," she said, astonished she was back where she wanted to be. She was home. "Impossible like your eyes."

"We'll get through it together." He leaned his head on her shoulder and she tilted hers to him. "Stay."

Chapter Thirty-Three

THE SUN WAS setting and Jude could see the last of the rays disappearing between the buildings outside the window. The tea she had made earlier was now cold and she debated warming it up. But she didn't want to move from Hazel's arms, so she scooted closer to him and his arms tightened around her.

Hazel was right. That paper didn't represent who they were to each other. Their souls were eternally bonded, and so here she would stay, his arms her safe haven.

"You're not going back," he breathed against her shoulder blade.

"There's nothing there that matters to me." She thought of Roman, but he wanted her to be free. Once she was, she'd find him to say goodbye. In the meantime, she rolled over to face Hazel. She looked at him. Really looked at him and leaned her head against his. "I will love you long after this life and into the next."

"I'm counting on you."

It was good to be counted on. She closed her eyes and in the comfort of their home, she fell asleep.

The next morning, Jude sipped coffee on one barstool. Hazel was on the other. The newspaper remained untouched between them. "Isla called newspapers antiquated," she remarked.

"That's why I like them," he replied. "I like that the ink comes off on your hands and the smell of the paper. It's real, not like reading online."

"That's why I like books. They give me something to hold on to when my emotions are unraveling from the story." She touched his thigh, and said, "We should talk about what's going on with me."

His gaze left the mug and went to her face. Leaning in, he kissed the side of her mouth, then sat up. "Okay. What's going on?"

"My mother fears for her life."

"Ironically."

"Yes. Ironically, but I've seen her twice. I might forgive her one day. I'm not asking you to do the same, but I might."

"Can you? Will you ever really be able to forgive her?"

"She was manipulated when she was at her lowest. Ryan's death devastated her."

"Your life should have meant more to her after that then."

"You're right. I'm not defending her. I'm only stating that she's a troubled woman who now fears for her life, but she fears for my life more and has offered to be there for me."

Taylor absorbed what she was saying. "You can't change the past so you want to change the future."

"Yes. I don't want to live with an angry heart. She's seeing a therapist a couple times a week. All I can hope is that she gets the help she needs and is there for me when I need her."

"You're an amazing woman, you know that, Jude Barrett?"

She smiled from hearing the name. She smiled from being near the man she loved most. "There's more. Caleb Monroe is filing a petition on my behalf today to win my rights back as well as including evidence to show wrongdoing by Bleekman's and Dr. Conroy."

Hazel dipped his head into his hand in astonishment and rubbed his brow. "Really?"

"There's more. My uncle left me his inheritance or what I call *guilt* money. We're suing for the entire amount back or what's left of it."

Taylor stared at her in complete awe.

"We have testimony from five different employees at Bleekman's who have recorded statements on my behalf that not only did they have their job security threatened but that they themselves would face repercussions if they spoke up. Well, they're willing to fight the good fight together."

"How did... when did... Caleb?"

"He took me on as a pro-bono client so my family wouldn't be able to trace any payments. And I've become friends with a nurse who works at Bleekman's. She set me up with a psychiatrist here in the city, who also worked with me for free. After two months of counseling, I have his professional opinion that I am not insane as claimed by my family and Dr. Conroy."

Taylor took a second to digest all that she just laid on him. "You've been doing all this by yourself?"

"Well, I had my friend Lacy, the nurse from Bleekman's helping, but I had to. I had to fight back."

Then irritation set in. "Why didn't you come to me? I would have helped you. I would have done anything for you. Why didn't you trust me?"

She touched his cheek, then kissed his chin. "I trust you with my life. I know you would have done anything for me, but I didn't know if you were being watched, I didn't want to give you false hope. *Annnnd*, I needed to do this on my own. I didn't want to come to you the same as I was before. I wanted to be whole, to be free, for you, but more importantly, for me."

Rubbing her knee, he found a renewed spirit in her words and a sparkle to her eyes. "I get that. I wish you would have come to me, but I understand the need to do it on your own. Do you have a date set?"

"I'll find out soon. Caleb said he'd call me."

"I can pay him for the time he's put in on your case if you want me to."

"He's about to have a windfall when we win, so don't worry."

"You sound confident."

"We are. There is no reason—legal or medical—for them to retain guardianship."

With a wide smile, he suggested, "We should celebrate."

"Let's wait for the final verdict first before the confetti comes out."

His hand slid down her waist and back up. "I was thinking maybe in the bedroom. A private celebration with just the two of us and a mattress."

Jude had missed his touch so much. She had missed *him* so much. There were nights back in the pink prison her body had yearned for him, her soul had ached for him.

Neither knew how long they would have to wait to see her conservatorship through and she didn't want to deny her heart or her body any longer. Feeling empowered by his presence, she stood up and walked to the couch. Bending over the arm, she reached for a cushion on the other side, then glanced back at him. "The mattress? And here I thought you were more adventurous, Mr. Barrett." She wiggled her ass, beckoning him to her.

Recalling their prior "adventures", Hazel knew they were always good together, passionate, but this new side of Jude was playful. He could definitely get on board with this game. He stood up, the barstool scraping against the wooden floor.

Jude watched the man who was kindhearted, handsome, and sporting some seriously sexy swagger come for her. This morning, with his mussed-up hair and dreamy eyes, he was absolutely drool-worthy. She added that to his never-ending list of attributes. His toned chest and chiseled arms synced nicely, the muscles working together to make her forget herself. She closed her mouth and lifted up, turning around and planting herself on the arm of the couch. She bit her bottom lip as anticipation formed under his smoldering gaze.

Bending his head toward her, his thighs bumped up against her knees, his fingertips running the length of her neck and under the strap of her bra. "What do you want, Jude?"

His eyes were intense, his lips seductive—so close and yet too far from her own. One of her straps was down and he was lowering the other. She reached around and unfastened her bra and he took it down her arms and tossed it on the couch. "I asked what you want," he repeated, his voice direct, committed to his purpose.

"I want you."

"How? How do you want me, pretty girl?"

Playful seemed to escape her tone as he built her desire from within. "Here. Now."

His fingers graced her face again and he tilted it all the way up. "I love you."

Her eyes went wide. His words were laced with seduction. Hazel had always been a dedicated lover, but right now, he stood before her a predator. "I love you, Taylor," she emphasized the T of his name, then licked her lips.

"What did I tell you about calling me that?" He abruptly lifted her to her feet, his hands under her arms and he leaned in dangerously close. "You've been a bad girl. A very bad girl."

She had no idea where this side of him was coming from, but he made her body purr with arousal. "Take those off," he directed. Without a pause, she lowered her underwear, then stood straight up in challenge, eyeing him. He eyed her right back, unabashedly. "Turn around and bend over."

There was safety in his tone, even if it was demanding. Jude had been a shrinking violet for too long. He gave her confidence and made her stronger. She was flaunting this newfound confidence. With her hands on the couch, she arched her back downward and stuck out her ass. With one sly glimpse back, she taunted his willpower.

The sight of her weakened him in ways he liked, in ways he craved. But he gained his strength and leaned over her. He licked the back of her neck and kissed her spine before pressing his hard body against her backside. "You're so naughty, but I'm going to treat you *so* nice." Dropping to his knees, he turned around and maneuvered between her legs, coaxing them apart with insistent hands.

Jude closed her eyes, the magnitude of his positioning was too much and she dropped her head down onto the cushion. His hands gripped her hips, while his lips caressed her, driving her mad with ecstasy while he situated her over him. With his tongue, he made her universe thunder and her thighs vibrate. Jude moaned from pure bliss as his hands rubbed down the outside of her legs. Gently, he kissed each of her inner thighs hesitant to leave a mark on her. Just before he was about to move, she asked, "If you could do anything to me, what would you do?"

He was about to speak, but she added, "Shh. Don't tell me. Do it."

His lips stroked her thigh and he sucked, closing his eyes, and marking her. Reaching down, her fingers scraped through his hair, encouraging him.

Moving out from under her, he stood up and put pressure on her back, running his hands from her shoulders to her ass until his cock was right there, where he wanted to be most. "How did you know?"

"I didn't. I hoped. Don't let the world taint what we have together. I love you."

"Remember how much I love you too." He thrust inside her without warning, needing her wet heat to swallow him. Their mouths dropped open, solicitous moans escaping.

"God, I missed this," he said, squeezing her as he stilled. His breath rolled over her skin, making her shiver.

She wanted to speak, but words were failing her so she squirmed instead, and he started moving again. Faster and faster until her breath caught and she cried out. "Oh God!"

Her body embraced him and he came thereafter, holding her hips for leverage. More kisses were followed though Jude felt helpless and sated, and loved. She opened her eyes when he stood up, taking her hand to help her up too. In one fast swoop, she was in his arms being carried to the bedroom.

Taylor set her down on the bed to recover, then joined her under the covers. Moments passed before their breathing evened. Jude stayed in his arms, never wanting to leave them again. They became a tangle of relaxed limbs, sleep starting to arise, but then she asked, "Why do we cry out 'God' when we come? We're not even that religious."

He burst out laughing. "I seriously missed you."

"I missed you too. But really, do you think it's because there's nothing more powerful in that moment? It feels that way to me."

Amused, he kissed her temple, and said, "Maybe it's because we're closer to Heaven when we're joined together."

"Oh, that's a really good answer."

"Glad you like it." He closed his eyes, still smiling.

A ringing made both of their eyes open. She sat up and swung her legs over the edge of the mattress. "I'll be right back."

"Is that your phone?"

"Yes."

He lay back with his hands under his head. "I still can't believe you have a phone. Do I get the number?"

"Yes, of course," she said, giggling as she ran out of the room. She grabbed it and answered it. "Hello?"

"It's Caleb. We got our expedited hearing. Monday at eleven."

"This is amazing news."

"It is," he said. "Now what are you going to do until then? Where are you going to stay? It's not safe for you to be there. They'll know in the next hour."

She looked over her shoulder and saw Hazel in all his naked glory leaning against the door to the bedroom. "I'm with Taylor."

There was a pause, and then Caleb questioned, "With *with* or talking with?"

"*With* with. For good. I'll stay with him."

"Are you safe there? They may come for you, like last time."

"This time they have no right to take me, correct? The order of protection is in place?"

"That's correct, but that doesn't ultimately protect you." He sounded worried, and said, "Don't go out on your own. Stay with Taylor. Just lay low until Monday. All right?"

"Okay. I will."

"And say hello to him. It's good to hear you so happy."

"Thanks," she said, smiling though he couldn't see. But she did feel happy. Happy in love. "And I will."

When she hung up, Taylor said, "I don't want you to think I'm prying, but I want to know."

She went to him. "You're not prying. You're my husband. I have no secrets from you. Caleb said we got our expedited hearing. Next Monday at eleven."

He hugged her. "That's great news."

With her cheek to his chest, she said, "He told me to lay low, to protect myself if they come after me. There's a restraining order in place, but he fears, like I do, that it won't stop them." Tilting her head up to look at him, she asked, "What do you think?"

He tightened his hold on her and spoke in a low tone, caught somewhere between anger and possessive, "We protect you."

The moment she went to shower, Taylor went to work to secure her safety. He alerted the doorman that no one, not even the police were allowed up to his apartment without a warrant. He called a locksmith to get a new bolt added to the door, and he didn't let her leave the apartment until she freaked out on him on Saturday because of her cabin fever. And then, with extreme caution, they went to the park, had lunch out, bought her a dress for court, and then returned home that evening. She was exhausted, but happy. And that made Taylor just as happy.

The next day and a half passed not so fast, but not too slow. It went by, taunting them with all the possible outcomes that could come of this hearing. They tried to distract themselves with blueprints and movies, books and light conversation. But Monday loomed and caused stress whether they thought about it directly or not.

When it was finally time for court, they walked in together, hand in hand, to face the hard glares of her family. Caleb walked to the right of them, making sure the respondents didn't talk to his client.

Right away, Jude noticed her mother was missing. Her aunt and stepfather sat down and spoke quietly with their lawyer while

Hazel and Jude sat down at their table with Caleb.

The introductions and background information were told by both parties and then they spent the next three hours dissecting all that was Jude, Taylor and Jude, Jude and her family dynamics, Jude and Bleekman's, and the evidence presented.

The other side made convincing, though fabricated arguments. When Jude took the stand, she happily rebuked them. She held her head up and her shoulders back. She wasn't meek anymore. She was prepared to face this alone, head-on. But Hazel being there made all the difference and she held strong in the belief that she would win by reason of sanity.

Caleb had told them to let the evidence speak for itself. And Jude only answered what was required of her. When she spoke, everyone in the court stared at her, trying to decide if she was crazy like the opposing counsel had claimed. She saw Dr. Robert and Lacy there and found comfort in their presence. After a grueling day, the judge took the information and retired to his chambers. It was over. Now they waited...

The next morning, Caleb, Hazel, and Jude, along with Dr. Robert and Lacy waited in the courtroom. Jude didn't have a way to contact her mother and she had been worrying about her absence all night. As if she knew her daughter needed her, the doors opened at the back and in walked Renee Boehler, her mother. She looked good—healthy, happier, and more importantly, happy to see Jude. Her mother took her side and sat behind Jude's table, in the closest chair to her daughter. Reaching forward, she rubbed Jude's back and said, "This is a good day. I can feel it."

Judge Lathrop walked in and with all eyes on him, sat down on his throne. His expression was unreadable, severity set deep in the lines on his face. Would he see the truth behind the lies? He didn't appear to be a man who would give a young girl her life back with a simple ruling, but she held on to hope as tight as she held on to Hazel's hand.

Nine months ago, Jude had no idea her life would be about to change its course. She had no idea that attending a party her parents had been invited to, but didn't attend—a party she attended without them knowing—would lead to this. She often thought of how she met Hazel, how he came to her and stood by her side, protective from the beginning. *"Feels like our whole lives."* And it did, even from the first moment she looked at the broken man with dashing eyes.

Theirs had not been an easy journey. No doubt at times he had hated her ability to stay, to try to weather the storm of her past. She had hated herself for that very same reason. But today she knew, *she knew*, she was not crazy. She had been wronged and today she would face her future, whatever may come. But not alone. Never alone again.

Hazel needed her as much as she needed him. She also knew this. A party invitation had led them to each other—to their destiny.

Her life for his.

His life for hers.

Together no matter if they had a piece of paper saying so or not.

Hazel squeezed her hand and kissed her temple.

Judge Lathrop found Bleekman's, Dr. Conroy, and Brewster Boehler liable for criminal charges that would be filed against them that day. All monies she was forced to sign away while at Bleekman's would be returned as well as additional monies for the abuse she endured. As the case continued, he ruled that Judith Boehler was the only one in charge of her life and that full rights to her own guardianship would be returned to her immediately. His final ruling was on an item that Caleb Monroe added after the case was scheduled. The judge had agreed to the addition over whisky and a cigar late Friday evening.

Taylor and Jude were already breathing easier on regaining her freedom, her independence, but both sat with their fingers entwined with each other's awaiting the final piece—the legality of their marriage.

As the judge spoke, the courtroom went quiet. "The annulment was forced due to lies told in the courtroom during the initial case. Those who instigated the lies and carried them forth will be held legally accountable. Based on the facts and what I've witnessed today, I'm overturning the annulment. The marriage is valid and a new certificate will be issued."

Taylor looked to Jude, a broad smile on his face. She smiled just as big. Life was becoming as it should be—perfect. Their love would always go beyond this existence, but it was nice to get the legal stamp of approval.

She was swooped into his arms and covered in kisses. Her laughter rang out, filling the courtroom. "Free," she said. *Finally.* She was free from evil, free to live, free to love.

When Taylor set Jude's feet on the ground again, Caleb hugged her. He wasn't a hugger but this was a wrong that had been righted and his emotions seemed to get the better of him. A loud commotion caused Caleb to release her and step out from behind the table. Taylor took Jude by the waist and moved her safely behind him.

Brewster Boehler stood in rage and yelled at his legal team. "She's crazy! She'll try to kill herself again. Her death rests on your shoulders." When Leslie touched his back, shock firmly implanted like Botox in her face, he knocked her hand away. "Get away from me."

Jude watched in horror as the dramatics played out. Had she never meant anything to him? He had raised her half her life. He had claimed this all started like most crimes—opportunity presenting itself. But watching him now, she knew there was never love in his heart for her. Like a burden that had weighed her down, knowing how he truly felt freed her from the guilt she felt for not loving him.

Slowly, a smile appeared. She couldn't stop it though she thought it was probably inappropriate. It grew even bigger with that thought until she laughed out loud, unable to hide her joy.

Hazel and Caleb looked at her, and like Hazel and Jude's determination to be together, her happiness was contagious.

Two light laughs were heard behind her and she turned to see smiles on Isla's and her mother's faces, along with tears in their eyes.

Isla's words were rushed as if she was racing the onslaught of tears before they fell. "I'm sorry, Judith. I had no idea, and then when I did, I didn't know how to deal with it." Some heavy emotion struck her suddenly and she grabbed her stomach as if she was going to be ill. "What my father did to you... I blamed you, but I should have blamed him. I'm sorry. Please forgive me."

When her heart hurdled over the betrayal and she left the deceit in the past, Jude's heart grew, as did the family she could rely on. With a small, sympathetic smile, Jude replied, "Let's move forward. The past is too ugly to dwell on." The cousins, who were divided by deaths and lies, were reunited in truth and hope. They embraced.

When they parted, Jude's mother was waiting patiently. Their eyes connected and both women became teary. She didn't want to play any more emotional games with anyone. She was too tired and was ready to be happy, so she just hugged her.

Her mother was behind her when it counted and that was all Jude needed to know to forgive what her mother considered the unforgiveable. The two women agreed they would rebuild their relationship at Jude's pace. But Jude never did anything slow, there was too much life to live for that. "Maybe the four of us can have dinner this week?"

Isla agreed and Jude's mother said, "We have a lot to celebrate."

Hazel's hand tightened around Jude's side, and he whispered, "It's time to go."

When they reached the aisle, Jude cut across the front of three chairs and hugged her mother once more. Her mother started crying and said, "I'm sorry."

"I am too," Jude replied. *I am too.*

Outside the courthouse, Caleb stood before the couple. "This might be the sweetest victory I've ever had."

Hazel smiled, but Jude spoke. "It might even be sweeter than ice cream."

"Or jellybeans," added Hazel.

She laughed. "No, love, nothing is sweeter than jellybeans. Now as for those popcorn ones, which are savory... well that's a whole other conversation."

"Indeed, a discussion for another day."

Caleb said, "And you have plenty of days ahead." He shook Taylor's hand and then took Jude's between both of his. "You're a strong woman. Always remember that."

She reached up and hugged him. "Thank you for everything."

"Thank *you.* Now go live your happiness."

Leaning against Hazel, she replied, "I already am."

Chapter Thirty-Four

THE TWO LOVEBIRDS, once married, then denied their love, then once again recognized as married, walked down the street holding hands a month after living in splendid freedom. They didn't speak, but their feet led them both to the same place. Like their hearts, they were in sync. Taylor sat on the bench and pulled his pretty little double dipper onto his lap, and asked, "Did you ever decide what kind of ice cream I was?"

"Of course. I knew the first day I met you."

"Was this before I ordered pistachio or after?"

With a wry smile engaged on her lips and her arms around his neck, she gazed into his eyes. "After, but the fact you ordered pistachio was wrong in the first place."

"Why are you so harsh on pistachio?" he teased.

"Pistachio is fine... but it's just not your flavor," she said with absolute confidence.

He rubbed the bridge of his nose against hers, then kissed the end of it. "What flavor am I, Jude?"

She stood up. "C'mon, let's go get ice cream and I'll let you decide if I'm right."

They walked to the nearest location of her favorite ice

cream chain and holding two fingers up, she ordered, "Two mocha chocolate-chip ice creams on sugar cones, please."

He asked, "Mocha chocolate-chip, huh?"

"Just wait."

When they walked out onto the sidewalk, they stopped and both took a lick, but Taylor took an additional bite as well. "So?" she asked.

"You used to be rocky road. What happened?"

"I found it too precarious. I thought mocha chocolate-chip suited me better."

"Why?"

"Because you're mocha chocolate-chip."

He grabbed her in a bear hug and brought her closer to kiss the back of her head as she giggled. "You know what?"

"What?"

"I'm okay with this answer. Now let's get going. I want to show you something."

She eyed him suspiciously. "Is this a penis joke?"

Taylor did a double take in surprise. "Wow, freedom suits you. You're just gonna let it all hang out."

She laughed and it was hearty, then she took another lick of her ice cream. "There's no stopping me now."

As they walked, he said, "And by the way, it's no joke when it comes to my penis."

"You're telling me!" She quirked a smile and kept walking, leaving him entertained, and entirely enchanted by her.

They had covered three blocks when she asked, "Can we make a pit stop before home?"

When he agreed he didn't realize her "pit stop" meant twelve Manhattan blocks and to the stoop of her past. "Why are we here?"

he asked, keeping her two doors down from her family's brownstone.

"I need to say goodbye—"

"To what? A room where you were held prisoner for years? A family that tormented you and stole your life? What Jude? What do you have to say goodbye to?" He didn't understand any of this and his anxiety of being here made his temper flair.

"I need to say goodbye to Roman."

Taylor's anger sank into remorse. He grabbed her and held her to him. "I'm sorry."

She wrapped her arms around him knowing he needed the hug more than she did. "No need to be. I understand your fear. I should have explained."

When they parted, they moved to the side so other people could pass. "I don't want you knocking on that door. I want you to stay here. I'll go."

She agreed and he left her waiting on the steps of another stoop. She watched as Roman answered and polite words were exchanged between them. Roman stepped out, looked past Hazel, right at her, and then came without being asked.

Remaining one step up kept her eye level with him. He smiled and said, "You look ravishing, Hummingbird."

She almost twirled in her happiness but didn't, knowing she didn't have much time. "Thank you. Life has a funny way of expressing itself through our hearts. My heart is so full and so happy."

"And you deserve it all."

Hazel came back, but kept a few feet back, giving them this time alone. She looked at him, but then to Roman, she asked, "How long are you going to stay?"

"I can leave now that I know you're safe."

"You know, I'm not very good at maintaining the house, but I try my best. I try to make you proud. Even so, I'd like you to be a part of my life."

"I'd be happy to help."

"Not to help me with my apartment, but as my friend."

He smiled even wider. "It would be an honor."

"Actually, it'd be mine."

They exchanged numbers and Taylor came forward. "Thank you for being there for her when she had no one."

"It was my pleasure, Mr. Barrett."

They shook hands and Taylor corrected him, "Please call me Taylor."

Jude and Roman hugged, two battle weary soldiers fighting on the same side of a righteous war. "Take care of my Hummingbird, Taylor."

"I will. I promise."

Roman nodded and stepped back toward the brownstone. Jude could tell he felt lighter than she'd ever seen him. He chuckled. "Guess I can give notice."

"Good luck," she called out.

"Good luck to you, too."

Back home, the air felt different to Jude and Taylor. Before it was stilted, now it was alive. A window in the living room was left open that morning and a cool fall breeze blew in, greeting them. When he shut the front door, the papers on his drafting table flew, filling the air like snowflakes. They both leapt into action, collecting the sketches and drawings, the blueprints, and the renderings.

As Jude caught one, the miniature blueprint drew her eye. Papers rained down around her, softly falling to the floor like feathers. She looked at the one that most interested her. "What is this?"

Taylor was on his knees sweeping the papers into a pile with his hands, but he stopped and looked up to see what she was referring to. When he saw what it was, he sat back with his hands casually on his legs. "It's our house."

"When did you finish it?"

"Last night, after you fell asleep."

She walked over to him and sat down on the sturdy coffee table. "Will you take me through it?"

He took the papers from the floor and stood up with a grin. "Yeah. I'd like your thoughts and suggestions." They walked to the drafting table and he set the other drawings aside, then centered the blueprint he took from her hands. "I have a bigger one." He eyed her suddenly feeling a bit shy on the subject.

"Yes, I want to see every detail. Get the big boy out."

"Are we still talking blueprints?"

She knocked him on the arm. "Silly, horny man."

While laughing, he pulled out the rolled-up, tube-shaped plans from a holder next to his desk, flattened them and clipped the corners down. "Where do you want to start?"

"At the front door." Jude settled into his lap and with his arms wrapped around her, he walked her through the entire design. The house included the extra large closet he promised her, the large tub—just for them, and a built-in window seat in the library for her to sit and daydream or curl up with a book.

They sat there for over an hour, the time slipping away, as they planned their future. For dinner, they went out. In a little Italian restaurant a few blocks from the apartment and after a bottle of Chianti, Taylor asked, "Where were you going to live in California?"

Jude was surprised by the question, only having spoken of it one time in what seemed like another life. "Somewhere in Los Angeles, anywhere we could afford, I guess. Since Ryan wanted us out of New York and he couldn't attend NYU, he wanted to go to USC. But he only got an academic scholarship to cover one year. And it's not like I could live in his dorm."

"If you could live anywhere, where would you live?" He picked at the noodles in front of him much more interested in her answer than the pasta.

"Anywhere but here." Sadness overcame her and he reached across the table to hold her hand. She looked up, her eyes meeting his, and said, "I love what's *us* about New York. I hate what's *them*, which is a lot. Even if they are locked away in upstate New York for what is considered a white-collar crime, too many reminders remain, my memories threaded together with a past I want to forget."

"So if you could live anywhere, it would be the opposite of here?"

"I want to live near the ocean. If I could live anywhere, I'd live perched above the water and walk the beach every evening with you."

Taylor loved that she saw their futures entwined. For him, it was from the moment he met her. "We should move to California."

Her eyes went wide, this time in a good way. With a gentle smile, she squeezed his hand. "You're more New York than California, Hazel."

"I would be California for you."

It was that moment, that moment right after the other 6,385,629 moments they had shared that defined their future and also defined them.

THE LOS ANGELES Dodgers were down in the third to the New York

Mets, but Jude and Hazel were still on cloud nine two years later, still going strong. It was the very beginning of September and they sat at a Dodgers game, their home team now. Lacy and her boyfriend, Troy, sat next to them. It was her second time visiting them in California, the two friends talked daily, but their visits were the best.

But Jude really loved going to baseball games with Hazel. Every time they came out to the ballpark she saw the spark return that New York had dulled. So she bought him tickets to his favorite season of all—baseball.

He turned to Jude, and said, "You never told me about Rayleigh scattering."

"You just want me to go on about your impossible eyes, don't you?"

With a smirk, he bumped his shoulder against hers. "Maybe."

"Before we were married, you weren't so self-assured. What happened, Mr. Cocky?"

"Before we were married, I was very self-assured. Trust me. All the ladies loved me."

"How did we get from Rayleigh scattering to 'all the ladies loving you'?"

"Simple. My impossible eyes." He was starting to sound a lot like Jude in the way his thoughts circled. That made her smile. He took a sip of his beer that left a little beer-stache above his upper lip. She watched as his tongue dipped out and wiped it away. Her body stirred in reaction.

"And why are they so impossible?"

Jude wrapped her arm through his and leaned her head on his shoulder. With a smile as they watched the Dodgers finally score after two innings, she tilted her head up, and said, "Because I never stood a chance. They were impossible to resist, like you."

Taylor smiled, enjoying his day out, smiling because the Dodgers, his new favorite team had scored, and loving that his life with his pretty wife felt complete.

Or so he thought...

JUDE'S EYES WERE closed as she lay on the large balcony that overlooked the ocean in the short distance. She loved this time of day—when day was turning to night, when the stars swallowed the sky, and she could hear the waves crashing. This was Heaven. This is what Ryan would have loved. This is what she *did* love, and Hazel gave her this Heaven on Earth with no strings attached. Well, one string was attached—from her heart to his. It might have been invisible, but it was mighty, and was strong.

Taylor walked outside and leaned his hands on the ledge. "I don't think I ever appreciated California until I lived here."

"Laguna is beautiful; more than I could have ever dreamed," she said, opening her eyes to see her husband haloed in the last of the day's rays. Her breath stopped in her chest, just short of release upon seeing how stunning he was as if it were the first time she'd ever laid eyes on him. This time, he might not have been wearing a suit. He had changed clothes already, but he was just as handsome as he was standing in the middle of that party on a cold winter's evening.

He offered her a hand up and she happily accepted, landing firmly in his arms. He asked, "I missed you today. How are you?"

"Gloriously happy."

"Are we allowed that much happiness in one lifetime?"

"I sure hope so or I'm going to burn through it fast."

He chuckled, understanding exactly what gloriously happy felt like, and kissed her head. Taylor's hands trembled less on the West Coast though he still aged. Maybe it was the weather or the laid-back lifestyle they chose to live. He had very strong suspicions it was the little brunette that gave him something to hold on to, something worth fighting for. He shared his bed, his house, and his life with her and it all became...

Their bed.

Their house.

Their life together.

And *they* cherished every minute.

She led him by the hand inside the house; the house he'd designed and had built for her. One hundred percent of the guilt money had been given away to various domestic abuse and child abuse charities, but the money received from her family for her "troubles" more than paid for the beautiful home. It felt like salvation—all light and sunshine, clean lines like he liked, bright colors like she loved, except for pink. She hated pink bedrooms. This house was Hazel and Jude inside and out. "My mother arrives tomorrow afternoon."

"I've hired a car to pick her up. She'll meet us there. Be prepared. She sounds excited."

"Beats the alternative," she joked, and walked into the kitchen ready to bake him something. "Are you hungry?"

"No, I'm still stuffed from the pancakes and bacon." Jude grinned, comforted by his satisfied smile when he added, "You're going to make me fat."

"Then we'll be even," she replied, rubbing her very round belly.

He came around and couldn't resist, like any other time he was with her. He rubbed the baby bump and kissed his wife. "I still can't believe we're having a baby. I can't believe you'd want to have a baby with me."

"The whole of you isn't Parkinson's, Hazel."

"When I die—"

"*If* you leave me, leave this earth—"

"It would never be by choice or without a fight. You know I'll fight, right?"

"I know you will, with all you have. I know you will."

They walked to the couch and sat down to watch the sun dip below the horizon. She was curled into his side and he had his arm wrapped around her. They didn't often talk about his disease, but they didn't deny it either. It was just a part of him. "If you should go," she started again, "this baby will always keep you close to me, a gift I couldn't have had without you. One of the many gifts I didn't experience until I met you."

"Like the disease, your stepfather, your aunt, and Bleekman's tried to destroy what was good. But once you were freed from them, you grew. You shone. You became the person you were always meant to be."

"After all we've been through, it only took a whole new life to create one."

He smiled, liking her perspective on things. "Yep, a whole new life."

She yawned and stretched her legs out. Taylor sat up, and said, "You should get some rest. We have to leave early in the morning."

"What time?"

"Six to make it to the hospital on time. You're supposed to be induced at eight."

Taylor couldn't pinpoint the exact moment. There were so many great ones they had shared throughout the last three years. But he had a feeling it was the night his parents threw that party one January, when he'd watched Jude twirl away from him while he'd stood there waiting for her to return. As he'd watched the petite little brunette in the chartreuse dress, deep down he'd felt... no, he'd *known* he'd follow her anywhere.

Tonight, it would be to their bedroom so he could love on her and she could make him feel invincible.

Tomorrow, it would be to the hospital to meet the child he never thought he'd meet.

But the day after that, he'd go buy the love of his life—whether it be a long or short life—mocha chocolate-chip ice cream, just because she likes it and he wants to see her smile.

Hazel, with the remote in hand, switched on the music. Through the speakers, Otis Redding began crooning, "Try A Little Tenderness," and Hazel took her hand, pulling her to her feet. He started walking away from the couch, but Jude stopped him and smiled with the most mischievous glint in her blue-green eyes. Taking both of his hands in hers, she asked, "Wanna dance with me?" She wiggled her hips back and forth to the beat, pursing her lips and hoping to entice.

Taylor laughed, loving this life too much to leave it anytime soon. He spun his sundress-wearing beauty out and then delicately whipped her back in, bringing their bodies together, their breath quickening and seduction growing. He dipped her and she squealed in pure delight. But with a solid hold on her, he kept her there, his eyes roaming over her body.

Jude found his gaze unhurried and comforting. When his lips were joined to hers, one breath shared between them, he said, "Let's go."

Quirking an eyebrow, she hoped they were heading into the bedroom, but asked just in case, "Are we going anywhere in particular?"

With the smile that always melted her heart—and her panties—he kissed her, and then replied, "The world is our rainbow, Jude."

A Personal Note

Dear Readers, I put my heart and all my emotions into this book. It tore me up during the writing process and then healed me through the story. It was a great honor to have shared time with these characters and to share them with you.

Dearest Adriana, Corinne, Danielle, Flavia, Heather, Irene, Jessie, Kellie, Laura, Lisa, Lynsey, Marion, Marla, Mary, Michelle, Ruth, and Sonia, I treasure our friendship so much. You touch my heart, make me smile, support me, encourage me, and inspire me daily. Thank you and Love You!

To my awesome FYW girls—You Rock! Now go write!

Dear Mom and Sis, thank you for always being my cheerleader, even when I write sexy scenes. Hehe

Dear Jennifer and Kerri, thank you for a life full of fun times and great chats. Love ya!

To my family and friends who are always there for me, supporting me as a friend and an author, I say thank you. It means more to me than you will ever know.

Love,

S.

About the Author

Always interested in the arts, S. L. Scott, grew up painting, writing poetry and short stories, and wiling her days away lost in a good book and the movies.

With a degree in Journalism, she continued her love of the written word by reading American authors like Salinger and Fitzgerald. She was intrigued by their flawed characters living in picture perfect worlds, but could still debate that the worlds those characters lived in were actually the flawed ones. This dynamic of leaving the reader invested in the words, inspired Scott to start writing with emotion while interjecting an underlying passion into her own stories.

Living in the capital of Texas with her family, Scott loves traveling and avocados, beaches, and cooking with her kids. She's obsessed with epic romances like The Bronze Horseman and loves a good plot twist. She dreams of seeing one of her own books made into a movie as well as returning to Europe. Her favorite color is blue, but she likens it more toward the sky than the emotion. Her home is filled with the welcoming symbol of the pineapple and finds surfing a challenge though she likes to think she's a pro.

Scott welcomes your notes to sl@slscottauthor.com

Available Books by
New York Times Bestselling Author
S. L. Scott

Hard to Resist Series

The Resistance

The Reckoning

The Redemption

Welcome to Paradise Series

Good Vibrations

Good Intentions

Good Sensations

Happy Endings

From the Inside Out Series

Scorned

Jealousy

Dylan

Austin

Stand Alone Books

Until I Met You

Naturally, Charlie
A Prior Engagement
Lost in Translation
Sleeping with Mr. Sexy
Morning Glory

www.slscottauthor.com